**HUNT +
GATHER**
Bookseller & Publisher
311 Aztec St., Santa Fe
New Mexico 87501
@HuntAndGather.net

By Lisa Goldstein from
Tom Doherty Associates

The Red Magician
Strange Devices of the Sun and Moon
Summer King, Winter Fool
Tourists

Tourists

*a
novel
by*

Lisa Goldstein

A Tom Doherty Associates Book
New York

TOURISTS

Copyright © 1989, 1994 by Lisa Goldstein

This book is printed on acid-free paper.

An Orb Edition
Published by Tom Doherty Associates, Inc.
175 Fifth Avenue
New York, N.Y. 10010

ISBN 0-312-89011-7

First Orb edition: September 1994

Printed in the United States of America

0 9 8 7 6 5 4 3 2 1

1.20.2004
Los Alamos

To Mikey Roessner-Herman
The Peripatetic Woman

Contents

Dr. Tamir's House

Dr. Mitchell Parmenter stood in the middle of a room in Amaz and looked around him. Why in God's name was it so huge? Was it supposed to be a living room? Did Dr. Tamir, with whom he had arranged to trade houses for a year, do a lot of entertaining? If so he was going to be disappointed with the size of the Parmenters' living room, that was certain.

The big room was crowded. Tall oak bookshelves, some with glass fronts, stood straight against two walls, the shelves stuffed with books, manuscripts, geodes, carved and crudely painted animals, an African thumb piano, a nest with two perfect blue eggs. Mitchell recognized a double birdcage from Indonesia made of jackfruit; the two halves, originally intended for the male and female birds, were being used as bookends. Against the other two walls and in the center of the room were long wooden benches, and on the walls hung swords, silk-screen tapestries and wooden masks.

Mitchell ran his hand absently over the back of one of the benches. He was a tall, large man with the heavy grace of a sea mammal, with thick brown hair, gray eyes, a fleshy nose, heavy lips.

The young man who had brought Mitchell to the house moved a little, and the polished wooden floor creaked beneath him. Mitchell turned suddenly; he had forgotten the man was there. "Well," Mitchell said. The word echoed a little in the vaulted ceiling. "I didn't really expect—how many bedrooms did you say it has?"

"Three, Dr. Parmenter," the young man said.

Three, good. One for him and Claire, one for Casey and one for Angela. He wouldn't have to worry about Casey, but what would Angie make of this strange country, this strange house?

The young man led him through a door at the far end of the room and down a long corridor. "The bedrooms, Doctor," he said. In contrast to the living room the bedrooms were small and plain, the hardwood floor scuffed, the white paint peeling in places. And they were too close together, two right next to each other and one across the narrow corridor. Angie was always talking to herself or laughing or screaming, and it would be hard to concentrate. Maybe he could do his work at the college—he'd have to see what kind of office they'd give him. And Casey could have the room next to Angie's— she didn't seem to mind her as much as he did.

The young man showed him the kitchen and the bathroom—one bathroom for the four of them, but at least all the fixtures and appliances looked new—and they went back to the living room. Now he noticed that the walls were made of massive gray stones, fitted carefully one on top of the other. He went closer to examine them. No mortar, everything cut perfectly to match. "When was this house built?" he asked the young man.

"Oh, it would be impossible to say—approximately three hundred years ago. Perhaps more," the man said.

"Doesn't it get cold in the winter?" Mitchell asked.

"Ah," the young man said, "but it never gets cold here."

The young man let himself out. Belatedly Mitchell remembered his manners. "Thank you for showing me around," he called after him. "And thanks for the ride from the airport!" The young man nodded and closed the thick wooden door, bound in brass, behind him.

The silence settled over Mitchell immediately. Despite the sun, despite what the young man had said, he was starting to feel cold. He wished he could remember the young man's name, wished he knew what he did. Probably connected with the college in some way. There had been a hasty introduction in the car at the airport, but Mitchell hadn't been used to the man's accent yet and the words had mostly passed him by.

He paced back and forth across the floor, the polished wood creaking loudly beneath him. Come on, he told himself. This isn't like you. At home you're always yelling for quiet, you need perfect silence to work. Well, here it is—perfect silence. Get to work.

He stopped and looked at a small light fixture shaped like a candle set into the wall. There were eight of the fixtures, he noticed, two on each wall. At least there's electricity, he thought. It must have been added long after the house was built. If that ever goes, we're dead. There aren't any windows in this room. He shivered suddenly.

I can't get to work, he thought. I have to show Dr. Jara the manuscript and get him to tell me if he thinks it's authentic. There's not much point in starting to work if it's a fake.

He paced some more. Too bad Claire isn't here, he thought. Another month, and then Dr. Tamir gets back from his field trip and goes to the States and moves into our house. I hope he likes it. I hope the family likes it here. Maybe this'll get us out of the rut we've been in.

The next morning Mitchell left the gray stone house and stood blinking in the sun, holding his briefcase in one hand and Dr. Tamir's letter in the other. "Across the street," Dr. Tamir had written, "is a statue of a man holding an egg."

Mitchell raised his eyes from the letter. Sure enough, the bronze man across the street stood holding a bronze egg carefully cupped in his hand. His shoulders were thrown back heroically, and he seemed to be looking out both at the future and at his egg. Why on earth would the people of Amaz want to honor a man and his egg? There must be a story behind it, one of those pieces of folklore that some of his colleagues at the university loved to collect. He made a mental note to learn more.

To the left of the statue a small knot of people stood silently, doing nothing. No, they were looking at his house—Tamir's house. He scanned the letter to see if Tamir had had anything to say about them, but there was nothing. He frowned. The group swayed slightly, like a small tide. What on earth were they doing? They were all wearing turbans.

He ignored them and crossed the street, following Tamir's directions. As he got closer to them he saw that only the men were wearing turbans. The women wore bright clothes of blue and red. In the fierce light it hurt his eyes to look at them. Neither the men nor the women said anything to him as he passed.

"Most of the streets in the city have no names," Tamir's letter went on. "Additionally, there was a devastating fire a few years ago, and small earthquakes occur frequently. It may seem to you, before you become accustomed, that the city is moving, that it has a life of its own. But you will soon be able to find your way to the major landmarks. Though if you wish to go anywhere else—I confess I have lived in the city all my life and can still lose my way."

Mitchell reread the paragraph and frowned. It had seemed straightforward enough when he had read it in the United States, but under the different sky of Amaz it took on a new character, a mystical tone. Was this the man who was going to stay in the Parmenters' house for a year? Maybe he should have asked for more references.

A man drove a donkey leisurely across the street and traffic came to a standstill. Cars honked furiously, a man leaned out of his car window and shouted, another man got out of his car and slammed the door angrily, shaking his fist at the man with the donkey, who was taking no notice of anyone. The air had quickly taken on the smell of exhaust fumes, but there was a hint of cinnamon and of something else. The sea?

Mitchell walked on. "Turn left at the empty field," he read. He saw no empty field anywhere on the street, but to his left there were rows of red woven umbrellas, diminishing with distance. A loud raucous noise came from beneath the umbrellas, something like the noise of a carnival—but like that of no carnival he had ever heard. Curious, he went closer. It was an animal market.

A fat woman sat under her umbrella surrounded by cages of parrots wearing the strange colors of tropical flowers. Under the umbrella next to her cages of monkeys were piled one on top of the other, and over them all a monkey hung from the supports of the umbrella as if he were the proprietor. Snakes in terrariums. An ocelot, pacing alone in a cage under an umbrella. And tethered to a stake at the end of the row, all by itself, an elephant raised its trunk.

Mitchell smiled to himself. Casey would love this place. And Angie—would she even notice that she was in a different country? As always when he thought of Angie he felt uneasy. He began to walk faster.

The animal market had to be Tamir's empty field. Mitchell turned left, turned right at the old railroad tracks sinking slowly into the asphalt of the street, walked past what seemed to be miles of stores displaying nothing but bathroom fixtures. "Money?" a beggar asked. He held a bowl firmly between two bare feet, and Mitchell, looking at him quickly and then looking away, thought he might be missing an arm, or two. "Money?" the beggar said again. "Hungry?" Mitchell hurried past him. On his left, on a vacant storefront, someone had scrawled something in unreadable jagged graffiti, and over that, nearly covering it, another hand had drawn stylized, almost circular letters.

Down a street to his right was the marble building that had to be the university, endowed by the silver barons at the turn of the century and since then fallen on hard times. The short street even had a signpost with a name on it in Lurqazi and English: University Avenue. He hurried up to the university and found the anthropology building—low and made of wood, as they all were, once past the impressive auditorium and administration building. The directory gave him the number of Dr. Jara's office and he went down the hall and knocked on the door.

"Come in," a voice—a familiar voice—said.

Mitchell opened the door. Behind the desk, in a tan coat and a brown silk tie, sat the young man who had met him at the airport yesterday.

It was the coat and tie that saved Mitchell; otherwise he would have taken the man for a secretary, and that would have been unforgivable. He walked into the room and stretched out his hand.

"Good morning, Dr. Jara," he said. Should he mention the airport? No, better to pretend the whole thing never happened. Maybe Jara would assume jet lag. Damn, why did he have to be so goddamned preoccupied all the time?

"Ah, Dr. Parmenter," Jara said, standing to take his hand. "Have you brought the manuscript?" He had the same accent as Tamir, Mitchell noticed now, as all the intellectual class of Amaz, slightly British, with a tendency to use a longer word if one was available. Casey had gone through a stage like that, Mitchell thought, smiling as he nearly always did when thinking of his daughter. Thank God she was over it.

But Jara was looking at him. Preoccupied again, Mitchell thought. "Yes, yes I have," he said. He set the briefcase on the desk, thumbed the combination and opened it.

Jara lifted the transparent plastic bag containing the manuscript carefully out of the briefcase. "And you say you discovered this—where?" he said. He was already looking at the colored web of calligraphy, the old Lurqazi letters before the switch to the Roman alphabet.

"At the university," Mitchell said. "In a box labeled 'Arabic Studies.'" He still could not believe his luck.

"Yes," Jara said. He pointed to a colored wheel of letters that seemed to Mitchell to swirl like a kaleidoscope. "That is called The Sun Upon the Waters. But of course you have researched this before you came here."

Mitchell nodded. His impatience took over and he said, "Do you think it's genuine?"

The young man sat back in his chair and placed the tips of his fingers together. "It is too soon to tell, of course," he said. "I shall have to perform tests—"

"It's been tested," Mitchell said. "Judging by the materials it was made some time around the ninth century."

"Ah," Jara said. "But my own tests. But as a guess, examining it now, I think that it may be authentic. It may be." He ran his fingers up and down the plastic. "And it seems to be, as you said, directions—"

"Directions to the Jewel King's sword," Mitchell said. He was almost whispering. "It might be—it might be the Book of Stones itself, mentioned in the epics."

Dr. Jara was silent for a minute, staring at letters as bright as the Jewel King's robes. "You know," he said finally, "I wrote my thesis on the sword. I examined its archetypal aspects, the similarity between it and Excalibur, the sword in the Arthurian stories. And now here you are saying that this sword is a real thing, that it exists. You will turn us all on our heads, Dr. Parmenter."

"Well," Mitchell said, unsure of what answer to give to this, "get back to me as soon as possible. Please. I'm anxious to begin work."

"I should imagine. Yes," Dr. Jara said, nodding. The nod was a dismissal. Now that it came to it Mitchell was reluctant to leave, to hand over the manuscript. He stood for a moment, a big man looming over the small desk, the slight form of Dr. Jara—how embarrassing that he hadn't caught his name at the airport yesterday!—but Jara said nothing more, and Mitchell turned to leave.

He spent a few hours at the library and in his new office, ate lunch at the university cafeteria, but there was really nothing he could do until Jara got back to him. He took out Tamir's letter and followed the directions home.

The crowd of people on the corner across from the house was still there, had if anything grown larger. Looking at them Mitchell realized that he hadn't seen anyone else in turbans in the entire city. He passed the statue, wondering again why the man was carrying an egg. Or was it a woman? The long hair made it hard to tell, and he didn't want to linger near the crowd, as silent and ominous as the sea. He hurried across the street.

The living room was cold and dim as he entered, and he fumbled for the lights and turned them on. Masks and tapestries sprang into existence around him. He frowned. Had that bench always been against the wall like that? Hadn't it been in the center of the room? He walked past the bench and down the corridor toward his bedroom, still frowning, but he had already forgotten about it. He was used to things moving around on him: it was what happened when you didn't pay too much attention to your surroundings.

The room looked as if it had been the site of one of Dr. Tamir's small earthquakes. His mattress had been tossed to the floor and slit down the middle; his suitcases emptied and their contents spread over the room; the few suits he had hung up in the doorless closet were sprawled on the floor, still on their hangers, with their pockets turned inside out. He moved forward like a disaster victim, stood uncertainly in the room, and then with an abrupt gesture he lifted the mattress back onto the bed, feeling it buckle in his arms. He left the mattress half on, half off the bed, ran outside and crossed the street.

The band of people was still there. He looked at them, uncertain of who was the leader, where to start. "Did any of you see anyone go into my house?" he asked.

They seemed to shuffle, to shift like the changing patterns of leaves stirred by the wind. Long years of teaching had shown him that the best way to deal with crowds was to single out an individual. He picked out a young man, drawn by the fact that his turban was on a little crooked, and said, "Did anyone go into my house while I was gone?"

He thought the group was moving at the edges, forming new patterns, but the young man and the people around him stood still. The young man looked at him like an anthropology student doing his first year of fieldwork, as if he expected something from Mitchell. Finally he said something softly in Lurqazi.

"Do you speak English?" Mitchell asked. The dialect of Lurqazi he could read had changed radically in the fifteenth century, and anyway he had never tried to speak it. "Does anyone here speak English?" he asked, spinning so that he could see everyone in the crowd. He stopped, feeling off-balance and out of breath. "Did anyone see anybody go into my house while I was gone?" Silence. He had the feeling they were mocking him, that they could all speak English fluently. "Why are you standing here?" he asked. "Why are you all looking at my house?"

He looked around. Dusk was coming on, though the traffic was as heavy as ever. Car horns called to each other and were answered. No one spoke. "I'm going to call the cops," he said. The crowd stared back at him, mouths open, eyes wide, as though fascinated. "And when I do I'm going to ask them if you have a permit to stand here all day like this. Do you understand?" He turned and left, hoping he had salvaged something from the situation, fearing he had made a fool of himself. He resisted the impulse to look back at the people he felt massed behind him, watching him.

Back inside he walked slowly through the living room and the empty echoing bedrooms, making sure they were untouched. The cluttered front room seemed the same as he'd left it, but how would he know if anything was missing? Damn, now he'd have to write to Dr. Tamir on top of everything else. Then he went to his own bedroom, picked everything up off the floor, rehung his suits, checked to see if anything had been taken. His traveler's checks were still there, and so was the watch Claire had given him for their anniversary. He had taken his passport with him when he'd left.

The floorboards creaked under his feet as he went back to the living room to use the phone. On his first try he heard nothing but static. He hung up, jiggled the button and listened to the gabble of another conversation. Finally he connected with the operator and asked for the police. When a man came on the line he asked for someone who could speak English. The English speaker told him they would be right over. He sat in the darkened living room, the dim lights unable to penetrate the dark of the groined ceiling overhead, trying to concentrate on his fourteenth-century Lurqazi dictionary. By eleven it became clear that the police were not coming. He remembered he'd had nothing to eat since the afternoon at the university. He sighed, put down the book and went off to his bedroom.

Sometime in the night he awoke, hungry and dazed, sure that he'd heard a noise. He rose, careful to make no sound, walked down the corridor to the living room, and turned on the dim lights. Everything was just as he'd left it. He opened the door, letting in the light of a million stars. Across the street, darker black against the black of the night, looking as if they hadn't moved for hours, stood the group of people in turbans.

· · ·

By morning everything was clear. His house had been ransacked for the manuscript. Funny how he hadn't thought of that last night. But who had known about the manuscript? Only Dr. Jara, and anyone Jara might have told. So it had to be someone at the university. Mitchell wasn't even surprised. He'd heard of similar things happening at his own university in the States, though never so violent. As he went toward the phone to try the police again he decided that he wouldn't mention the manuscript or the university unless he was asked. It didn't do to get one's hosts in trouble, after all.

He reached the police on the third try. "Hello?" he said. "Hello, does anyone there speak English?"

"Hello?" someone said. "Yes, I would receive enormous pleasure to practice my English with you. Please continue, please."

Mitchell sighed. Another damn intellectual, though what he was doing working with the police Mitchell couldn't imagine. "My house was broken into last night. I called the police—called you—last night and someone promised to come, but no one did."

"Ah," the man at the other end said. "And what was taken during this breaking-in?"

"Well, I don't think anything was, but—"

"Well you see, that is why we did not come," the man said. "If there was nothing taken, then it is not a crime, and if it is not a crime, then we do not come. You see?"

"You mean—you mean breaking and entering isn't a crime?" Mitchell asked. "My mattress was cut open, my things were thrown all around the room, but that's okay?"

"Yes, exactly, sor," the man said.

"But what if they come back?" Mitchell said. "What if they were looking for something, and they come back because they didn't find it?"

"Ah," the man said, "then it becomes a matter for the police. Then you call us, sor."

"But don't you want to—to take fingerprints or something? Check the locks?"

"I don't know how you do these things in America, sor," the man said. "But we do it differently here. You must try to be tolerant of other customs."

Even through his anger Mitchell recognized the irony—a police-man telling a professor of anthropology to be tolerant of other customs. "Well, what about last night?" he asked. "When the policeman I talked to promised to come to the house? You mean he had no intention of coming over?"

"That is precisely what I do mean, sor," the man said. "No intention whatsoever."

"But why the hell—why did he say he'd come?"

"Ah, well, this is Amaz, sor," the man said. "You must be tolerant—"

Mitchell swore and hung up. Now that he thought about it, he realized that he'd probably been too distraught to give the man he'd talked to last night an address. No, he definitely hadn't given him the address, because he didn't even know what the address was. Whenever he'd sent Dr. Tamir a letter he'd had to write a whole series of complex instructions on the front of the envelope, instructions that seemed to be directions from the post office to the house. He had no idea how anyone would get to the house from the police station.

He swore again, went over to the heavy wooden door and examined the lock. It didn't seem to have been tampered with. He opened the door and looked outside. Across the street, like a parade unaccountably come to a standstill, stood the group of people, waiting, expectant. It appeared to have grown larger since the day before.

Mitchell slammed the door. If only Claire were here, he thought.

War in Borol and Marol

*A*ngie screamed from upstairs.

"Oh dear," Claire said in the kitchen, looking up from her newspaper. She's still staring at the same page, Casey thought. That could be some kind of record for her, over half an hour. Maybe I should time her. Claire took another sip of her drink and said, "Casey, could you go and see what's wrong?"

"Sure, Mom," Casey said. She put down her physics book and went upstairs.

Angie was sitting quietly on the floor of her room, her black notebooks spiraling around her. As always, Casey couldn't help noticing, with a little envy, how beautiful her sister was, her long white-blond hair and blue eyes. "What's wrong?" Casey said.

Angie looked up at her slowly. "What are you doing here?" she asked. "Borol and Marol are still preparing for war. Are you here to discuss treaty terms?"

Casey thought quickly. It was one of those days, then, when Angie would not come out of her imaginary kingdoms. The kingdoms had been fun even as recently as last year, but now that Casey was fourteen and Angie fifteen Casey thought it was time to put them away. But when she'd told Angie a few months ago that she was no longer interested in playing there had been fires in Borol, Angie's country, plagues and invasions in Marol, Casey's country, and at the end of it the two kingdoms had declared war. "No," Casey said, still determined not to humor her sister, to try by harshness to bring her back from wherever she had gone. "I'm here to find out why you screamed."

"A messenger from Marol has opened the War Gate in the Twelve-gated City for the first time in over four hundred years," Angie said. She used as many words as she could in the language she and Casey had made up together: messenger, war, gate, city. "The war has begun."

"So it's nothing important then," Casey said. Angie flinched a little at the severe tone but said nothing. "Good. I've got to get back to my homework."

"Your kingdom is doomed," Angie said in Bordoril, the made-up language. Her eyes were hard as stones. "You have put off your preparations for war for too long." This time the only words she could manage in Bordoril were "you" and "war."

"So slaughter me," Casey said, trying to sound light. She left Angie's room and closed the door behind her.

As she went down the steps she wondered if there was something more she could be doing to help her sister. Maybe I could have cooperated more with that psychologist Dad found, she thought. Well, but he didn't want to learn Bordoril, even though I offered to teach him, even though that's all Angie was speaking to him. And he didn't want to discuss Freud's *Jokes and Their Relation to the Unconscious* with me. You'd think they'd teach psychologists about precocious adolescents. Apparently not. Anyway he wasn't too bright. He gave up on Angie after only a few weeks.

I can't think of anything else I could be doing for her. Mom and Dad say she'll grow out of it. I did. But there's a lot Mom and Dad don't know.

She went back into the kitchen. Her mother had almost finished her drink and was still looking at the same page in the newspaper. "What happened?" Claire asked absently. She hadn't combed her fine pale hair yet, Casey saw, and it hung in wisps around her face like a tangle of thread. Her round face was unlined, but when she bent her head, as she was doing now, Casey could see the soft web of wrinkles in her double chin.

"Oh, you know," Casey said. "The usual thing."

Claire lifted her hands softly, fingers spread as though she had just polished her nails. "I can hardly wait until we leave," she said. "Your father knows how to deal with her. Sometimes I think he's the only one holding this family together. God knows I can't."

Oh Mom, Casey thought, sitting at the kitchen table and picking up her book. Don't you know I'm the one holding everything together?

Angie made a mark in one of her notebooks and the messenger at the gate was dead, killed by a watchman on the walls. There, she thought with satisfaction. The first casualty in the war, and he was from Marol, one of Casey's. If Casey had been here she could have retaliated, there could have been a good border skirmish, but since she wasn't... Angie shrugged. Casey hadn't even built up her border defenses. The war would end with Marol conquered by Borol and lying in ruins, probably. And then she wouldn't need Casey for anything. Then she could explore both countries on her own.

It would have been more fun with Casey, though. The thought sneaked past her defenses like a spy in the Twelve-gated City. Casey had had some of the best ideas, had made up Bordoril's grammar, had, after looking through their father's anthropology textbooks, come up with the Winter Solstice festival that the two of them celebrated every year. This would be the first year she would celebrate it alone.

Damn Casey anyway! She hadn't said anything, but Angie knew that she preferred to be outside, out in the world. But what was out there for them anyway? They had talked it over many times, and each time they had come to the same answer: Nothing. Kids who made fun of them because they did so well in school. And lately something even worse, boys who followed Angie home after school, whistling and howling and calling to her. Why? Because she had long blond hair and breasts? Didn't Casey see how stupid that was, how stupid everyone was?

Well, she'd solved one of her problems, anyway. She had stopped doing her homework, stopped doing anything that didn't involve the Two Kingdoms. No one could call her brainy or good in school again. She knew that her parents had been called in to talk to her teachers but she didn't care. School had nothing she wanted, none of the poetry or glittering complexity of the long histories of Borol and Marol. "But Borol and Marol aren't *real,*" everyone said, sooner or later. But what did that matter? They were beautiful.

So why didn't Casey want to play any more? She didn't care what anyone else said, but Casey had been her only friend for so long. Her laughter and cutting remarks were like a reproach. Angie bent over another notebook, her long hair falling like a curtain over her face, and counted her troop strength.

The next day was Monday, a school day. At lunch Casey was allowed to leave school and take a bus to the city college. She remembered the rising excitement she had felt when her counselor had taken out the college catalog and shown her the list of courses. "You mean—I can take any one of these classes?" she had asked.

That had been a mistake, letting him see how thrilled she was. They spent more time on the problem kids, the ones who didn't react, just like at home. Finally she'd chosen a beginning physics class. At first it had been a relief to leave school, to skip lunch, the slow and shallow kids talking about trivia, the teachers even stupider than the kids. But in the last few weeks she started to suspect that the students at the city college were just as slow. She felt cheated. She'd thought that at last she'd have access to a whole other way of life, to a place where people finally understood her. But nothing had changed.

Last week she had confronted the counselor. He mumbled something about the school's giving her credit for next year in Amaz, and letting her start at the university when she came back. It would depend on her SAT scores, he told her, and on her behavior. She wondered what he meant by that. Did he know that she went out after class with some of the kids, drinking coffee, smoking dope? No, that was ridiculous, how could he know? She could hardly wait to go to the university, the place where her father taught, but she wasn't going to be blackmailed. Her SAT scores would be good, she knew. She continued to hang out with the kids at the college. What the hell, she wouldn't see any of them ever again after next month.

The first thing she had done, when her father had said they would spend a year in Amaz, was to go to the library. Her neighborhood library had had only two books on Amaz, but the librarian, seeing her interest in the country, had put her in touch with a worldwide network of pen pals. She had chosen Rafiz at random from a list at the back of a magazine. Now, sitting by the window on the bus to the college, she took out her letter to him and reread it.

Dear Rafiz,

I'm sorry to tell you that most of your guesses about what I look like were wrong. I'm fourteen years old, not in my early twenties, as you thought. I'm very mature for my age, though, and will probably be starting at the university next year. I hope you're not disappointed.

I have medium-length brown hair, red in certain lights, or so I'd like to believe. In fact I dyed it red for a while, but a book I read on Amaz says that women with dyed hair are considered loose, so I stopped.

I think my best feature is my eyes, which are large and gray. My worst feature is my nose, which is too fat, like my father's. But you can judge for yourself—I'm sending you a picture.

Now it's your turn. What do you look like? I imagine you in your early

twenties, tall, lean, with a narrow face and dark eyes. Am I right? Send me
a picture if you have one.

I can't wait to get to Amaz and see for myself what I've been reading
about for so many months. My father is already there. And of course I can't
wait to meet you.

As always,
Casey

P.S. Is it true about the women with dyed hair? If the guidebook was
wrong I can go back to dyeing my hair.

The bus was coming up to her stop. She folded the letter, sealed it
and a picture in the envelope and got off the bus.

She had fifteen minutes before her class started. The counselor had
suggested that she use the time to eat lunch. Instead she went to the
bathroom and put on makeup she had stolen from Angie. She knew
her sister would never miss it; her mother had gotten it for Angie
back when she had been trying to get her to socialize more. As if
Angie needed makeup to look beautiful. The makeup and her height
(Casey was tall for her age) helped to make her look a little older.

As she walked into class she felt the letter in her purse like heavy
treasure. Only a few more weeks, she thought. A few more weeks
and I'll be in another country. Somewhere else.

Then, suddenly, it was time to leave. Casey packed her physics book,
a guidebook to Amaz, a Lurqazi dictionary and phrase book, and five
or six other books she'd gotten at the campus bookstore. Angie
packed all her black notebooks, the long history of Borol and Marol.
Claire packed clothes for all of them, unpacked when a phone call to
her husband told her how hot it was in Amaz, unpacked again when
she decided it might turn cold in winter. Casey said good-bye to
everyone at the city college, slept for about two hours the night before the flight, slept again in the cab to the airport, and woke to hear

her mother say, "We're going to leave you here if you don't wake up, I mean it."

Mitchell stood in the terminal, watching as groups of people left the plane. Almost immediately he saw Casey running down the steps and to the line on the landing field to have her passport stamped. She looked up and he waved to her through the window. The landing field, paved with tar, seemed to be melting in the heat. A few moments later she ran inside and hugged him so hard she nearly threw him off-balance.

"Hi," he said after she let him go. He sneaked a close look at her when she turned away for a moment. Hadn't her hair been redder? "Where's your mother and Angie?"

"Oh, they're still on the plane," Casey said. Groups of tourists moved to the left, almost as if they were being processed by an invisible hand, heading for the taxis and air-conditioned buses which would take them to the hotels and beaches up the coast. "I couldn't wait."

Claire and Angie came inside the terminal, Claire waving, Angie expressionless. At least one of his daughters had turned out all right, Mitchell thought for what must be the hundredth time. He looked at Casey again as she stood by the terminal window, and he felt the familiar love for her, as though his rib cage had turned to soft jelly. If anything happened to her . . . But nothing would; she could look out for herself. Angie was the one they had to worry about.

He hugged Claire and led his family to the luggage carousel and then out the glass doors to the cab waiting for them by the curb. Angie walked a little apart, as if pretending they were someone else's family entirely. In the cab he turned to the back seat and asked Claire, "Did Dr. Tamir get in all right?"

She nodded, looking past Angie at the maze of the city streets. The cab stopped abruptly and the driver started to honk, joining the rising crescendo of other horns up and down the street.

"Did he get my letter?" Mitchell asked.

"Letter?" Claire asked, not looking away from the street.

"What's that?" Casey asked from Angie's other side, pointing to a group of wooden stalls on the sidewalk and halfway into the street.

Traffic started to move again and the cab swerved around the stalls, coming within inches of one of them.

"I don't know," Mitchell said, then to Claire, "The letter I wrote. His house was broken into. Don't worry, none of our things were taken," he added quickly, though Claire hadn't looked worried at all. "But the police won't come unless something was stolen, and I sent him a list of everything that I thought was valuable. . . . If he can spot something missing then I can finally get the police out here."

"I don't know," Claire said. "I don't know anything about a letter."

"What are those?" Casey asked. "All those buildings over there, by the hills?"

Mitchell looked up toward the hills and saw pale spires, marble domes, golden roofs flaming in the sunlight. He couldn't remember ever seeing them before. Maybe Casey had conjured them up. "I don't know," he said.

"Is it always so hot here?" Casey asked.

That one he knew the answer to. "It's been like this ever since I got here," he said.

"Where's Twenty-fifth November Street?" she asked suddenly, leaning over the front seat. She looked at the driver and said, *"Lok tol—"*

"Streets don't have names here," Mitchell said, glad that he was able to tell her something. "You have to find your way around by directions."

The driver had abandoned all pretense of watching the road and was looking at Casey in amazement. He said something to her in rapid Lurqazi. She shook her head and haltingly said a few words. "Little, yes," the driver said, finally, in English. "Yes, I speak little English."

The driver hadn't spoken any English when Mitchell had flagged him down earlier. He'd had to pantomime "airport" and "airplane," feeling very foolish, and he'd half expected to be taken to a bird sanctuary. Where on earth had Casey picked up a Lurqazi phrase book? He wondered if he would ever stop being astonished by his daughter.

"Twenty-fifth November Street, yes, I can find," the driver was saying. "Stores of—stores of—" But here his English deserted him and he shrugged and, to Mitchell's vast relief, turned back to the road.

"What are you looking for?" Mitchell asked.

"My pen pal," Casey said. "That's where he lives."

"Oh," Mitchell said. And how did you go about finding a pen pal from Amaz? "Over there—I saw an animal market there once," he said, pointing out the window. "My second day here. I never saw it again."

"Who are those people in turbans?" Casey asked. "Is that some kind of religious group?"

Dr. Tamir's house was on the left. The knot of people was still there, standing silently across the street. Mitchell had called the police about them one night, and a policeman had politely explained that the group was breaking no law. "That's where we're staying," Mitchell said, pointing to the gray stone building. "Over there."

"It looks like—it's a church, isn't it?" Casey said. "Or it was a church, and it was turned into a house for some reason, but it's still holy to those people across the street. And that's why they're standing there watching it. Right?"

The driver parked the cab in front of the house and Mitchell covered his embarrassment by paying him. Casey got out of the cab. The driver said something to her in Lurqazi and she giggled and blushed. She's really very young, Mitchell thought. That's what we keep forgetting.

Once inside Mitchell turned on the lights in the living room and showed the family the masks and tapestries and figurines, proudly, as if he had personally collected them from around the world. Only Casey went over to look at the bookshelves and tried to read the titles of the books. "I guess he reads German," she said, turning away.

"I guess," Mitchell said. "Is anybody hungry?"

"Yeah," Casey said. Claire and Angie said nothing, but he thought he saw Angie nod.

"Okay," he said. "Next stop, the kitchen." He had gone to the corner grocery store before picking them up and had managed to piece together a small snack of bread, cheese and milk. It had been a major effort, involving a long bargaining session with the clerk and no small amount of pantomime, but none of the family seemed impressed with his ingenuity.

"Are you sure Tamir didn't mention the letter I sent him?" Mitchell asked Claire.

Claire sat opposite him at the small kitchen table. She lifted a piece of cheese and then stopped halfway to her mouth, as if she'd forgotten that she held it. "Wait a minute," she said. "That's right, he did. He said to tell you not to worry about it, that when he came back he'd see if anything was missing. That he couldn't possibly remember everything he owned anyway." She put the cheese down.

"Are you sure?" Mitchell said. If it had been his house he would have certainly sent along a list of the most valuable items.

"Sure I'm sure," Claire said. She smiled at him and for a moment she looked like a young girl, mischievous, almost daring him to contradict her. It was the smile of a wild child, the same smile that had attracted him in college, and he looked back, letting himself relax. Then she said, "Did you get anything to drink?"

"No," he said. "They didn't have anything at the store. But once you learn your way around the city I'm sure you'll be able to find something."

"Oh dear," she said. "I hadn't thought—I guess I'll have to go out in the city to do the shopping."

"It won't be that hard," he said. "And Casey can help you. I didn't realize she spoke Lurqazi like a native."

"It's just a phrase book, Dad," Casey said. "I got it at the campus bookstore. You can borrow it any time you want, Mom. You too, Angie."

Angie peeled the crust away from her slice of bread and said nothing. One of those silences that had been so characteristic of their dinners at home settled over them. Mitchell looked from one of his daughters to the other, trying to think of something light to say, trying to move away from Angie's domain of silence. Finally Angie stood up and went back into the living room, leaving the bread, crust neatly separated, on her plate.

Mitchell badly wanted to say something to Claire and Casey about Angie's behavior, wanted even to make a joke at her expense. But he couldn't. A kind of etiquette had grown up around Angie's problems, and Claire's, and even Casey's. No one was allowed to mention them, because it was felt that mentioning them would somehow make them worse. No wonder, he thought, he had thrown himself into the work of decoding words.

After dinner he showed Claire and Casey the bedrooms. When he went back into the living room he saw that Angie had settled on one of the long wooden benches and was writing furiously in a thin black notebook.

Twenty-fifth
November Street: 1

On the street of the junk shops, every day begins the same way. Early light strikes the awnings on one side of the street and draws shadows beneath them down the fronts of the buildings. In the shops without awnings the light battles with the blackened, grimy windows and loses. Whatever is behind them remains a mystery, secrets not to be penetrated from the outside. On the other side of the street the buildings still sleep, drowned in darkness. By afternoon, light and dark will have traded places, and the afternoon shops will stay open into the evening while the shops on the morning side fade into the twilight and the shopkeepers lock the shutters and draw the awnings. The older residents of the street all have their shops on the afternoon side.

Mama, who has been on the street the longest, awakens in the room where she sleeps with her twelve children, dresses and goes downstairs to unlock the shop. Although her store is on the afternoon side she is always the first one to open. A few birds sing, a few cars rattle over the uneven cobblestones. She takes whatever she sees first out with her into the street—a lamp, a fireplace screen, a flower press. In three or four trips she is done, and on her last trip from the store she pushes out her easy chair, an old reclining leather chair that over the years has molded itself to fit her body. She will stay in her chair, a fat woman wearing an embroidered blouse and a skirt with coins sewn to every available surface, for the rest of the day. One of her children will take the money, should anyone want to buy something.

If it rains (but it rains very seldom) she will drag her chair back inside the shop. If no one has come to buy anything by late afternoon she will wander up and down the street, trusting her children to keep an eye on the shop, buying and trading and selling with all her neighbors, except, of course, Blue Rose. (Sometimes an object travels up and down the street for months, like flotsam, until it disappears.) Otherwise she sits in her chair almost every day of the year. There are only two things that can make Mama close the shop for the day.

The first is an English-speaking tourist. Mama has nothing against the Americans, unlike some of her neighbors on the street, but she was educated by an American missionary, and to her mind English is the language God speaks. When an American talks to her she is so flustered by the thought that she could be speaking to Jesus himself that she forgets every word of English except the Our Father. She stammers, blushes, shakes her head and finally retreats into the darkness of the store and closes the door on her customer, the coins on her skirt jingling and flashing.

Mama's other peculiarity is her method of divination. While her neighbors pore over their cards each day before opening their stores, Mama sits on her chair and studies the letters and numbers on the license plates of the cars driving by. No one knows how Mama receives her answers from the license plates, but on some days, though this happens rarely, she shakes her head, pulls herself to her feet and goes into the store. Mama's influence on the street is so great that if she goes inside some of the other shopkeepers will shake their heads and close their stores too.

Usually the second person out on the street is Blue Rose, Mama's neighbor, who got her name from the blue roses tattooed on the palms of her hands. Blue Rose has been on the street nearly as long as Mama. She is as thin as Mama is fat. Her curly hair shakes when she talks. She unlocks the grille in front of her store, and it makes a hellish clanking noise, shattering the silence of the street, as she raises it above her storefront. Mama lifts her eyes silently to heaven.

Mama and Blue Rose have not spoken to each other for seventeen years. No one else has been on the street long enough to know why. Blue Rose says a tourist once returned something she had sold him to Mama by mistake; that Mama recognized the object's value and said nothing to the tourist about his mistake but turned around and sold it to a wealthy Greek. Sometimes when Blue Rose tells this story the object is a necklace. Sometimes it is a vase. Mama has never contradicted Blue Rose; she has never told her side of the story. When people ask her, she is suddenly too busy to talk.

Around Mama and Blue Rose more stores are opening, more objects being dragged out into the street. People greet each other, wave good morning. Someone sees a pair of bookends in a store across the street and goes over to talk with the proprietor. A stranger comes up, the first customer of the day, and suddenly everyone is bargaining with his neighbor or straightening up her wares. No one likes to appear to be too eager.

On this day, life on the street—which is called Twenty-fifth November Street, after a revolution only one man in Amaz is old enough to remember—started the same as any other day. By mid-morning Mama sat in her chair, narrowing her eyes to watch the cars go by. Three of her children were in school. At some time the government had recorded that Mama had three children of school age, so every day Mama sent three different children off to school. The teachers never seemed to notice. The other children ate breakfast or ran up and down the street or played in the vacant lot on the next block.

At noon one of the daughters came out of the house with Mama's lunch. Some of the shopkeepers, including Blue Rose, closed for a nap after lunch, but Mama stayed open. Out of habit she counted the children: three at school, two shouting at each other on the next block, five somewhere on the street, one serving her lunch. Her oldest was missing.

"Where's Jarek?" Mama asked her daughter.

The daughter shrugged.

Just then a man came up and asked Mama if she had a top hat. Mama jerked her head toward her daughter and said, "Show him." The daughter took the man into the shadowed, dusty store, and Mama forgot about her oldest son for a while.

Two hours later an old Volvo drove noisily down the street, and Mama looked at the license plate and frowned. With an effort she got to her feet and went inside the store, where her daughter was still talking to the man who wanted the top hat. "Outside," she said to the daughter, and started up the steps to the bedroom.

The bedroom was empty. She rummaged through an elephant's-foot umbrella stand near the top of the stairs and found a torn lace parasol and a rusty sword before she found the heavy wooden cane she was looking for. Breathing heavily, she went downstairs. Then, for the first time in seventeen years, she went next door and knocked loudly on Blue Rose's door.

No one answered. Mama tried the door but it was locked. Cursing softly under her breath, she knocked again, then took out a ring of keys she kept tied to her skirt. The fourth key opened the door. She looked around briefly at Blue Rose's store. All the lights were off, and so was Blue Rose's electronic cash register. The cash register, with its electric-blue numbers that looked like veins, had been the marvel of the street three years ago, but Mama had never seen it. Disappointed at not seeing it lit up now, she picked her way carefully up the stairs.

The door to the bedroom wasn't even closed. Inside, Jarek and Blue Rose lay naked on the bed in a tight embrace. Jarek opened his eyes, opened them wider when he saw who was standing at the door. He shouted, jumped off the bed and ran past Mama out into the street. Blue Rose looked up at Mama under nearly closed eyelids and smiled a little.

"Huh," Mama said and started down the stairs after her naked son.

She found him in their bedroom. He had put on a younger brother's pants, which ended halfway down his calves. "Mama, I—" he said.

"Turn around," Mama said.

"I—she made me," he said.

"Turn around," she said again.

Puzzled, Jarek turned his back toward Mama. Was she going to beat him with the cane? She pinched one of his ears tightly and dragged him toward the mirror in the tarnished gilt frame on the bedroom door. "Look," she said.

Jarek looked awkwardly over his shoulder at his back. There, just below his shoulder muscles, were Blue Rose's tattoos.

It was Blue Rose's turn to take in Rafiz. Rafiz moved, slow as constellations, up one side of the street and then down the other, taking about a year to complete his circle. He replaced broken windows, tuned cars, built wooden toys for the children, added wiring. When someone was sick he would listen to heartbeats, peel back eyelids, ask questions, prescribe an herb or two. Occasionally he would send someone to the doctor. He always did this when he saw death written under the eyelids; he had never gone to the land of death, and the doctors, he was sure, went regularly. Or else why did they have such glorious offices, such elegant cars? No one on the street had ever complained about Rafiz after one of his visits.

Jarek wasn't sure how he felt about Rafiz staying with Blue Rose. Rafiz had been as much a part of his childhood as his mother's leather chair, and he knew that Rafiz was very old. Still, he felt uncomfortable with the idea of Blue Rose living with another man. He wondered if Blue Rose never spoke to him because she was sleeping with Rafiz now, wondered if she would ever want her tattoos back. Because he was very young, and because Blue Rose was the first woman he had gone to bed with, it would be ten years before he realized that she had had sex with him to score in a complicated game against his mother. Meanwhile he was too tired to give it much thought. Mama had started getting him up early and sending him to school every day, even though he was older than everyone in the school except the teachers.

Blue Rose, too, was unhappy that it was her turn for Rafiz, but for a different reason. She had been one of the first people on the street to take him in, and he had asked if he could use her house as a mailing address. Nothing was delivered for him for years, and then suddenly a letter came for him from the United States, and another letter every month after that. She wondered if he would be able to tell that she opened his mail.

Rafiz looked briefly at her pale-blue gloves when she gave him the letter. She had taken to wearing the gloves even during the heat of the day because the palms of her hands felt naked. He smiled a little as he turned over the envelope. If he noticed that it had been steamed open and glued back a little clumsily, he said nothing. Then he took a wooden stool from her shop and went out into the street to read his letter.

He smiled again as he looked at Casey's photograph, and a third time when he read her guess about what he looked like. He wondered how surprised she would be when she met him, an old man with thick white hair that stood straight up like weeds and eyes so black it seemed the pupils were missing.

The postmark on the envelope was over a month old. He closed his eyes, feeling the sun on him like warm, soothing hands. Even without the postmark he would have known that she had to be in the city by now. The cards had said so this morning.

His eyes still closed, he sank down past older memories like an archaeologist digging through layers of history. The Americans, and before them the British, and the Dutch, and the Spanish. No one had ever tried to start a nationalist movement in Amaz because no one but he remembered what it was like not to be occupied. You might as well start a movement to make the sun cooler, the people of Amaz would have said, and shrugged.

He opened his eyes and tried to stand. His legs felt as if they were made of string. Too old, he thought, his mind always shying away from thinking how old he was. Old enough that the doctors would come with their needles and iron instruments to test him if he ever told anyone how far back his memories went, and he had no desire to be special, to be singled out, again. He had been special as a child, treated with fear and pity and a little awe, when his mother realized that there were some colors that he was unable to see. A long time after that, but still a long time ago, he had discovered the word for what he was in an old book he had found somewhere. Color-blind. Reading the word, he felt as if a huge burden had been lifted from him. He was not alone, there were others like him, enough of them so that their malady was given a name and written in a book to be read by doctors and other learned people.

After that he thought that surely he must die, having discovered the secret of his existence. But he lived a long time still, tens, dozens of years. He began to think that death was like a color that he couldn't see, to wonder if maybe death had beckoned him many times through the years but that he was just too blind to notice. Death-blind. And at the same time other people, seeing how long he had lived, assumed that he knew death well and brought him their illnesses and accidents to cure. He had laughed a little to himself at first, since each of those people knew death far more intimately than he did. But they expected something of him, and so he had to live up to their expectations, pretending that he knew what they meant when they talked about dying much the same way he pretended to know the mysterious words "red" and "green." And over the years he had learned a little about herbs and symptoms, enough so that he could help most of the people who came to him.

He tried to stand again and this time was able to do it. Blue Rose wanted him to fix the back stairs and change the locks on her doors. And Casey would come to see him soon, sometime this week for certain. He looked at her picture one more time, wondering why Blue Rose had wanted to read his mail. Then he put the letter in his pants pocket and went inside.

In the City

Although Amaz had no formal ties with the United States, it had a large American community, large enough that there was a school for American children. But the school semester had just ended, summer vacation had begun, and Mitchell wondered what to do with his children until school started again in the fall. He was busy, though, working with Jara on a translation, trying to match the descriptions of places in his manuscript to actual locations in the city, talking to experts on the history of Amaz. The next time he thought about his children he realized that both of them had left the house and had gone out into the city on their own.

Was that safe? he wondered. Well, probably Claire was keeping an eye on them. And it was good that Angie was getting out. He had been worried that she would do nothing but sit in her room and write in those stupid notebooks of hers. Maybe she had changed in the time he'd been away, or maybe the city had changed her. He hoped so.

Angie walked slowly through the fish stalls, holding a notebook tightly against her breasts. She hadn't realized that her white-blond hair, in a city where nearly everyone's hair was black, would attract so much attention. Men called to her, laughing, made chirping kissing noises, rubbed their fingers together in a gesture she didn't understand but which she knew was clearly obscene. She should go home, continue the war. The son-in-law of the king of Marol, third in line for the throne, was about to be won over by a courtier from Borol, and his treasonous activities could bring the war to an early end.

But something kept her in the fish market, and after a moment she realized what it was. There was a fish market just like this one in Marol, which was called the Kingdom of the Sea, just as Borol was the Kingdom of the Plains. Before the war traders from Borol would come every week on market day to exchange fish for cattle. Now that relations between the two kingdoms had broken down Marol must be eating only fish, and must be heartily sick of it. "Would you throw in your lot with the fish-eaters?" the sly courtier asked the king's treacherous son-in-law in Angie's imagination.

"Silk, silver, jewels," a man said to her, and she looked up. "Special today, just for you. Gold to match your hair."

"Um, no, no thank you," she said, disoriented. Marol had gold mines too, and in friendlier times had made one of Borol's twelve gates, a gate of amethysts and beaten gold. But this wasn't Marol, this was—this was a country her father had taken them to, she couldn't remember the name. Why did it seem so familiar, why did she think she had been here before?

"Gold, very cheap," the man said, insisting, and unfurled a sparkling chain.

Another man hurried over. "Cards," he said, reaching into his sack and taking out what looked like boxes made of cheap cardboard. "Very new. I give you good price, very good."

"No," she said, walking away, looking at the ground and trying to ignore the men. Lines of graffiti, strange jagged letters almost completely covered by more rounded characters, had been spray-painted on the cement.

A strange sound made her look up. At one end of the marketplace a herd of cattle was being driven into pens. They lowed sadly, as if they could see the future and knew what was in store for them. "Ah, leather," the man who had tried to sell her gold said. "You wish leather, yes? I have a friend, a very good friend, come this way. . . ."

She barely heard him. She felt more strongly disoriented than ever, as if there was another world superimposed over the one everyone else saw. Suddenly she felt dizzy. The hot sun, the smells of cattle manure and fish, the buzzing of flies, the screaming of little children and lowing of cattle, the men's unwanted attention, all made her nauseous. She brushed past the men and started to run, hoping she remembered the way home.

After a few blocks she found a street that looked familiar. She ran past the monument, past the small crowd of people on the corner. Some of them turned away from Dr. Tamir's house across the street to watch her run, her hair flowing behind her like silk. She ran into the house and down the hallway to the bathroom, and vomited into the toilet.

That's it, she thought, sitting back shakily. I'm never going out again. I should have known there was nothing for me out there. Why should this place be any different than home? And I've got enough work to do on the Two Kingdoms to keep me busy until we get back.

A cab stopped in traffic in front of Dr. Tamir's house and Casey ran toward it. "Twenty-fifth November Street?" she said to the cabdriver through the window.

"What?" the cabdriver said in Lurqazi, rolling down the window.

"Twenty-fifth November Street," Casey said, louder.

"No," he said, this time in English. "The ruins, yes? You wish to go to the ruins?"

"No," she said. Cars behind the stopped cab were honking loudly. "Twenty-fifth November Street."

The driver shrugged. "I do not know," he said. "Colonial House? Very nice. Or the ruins, yes?"

Casey stepped back and the cab drove away. She wondered where the driver who had picked them up from the airport was. He had known where the street was, and she had thought it would be easy to find. But no one else seemed to have heard of it, and it wasn't on any maps.

One more try, she thought, running recklessly out into traffic toward an empty cab. "Twenty-fifth November Street?" she said, shouting.

"Yes, of course," the cabdriver said, and leaned over to open the passenger door. At last, she thought, getting in.

She sat in front and watched the street unfurl before her like a bolt of cloth. They passed beggars, street musicians, a man driving half a dozen cows, monuments, hotels, shops, burned-out houses and houses being rebuilt. A man slept half on the sidewalk and half in the street, and the driver's brakes squealed like a pig as the car swerved around him. She smelled cinnamon and ginger and fish, exhaust and manure. A man ran out to the car and thrust a cardboard box at her and said something in Lurqazi, but the driver slapped his hand away and drove on.

"What was that?" Casey asked. "What?" she said in Lurqazi.

The driver said nothing. He stared intently at the road as though determined to set some sort of speed record. She looked out the window again. Hadn't they passed that hotel before? And here was the same man lying out in the road, miraculously still alive. Should she say something? But the driver might get angry if she suggested that he was trying to cheat her, might not take her to the street after all. And she was eager to see Rafiz.

Up ahead she could see a group of people in turbans, and she turned her head in time to see Dr. Tamir's house go sailing by on the other side of the street. She was starting to get angry. Did he think she wouldn't recognize her own house? She stared pointedly at the house, hoping he would get the message. The driver made three left turns, a right, another left, and somehow there was Dr. Tamir's house again, this time on her right side instead of her left.

She couldn't help laughing, loudly enough for the driver to hear her, though he never looked away from the road. What if there were three houses like Dr. Tamir's in the city, ten, twenty, all with their little groups of pilgrims, all with American families, all with a daughter like Casey? All converging right now, after a crazy cab ride, on Twenty-fifth November Street? What if the city mirrored itself, ten, twenty, a hundred times, like a kaleidoscope? The laughter was enough to give her courage, and when she saw the man sleeping in the street for the third time she said, "It's all right, you can let me out here."

The driver didn't seem to have heard her. She said, louder this time, "Please let me out here." The driver stared at the road. For the first time she felt afraid. This wasn't her home town, where she knew all the bus lines and the phone number to dial in case of emergency. This was a strange city, a foreign city, in a country that, her father had told the family several times, had no formal ties with the United States. Maybe she shouldn't have gone off by herself after all.

There would be a traffic jam somewhere, and then she could open the door and walk away. No, run away, because he might come after her and try to collect his fare. She could get her money ready and throw it at him as she ran from the car. But he might become suspicious if she opened her purse. Just a few years ago she had carried everything in her pockets, and then her parents had given her a purse for her twelfth birthday. If only she had never gotten that damn purse. But there was no time to think of that. She would just have to run faster.

For the first time since she'd come to the city the streets were deserted. The driver seemed to be mocking her now, circling several times around the same block, taking the corners so fast she felt sick, writing his own calligraphy on the streets of the city. She thought he might be smiling, his lips turned up just a little at the corners, but she knew that that could be her imagination. She tried to look at him now, memorizing his features so that she could tell someone when she got safely home, but she was too terrified to concentrate. Where was he taking her? And who could she tell, anyway?

Suddenly the car stopped. "Here," the man said roughly. She opened the door quickly, afraid that he might change his mind, that this was one last joke. By the time she turned around to pay him the cab was already halfway down the street.

Okay, she thought. She took a deep breath, feeling shaky. A small woman in a torn skirt and blouse, holding an armful of dirty rags, stood up from where she had been sitting on the sidewalk. She was barefoot, her feet covered with dirt. "Please, mem," the woman said, holding the bundle out to her.

With a slow wash of horror Casey realized that the woman was carrying a baby. "Please, you want to buy him, yes?" the woman said. There was a scab down one side of the baby's face and dirt caked along the sore, and with one part of her mind Casey was thinking, You'd better clean his face, that could get infected. She backed away, shaking her head. "I can't—I can't buy a baby," she said.

The woman came after her. Casey raised her hands a little as if to stop her, then lowered them. "Okay," the woman said. "I give you, then. You don't buy him, I give. Okay?"

"No," Casey said. The cabdriver was probably the baby's father, she thought. And he'd picked her up because she looked prosperous and healthy. Maybe he'd even seen her around with her family. But why the strange ride through the maze of the city? Was he reluctant to give up his kid? "I—I can't take your baby. I'm only fourteen."

"Me, too!" the woman said, smiling widely. She had only four or five teeth. "Me, too. Fourteen!"

Even allowing for the woman's wretched condition Casey didn't think she could possibly be fourteen. Maybe she hadn't understood the English. "I can't take him. I'm sorry," she said.

"Here," the woman said, holding the baby out to her once again. "You take. You give to your family, okay?" She smiled again, as though Casey had already agreed.

"No," Casey said, but she was starting to think the idea might not be so preposterous after all. The baby would probably die if she didn't take it, or at the very least grow up stunted and malnourished. But how would he do in her own family? And even more important, what would her parents say if she came home with him? Maybe she could hide him for a few months and then say he was hers. No, it was ridiculous. "Look. I'll give you some money for food, all right?

Here." She opened her purse and took out a twenty. The woman's smile grew wider. Oh God, Casey thought. She thinks I'm going to buy him after all. "No. No, don't give me the baby. No, you keep, okay?" I may not learn any Lurqazi on this trip, but my pidgin English is getting much better, she thought. "No," she said in Lurqazi. "Here. Take."

The woman took the money and walked a few steps away, shifting the baby from one arm to the other. Then she sat back down on the sidewalk and started to cry. She's trying to make me feel guilty, Casey thought. Probably all she wanted was the money. Ignore her.

She walked a little distance away from the woman. How am I supposed to get home? she thought. Her parents had planned a dinner for a retired colleague of her father's and his wife who were in Amaz on vacation, and no one would look for her until then. But suppose she couldn't make it home in time? That would be the last time she would be allowed to go off by herself, at least until they stopped paying attention to her again. She wondered what time it was. The woman's sobs were louder now.

She didn't see any cabs driving by. Probably they didn't come to this place, which looked like one of the poorer parts of town. Houses squatted along the street like derelicts, paint peeling, windows gone or boarded over, roofs sagging. She had her guidebook in her purse, but she had no idea where she was, and the street probably didn't have a name anyway. She started to walk.

The streets twisted and flowed together like rivers. She felt as if she were walking a maze to which she had lost the key. The only people she saw on the sidewalks were beggars, and the cars went by too fast for her to ask the drivers for directions. After fifteen minutes she felt she had been walking for several hours and had gotten nowhere near the end of the maze. Then, finally, just as she was starting to panic, she came to a street completely destroyed by the fire, and she could see the hills in the distance, encrusted with glittering domes and spires. If she kept walking toward the hills, she knew, she would find a main street. After a few minutes the streets opened up before her and she saw a main avenue, clotted with cars and people.

She ran toward it, waved down a cab, and, after checking to make sure the driver was not the same one who had gotten her lost, she got inside. "The university?" she said in Lurqazi, and to her great relief the driver nodded. She could walk home from there.

It was only after the driver had dropped her off at the university that she realized the danger she had been in. She started to shiver. That first driver could have robbed me, she thought. Raped me, stolen my passport. I could still be lost.

But she had told Rafiz when she'd be in town, and he was probably wondering what had happened to her. And she wanted to see him. Okay, she thought. Try again tomorrow, but this time *be careful*.

When she got to Dr. Tamir's house she went straight to her room and lay down on the bed, trying to forget the intent look on the cabdriver's face.

Claire checked her purse for her wallet, her passport, her traveler's checks, her keys. She picked up her shopping list, put it in her purse and went through her purse again: wallet, passport, checks, keys. She opened the front door, locked it behind her, checked it and checked it again. Her fingers shook as she put the keys back in her purse.

She had had only one drink a day since they'd gotten to Amaz. She'd cut down not because she felt she was drinking too much or because anyone had asked her to—no one ever seemed to notice, let alone mind, how much she had to drink—but because she'd hardly been out of the house since they'd moved in. She was afraid of the city. Mitchell and Casey helped her do the shopping at a corner grocery store that seemed to sell only milk, fish, and a kind of sticky sweet bread. The thought of trying to find a liquor store by herself in the great maze outside made her turn cold. Every day she watched Angie and Casey leave the house to go exploring, and she'd been at first amazed, then envious, and finally irritated. Everything seemed to irritate her lately.

During the day she cleaned up after Mitchell and the kids until noon. After that she would stalk up and down the house, her fingers shivering as though they were beginning to have an existence apart from her, or she would go back to bed and try to sleep. There was nothing to do in this damn city. There was no television, and, for some reason, no newspapers. The radio had several broadcasts in

English, but in the past few days she'd gotten impatient with the music they played and had turned them off.

Then Mitchell would come home at six o'clock and they would all go out to a McDonald's a few blocks down between a fabric shop and a garage. It was the only McDonald's she'd ever heard of that served wine, and she would order a glass with dinner and feel the tension drain out of her as she drank it gratefully. Lately she'd needed to order another glass after dinner; the first one didn't seem to do much for her. She had been out of the house by herself only once, to find the McDonald's, but she had gotten hopelessly lost.

But now Mitchell's friend from the university, Dr. Wiley, was coming to visit, and they couldn't very well take him and his wife out to McDonald's. She would have to find a good grocery store, not the tiny one on the corner. And once she found it there was no reason she couldn't stock up on some liquor—after all, she would be entertaining guests that night.

Casey had looked up "grocery" in her Lurqazi dictionary and told her the word, but as usual Claire had forgotten it as soon as she'd heard it. "What's it like to have such a clever husband?" people from the university often asked her, and, at Casey's school, "What's it like to have such a bright daughter?" She usually smiled and made some inane answer, but what she wanted to say, what she would say some day, was, "Infuriating. They always *know* everything. And they expect you to know everything too." It didn't matter, really, what she said. They smiled at her tolerantly, thinking, Poor woman, little knowing that there had once been a time in her life, a long time ago in college, when she had known everything too. But it didn't do to think of that. . . . How was she supposed to find a grocery store when she didn't even know the word for it?

"Stop a cabdriver," she remembered Casey saying. "Ask him if he speaks English. Don't assume that he does or he'll be insulted. But a lot of them do. They'll probably know a good grocery store to go to."

A hot wind was blowing from the south. Somewhere someone had turned up a radio and she could hear a broadcast in what sounded like Chinese. Someone else on the street was cooking fish. Claire raised her hand timidly and stepped up to a cab that was stopped in traffic. "A—a grocery store?" she asked through the passenger window. Damn. She'd forgotten to ask the driver if he spoke English first.

But the driver was rolling down the window. "Yes, yes, of course," he said. She opened the door and got inside. "A grocery store, yes, of course," he said. "A store for alcohol."

She blinked, startled. He pulled out into traffic without looking behind him. Someone honked loudly. Maybe he hadn't understood the English, Claire thought. "Groceries," she said. "To eat?" She pantomimed eating, lifting a fork from a plate and chewing.

He looked away from the road to watch her. "Groceries, of course," he said. "And alcohol."

She shrugged and leaned back in her seat. Maybe every tourist who came to Amaz ended up looking for something to drink. She couldn't blame them, really.

Five minutes later the driver pulled up in front of a large glass-fronted building. The glass belled outward a little, shimmering, making the reflection of her cab and the other cars in the street rock like ships at anchor. Beyond the glass she could make out aisles and aisles of bottles, each one, it seemed to her, sparkling like a diamond. The stores on either side had burned down a long time ago, it looked like, and spray-painted graffiti covered the walls still standing. "Super Shop," the sign over the glass door said, and something in Lurqazi.

She got out of the cab quickly, paid the driver and went inside. When she closed the glass door behind her, she felt as if she had entered a dream. The sounds of the city—cars, strange languages, animals, discordant music—dropped away. The store was even air-conditioned. The bottles reached out to her like arms. She walked slowly up and down the aisles, pushing a cart she had found somewhere, taking bottles off the shelves almost at random. She had almost forgotten the Wileys and the dinner she was supposed to make that night, but at the very end of one of the aisles she found wooden shelves holding bread and vegetables, and a freezer with packs of cheese and cuts of meat. Without stopping to think whether the food was sanitary enough to eat, she took enough for a meal and went to the checkout counter. She picked up another bottle on the way out.

At Dr. Tamir's house she took out a glass, sat down at the kitchen table and opened one of the bottles. A hard knot in her stomach that she'd had ever since they had come to Amaz dissolved with the second drink. The afternoon seemed to swim in a golden light. It's almost like home, she thought, like when I used to sit at the kitchen table and read, or it would be if there was anything to read. She laughed a little. And soon the Wileys would come, and she wouldn't be nervous about meeting people from the university the way she used to be, because after all there was nothing to be nervous about. She poured another drink. Casey was sure wrong, she thought, and laughed again. If I'd asked him for a grocery store in his language he'd've taken me to a grocery store. Super Shop, she thought. I can remember that.

"And then he made a stop to pick up his girlfriend," Mrs. Wiley said. Claire blinked. Her eyes looked unfocused and a little too bright, Casey thought, suddenly depressed. She's found someplace to buy her drinks. Now she saw that her mother had set a drink behind her on one of the bookshelves, hidden almost out of sight. Another one of her tricks, Casey remembered. And she's been so good for so long. I guess it had to happen.

"Well, I said I wasn't going to pay for the extra mileage," Mrs. Wiley said. "I said he picked the wrong tourist to cheat, because when I got in the cab I asked him to take me to the ruins, and I happened to know that he'd driven miles out of his way just to pick up this woman. Actually I don't know where the ruins are, but he believed me and he took a five off the fare. You have to watch them all the time, you see. He wasn't the only native who tried to cheat us, right, Al?"

She sat up straight and reached for a slice of the local bread, changed her mind and took a piece of cheese instead. She was young and tall, with tinted brown hair brushed back in a fashionable cut. She wore a dark-red evening gown trimmed with dark gold, and diamond earrings that winked in the light like a second pair of eyes when she turned her head. Casey watched her and tried hard not to dislike her. Whenever she blinked she saw not Mrs. Wiley, thin and sleek in her red gown, but the barefoot woman offering her the baby that afternoon.

Casey thought Dr. Wiley had heard this speech before. He looked around at the masks and tapestries and swords glinting on the wall and then back at the appetizers Claire had prepared using one of the benches as a table. "How do you like it here in the city?" he asked. He was much older than his wife but still handsome, with white hair and black-rimmed glasses.

"Oh, very much," Claire said. "It's so interesting."

"I don't know," Dr. Wiley said. "We couldn't do it. It's so much cleaner up in the tourist city, and the service is much better, everything works, and when you step out of your hotel, there's the beach, right at your doorstep. I admire you in a way, Mitchell."

Mitchell shrugged. "It's closer to my work, that's all," he said. "The commute between the hotels and the university would have taken hours, so when Tamir offered us this house we jumped at the chance. And the kids like it."

Dr. Wiley looked around at the far walls, the high ceiling. "It's— interesting," he said.

"So what's there to see here?" Mrs. Wiley said. "We've done the ruins and the beaches, and what else is there?"

"I'm afraid my wife doesn't like traveling very much," Dr. Wiley said.

"Oh, that's not true, Al," Mrs. Wiley said. "I did see something I liked today, when we were coming into the city. You remember, we saw those natives on the outskirts, living in huts, washing their clothes in the stream. I always like to see the way people really live."

"I don't know—I sort of feel sorry for them," Claire said, reaching back for her drink.

"Oh, but they live that way because they want to," Mrs. Wiley said. "They're probably happier than we are. Why do you feel sorry for them?"

Claire took a sip of her drink and said nothing. "Because they're hungry," Casey said.

Mrs. Wiley ignored her, as Casey knew she would. When I grow up, Casey thought for the hundredth time, I'm never going to ignore anything people's kids say. I'm going to talk to them as if they were adults, as if they had brains too. "Al was talking about renting a car and going down the coast," Mrs. Wiley said. "I hear you can get good bargains on leather in Qarnatl. There's no place in the tourist city to shop, really. Everything is just as expensive as at home. But I don't know." She took another piece of cheese and sat back. "The idea of breaking down on one of those roads out there, so far away from everything... Well, maybe I'll just stay on the beach and work on my tan." She smiled at everyone, even Casey.

Casey looked at her mother's watch. "Mom," she said, "I bet dinner's ready."

They went into the kitchen to eat, the six of them barely fitting at the kitchen table. Claire offered everyone a drink and then took the roast out of the oven. Dinner was delicious; Claire was a good cook. She can function when she wants to, Casey thought, watching her closely. Dad would probably divorce her if she couldn't. What would that be like, divorce? No, better not think of it.

Mitchell and Dr. Wiley talked about university politics during dinner. Dr. Wiley had been in the biology department. Casey felt enormously glad to hear it; she would hate to think that someone with his attitude toward the people of Amaz could be an anthropologist.

After dinner Dr. Wiley sat back and said, "That was wonderful, Claire. I don't know how you did it. I couldn't begin to find a grocery store in a strange city."

"Oh, it was easy," Claire said.

"Who are those people out on the corner, the ones in turbans?" Mrs. Wiley said. "They looked like they were staring at your house. Are they dangerous?"

"Oh," Claire said, laughing. The wine had made her expansive, Casey saw. "No, they're not dangerous. We're not really sure what they are, but we think they're some sort of a religious cult. This house used to be a church, you know. Casey figured that out."

Somehow the talk turned to Casey. She had seen her parents in this mood before. All the anecdotes from her childhood were brought out like treasured baby pictures, the ones she had devoutly hoped everyone had forgotten. Look at us laughing and talking, Casey thought.

The Wileys are probably going to go home thinking we're a model family. No one will notice that Angie hasn't said a word all evening, or that Mom drinks too much, or that Dad has hardly been home since we got here.

"And then the kindergarten teacher said, 'That must have been a frightening experience for a young child, having to jump out of an airplane like that,'" Claire was saying. "And I said, 'What?' and the teacher said—well, apparently Casey had told her this story, that Mitchell was a pilot with the air force, and that he'd taken her for a ride but the motor had conked out, and she and Mitchell had to jump from the plane. But there wasn't a parachute small enough for Casey, so Mitchell had to hold her in his arms as they fell."

"What did you say?" Mrs. Wiley asked.

"Oh, I just laughed," Claire said. Her face was very red now. "What could you say? And then one time Casey was very sick, and she was sure she'd eaten something that was poisoned, but she didn't want to wake us up in case she was wrong. So she got up and wrote us a note that said, 'If I die, it was the chestnuts.'"

Everyone laughed. No one had looked at Casey the entire time her mother had been talking. I might as well not even be here, she thought. Maybe I can get away, go to my room and study Lurqazi.

Angie stood up. She leaned over to talk to Casey, her head so close that her blond hair brushed Casey's cheek. "You will die in this war," she said in Bordoril. "Soon."

Casey watched her as she walked down the corridor to her room. Mrs. Wiley watched her too, a puzzled look on her face. Of course, Casey thought, angry at herself for not seeing it before. Angie always hates it when they talk about me. She's always been the quiet one, the one nobody notices. I should have said something about her.

The Wileys were saying their good-byes now. "We'd better get back before it gets really dark," Mrs. Wiley said. "And we have to look for a cab, and you know what that's like."

"How long are you staying here?" Mitchell said.

"Four more weeks," Dr. Wiley said. "Why don't you come on up and visit us? We can show you the beaches, and we'll take you out to dinner. Bring the kids."

Kids, Casey thought, disgusted.

After they had gone, Mitchell put his arm around his wife absently and looked down at the empty plates on the table, as though he believed the facade of the happy family he had shown the Wileys. Then he turned and walked down the hallway to his room to study his manuscript.

Casey and Rafiz

Casey waved at a VW Bug with the word for taxi painted on it unsteadily in half a dozen languages. The cab pulled up at the curb and stopped abruptly enough to stall itself out. Casey looked at the driver carefully, trying to decide if she could trust him. "Twenty-fifth November Street?" she asked. The driver nodded and Casey got inside.

The cab jerked forward. Up ahead, two cars were blocking an intersection, honking loudly at each other. Without slowing down the driver pressed a button mounted near the shift lever and a loud police siren sounded from the cab. The two cars backed away and let the cab through.

"But—isn't that illegal?" Casey asked.

The cabdriver looked at her and grinned. When he looked back at the road they were a few feet away from another, larger, traffic jam. How is he going to get us out of this one? she thought, holding tightly to the door handle. The driver sounded the police siren again and drove up onto the sidewalk and around the stopped cars. "Okay!" he said to her, still grinning. She noticed that he was missing two fingers on the hand that pushed the button.

Fifteen minutes later he stopped at a street and let her out. She looked around her cautiously. The sidewalks sprouted strange junk like fantastic gardens. Shops stood shadowed and mute behind them. Was this what the first cabdriver had meant, a street of junk shops? Did Rafiz really live here?

She went up to a large woman sitting in an easy chair in front of one of the shops. "Excuse me, do you speak English?" she asked. "Do you know a man named Rafiz?"

But the woman was shaking her head and pushing herself off the chair. "Wait, please!" Casey said, frantically trying to remember the Lurqazi words for what she wanted to ask. The woman backed into her store, still shaking her head, and closed the door behind her.

Well, that was strange, Casey thought. If they didn't like Americans she was going to be in a lot of trouble. A thin girl, thick black hair like smoke almost covering her face, came and sat in the old leather chair, looking regal. Her skinny legs, which looked to Casey like the sickly legs of March of Dimes poster children, did not reach the ground, but she didn't swing them back and forth the way other children would have. Now Casey remembered the Lurqazi phrase: "Do you know Rafiz, please?" she asked the girl.

Three or four other children came up behind the chair and climbed on the back and armrests, giggling. "Satl," one of them said to the girl in the chair, and then a Lurqazi phrase Casey didn't understand. The girl in the chair—Satl?—pointed to the shop next door. The other children giggled loudly. The girl sat back, a bright amused expression on her face.

"Next door?" Casey asked, pointing. The girl nodded once, slowly.

No one sat in front of the store next door, and Casey went inside hesitantly. She blinked a few times, waiting until her eyes adjusted to the light.

"Can I help you?" a woman at the cash register asked in surprisingly unaccented English.

"Yes, I— Do you know a man named Rafiz?" Casey asked.

"Yeah," the woman said. "Just a minute." She stepped behind a curtain at the back of the store and Casey heard her yell, "Rafiz!" and a few words in Lurqazi. "He'll be right out," she said, reappearing in front of the curtain like a magician's assistant.

"Thanks," Casey said. "Do you know—Why was that woman next door so unfriendly to me?"

Casey thought she saw the woman's expression change a little, open up, as if she were leading Casey past the entryway of her mind and on into the next, more spacious, room. "Oh, that's just Mama," the woman said. "Don't worry about her. She's a little crazy, that's all. But don't go into her shop—she'll rob you blind."

"Really?" Casey said.

"You bet," the woman said. "When I first came to this street I sold someone something very valuable, a very valuable book. I was young, I was new at this business, and I let him have it for almost nothing, you see. And then he came back—"

An old man walked out from behind the curtain. "Hello," he said.

"Rafiz?" Casey said. His appearance, so different from the lean young student she had imagined from his letters, was like the punch line of a joke, and she laughed out loud. His pants and shirt, both the same brown color, looked clean and new, but when he bent under the counter she saw he used an old fraying rope as a belt. His sandals were made of the same kind of rope. "Hi," she said. "See, I found you at last."

"Hello, Casey," he said, holding his hand out to her. "It's good to meet you finally. Come—we will go out to the street and talk. I can show you around."

"How come you never answered my last letter?" Casey asked, taking his hand. It felt warm and dry, not at all the way she would have expected an old man's hand to feel. He smelled of burnt cinnamon. What luck, she thought. He probably knows the city intimately. I'll have great stories to tell everyone back home.

"I just got your letter," Rafiz said. "You looked different from what I expected too."

"You never answered me about my hair," she said. "I let it grow out anyway. See, it's not so red any more."

He nodded without looking at her.

"Is that woman your wife?" she asked.

"No, she is not my wife," he said. "I live with her for a few weeks, fix things for her, and then move on to the next house. That is what I do. Where do you want to go today?"

"I don't know," she said, looking around her at the street. Someone had put a rusted postcard rack out on the sidewalk, showing old postcards, bloated with water damage, of the Arc de Triomphe, the Taj Mahal, the Golden Gate Bridge. Clustered around the rack, making it impossible to get to the postcards, were a radiator, a dentist's chair and a clothes wringer, none of them younger than fifty years. "Don't you have to work?"

"I have the day off," he said. "Because I knew you would be coming."

"How did you know that?" she asked. The fat woman was coming back out of her store, the coins on her skirt glinting like moons. She dropped like a weight into the leather chair, not looking in Casey's direction. "I tried to get here last week. This crazy cabdriver took me around in circles, and then dropped me off somewhere, and this woman, I guess she was his girlfriend, she wanted me to buy her baby."

She had thought he would laugh at the story. Perhaps the young student whose imagined face she still saw superimposed over Rafiz's face would have laughed, but Rafiz only nodded solemnly. She could have kicked herself for being so stupid.

"Yes, some women in the city will do that," Rafiz said. "They will sell their babies, because they have no food for them."

"I gave her some money," Casey said. She realized how inane she sounded, the well-fed pampered American liberal.

"Good," Rafiz said. "We will go for food, is that all right? Are you hungry?"

She looked at him carefully for irony, saw none, and said, "Yeah. Yeah, I am."

He led her down past the storefronts to what looked like a dead end. At the last instant he ducked between two tilted buildings which nearly met overhead, and she saw that there was a small alleyway there, at first large enough for only one person, but then widening out into a street nearly as big as Twenty-fifth November. On both sides of the street stood houses the fronts of which had been peeled away by fire, displaying rooms and furniture, mirrors and carpets and old, faded photographs. "There was a terrible fire here," Rafiz said. "Long, long time ago." As he spoke Casey realized with a shock that people hadn't moved from those houses, that they stayed and lived their lives here, naked and exposed to the street. "They were too poor to move," Rafiz said, as though reading her mind. The different bright colors of all the walls made the buildings look like a paintbox.

"Where are we going?" she asked. They passed a woman sitting on the sidewalk, her head between her knees and her hand stretched out, a cardboard sign in the old Lurqazi script at her feet.

"Right here," he said, opening a door on a room that had miraculously escaped the fire. As they went in Casey looked up to see a section of the roof overhanging the gutted second floor, pointed downward like a knife. "The Sun and Stars," Rafiz said. "Because you had better have good luck to eat here. How is yours?"

"My what?"

"Your luck," he said. "Is it good?"

She frowned. She had noticed this strain of mysticism once or twice in Rafiz's letters and she hoped that he wasn't too superstitious. Of course, his customs probably differed from hers. When you're the daughter of an anthropologist you have to learn tolerance, if nothing else. "I don't know," she said.

"Well, mine is good enough for two of us," he said. "People on the street sometimes buy me a meal just to be able to eat here."

"Is the food that good?" she asked dubiously.

"It is not the food," he said. "It is the—to be able to say you have eaten here. I do not know the word."

"Courage?" she said.

"Perhaps." It was clear he didn't understand.

The one-room restaurant was hot and smoky, and deserted except for three men and one woman sitting at a table drinking. One of the men shuffled cards and dealt them slowly around the table, stopping to puff on a cigarette wrapped in leaves. He looked completely unconcerned as to how the game would come out. Calendars for the last eight or ten years and posters for Coca-Cola showing pale American families walking through tame forests, holding bottles and each other's hands, covered the walls. Overhead a fan turned lethargically, stirring the smoke only slightly.

Rafiz greeted the four people playing cards and sat down at the table next to them. As Casey passed them she noticed that the cards were nothing like the ones she knew. Each card showed a different picture, a woman, a man, a ruined building by moonlight.

Rafiz called something to the woman who had stopped to pick up the cardplayers' empty beer bottles. "That is okay?" he asked Casey. "You will have the same thing that I am having?"

"Sure," she said.

One of the men slammed his hand down on the table, said something and then threw back his head and laughed. In his hand had been a card, now face up on the scarred wooden table, with a picture of a young woman stepping down from a train. The others dropped their cards on the table, looking disgusted or indifferent, and the man who had won raked the money on the table toward him with his forearm.

"That card?" Rafiz said, nodding to the winning card on the table. "That is the Traveler. I saw it in the deck this morning. That is how I knew you would come today."

"By the cards?" she asked. "Those cards told you I was coming today?"

"Of course," he said. He reached into his back pocket and took out a small dirty cardboard box. "Here." He pulled the cards from the box and spread them in a rainbow arc across the table. "The Traveler," he said, pointing to one of the cards. "That is you."

"Well, she looks a little like me—" Casey said. The picture of the young woman stepping down from the train, eyes widened in anticipation, made her uneasy.

"Not a little," Rafiz said. "She is you. See?"

"Well, it's an interesting coincidence," Casey said. She took the box and turned it over, looking for a brand name, a manufacturer's mark, but it was blank. A strange pattern, a maze of interlocking letters, covered the backs of the cards. "Where did you get this?"

"The street vendors sell them."

"But where do the street vendors get them?"

Rafiz shrugged. "We do not know."

"Well, then, how—" she said, exasperated—"how could someone —you don't even know who—know that I was coming today? Not only that, but know what I look like?"

"We do not know," Rafiz said again. "But that is the way the cards work."

"It's hard to believe, that's all," she said.

"Ah, well," he said, smiling broadly. His teeth were even and very white in his brown face. "Sometimes I do not believe in television either. After all, I have never seen it. Pictures from all over the world, right there in the living room? No—you are asking me to believe the impossible."

She noticed that he said "the living room" and not "my living room" the way other people would have. She wondered if he had always lived in other people's houses. "But I can show you a television," she said, trying not to become impatient with him. "I can take it apart and explain to you the way it works, and it'll work the same way every time. But cards—"

"But here—I am showing you the cards," he said, running his hands across their bright colors. "I am showing you how they work. Here is the Traveler, your card, and here you are. There is nothing mysterious about it. The cards are the way we get our news—our television, if you like. And at the same time they are, like television, our entertainment. We play our games with them. And furthermore, we can tell the future with them, which is something you cannot do even with television."

The waitress came over and set what looked like fried fish in front of them. Casey took a bite of hers. The fish tasted bland as water.

"Look," Rafiz said, nodding to the cardplayers. The woman, smiling a little, set down a card showing the sun surrounded by a dark-blue sky set with stars. "Ahh," everyone at the table said, a sound of satisfaction, leaning back in their chairs.

"The Sun and Stars," Rafiz said. "It is always lucky when it appears. Another sign that the roof will not fall on us."

The other players pushed their money eagerly toward the winner. "But you didn't show me how they work," Casey said, not willing to let go of the argument. She took another bite of her fish. "You showed me one card that looks like me, that's all."

"All right," Rafiz said. He gathered up the cards in his hand, shuffled them and held them out to her. "Take one."

Casey pulled a card from the deck. It was the Traveler, her card. "You do magic tricks," she said, smiling.

He shook his head. "Another one," he said. "Where are we going today?"

She took another card from the deck, this one showing a large ancient stucco house. A porch ran along the entire front of the house, and tiny people, represented by five or six dots connected together, stood in a line that trailed down the porch's steps.

"Colonial House," Rafiz said. "A good choice. Many tourists go there. Where next?"

"Put the deck down," Casey said. Rafiz set the cards on the table and Casey picked another one, a card filled with clouds and a heavy rainstorm.

"Ah," Rafiz said. "We will have time for only Colonial House then. The rain will drive us home."

"It's not going to rain," Casey said, indignant. "Look at the sky. There aren't any clouds."

"But the cards say it will rain," Rafiz said.

"I'll bet you," Casey said. "I'll bet you it won't rain."

"Only a fool bets against the cards," Rafiz said. It had the finality of a proverb.

"Okay, then I'm a fool," Casey said. "Come on. If you believe in the cards so much, what have you got to lose?"

He started to say something, stopped as a small shabby man came in the door. The man held something cupped in his right hand, shaking it like dice and then bending over to peer through the closed cage of his fingers. The four players threw down their cards, gathered up their money and left.

"Sotano," the waitress said warningly, and then something in Lurqazi. Sotano stood his ground, holding up his closed fingers like a talisman. The waitress called to someone in the back.

Rafiz stood up. "We should go now," he said.

"Now? Why?"

"The—the roof," he said nervously. His tanned face had gone the color of newsprint. He grabbed her hand and pulled her out the door.

The cardplayers stood in the street outside the restaurant, nervously watching the beam poised to break through the roof. One of the men started to pace back and forth.

"What's wrong?" Casey said. "Did you hear something?"

"Sotano," Rafiz said. "He is very unlucky. It is bad luck to be in the Sun and Stars with him."

"You mean we left just because some guy came in?" Casey said. "You mean the roof isn't going to fall down after all?"

"Quiet," Rafiz said. His black eyes darted like fish. "That is bad luck, too, to speak of it. And Sotano is not 'some guy.' He is—"

"Very unlucky, I know," Casey said. "I wish I could have finished eating."

"You do not believe me," Rafiz said. "But if I tell you his story you will agree. He was not always unlucky, Sotano. A while ago, nine, ten years—"

Someone in the restaurant shouted. Sotano fell out the door and hit the street. His fist came open and Casey moved forward, fascinated, to see what he had in his hand. It looked like a bunch of small brown twigs. Disappointed, she went back to Rafiz. "Now we can go inside and finish our meal," he said.

Sotano got to his feet, dazed. He closed his hand and Casey heard a small clacking sound, like two billiard balls just barely touching each other. Rafiz shuddered as they went inside.

Sotano had taken all the sound and excitement of the Sun and Stars with him. The cardplayers dealt and discarded in silence. The waitress disappeared into the back of the restaurant. Even the overhead fan seemed softer. The quiet felt oppressive to Casey. She and Rafiz finished their meal without speaking.

"To Colonial House?" Rafiz said when they were done.

"All right," Casey said.

They walked back to Twenty-fifth November Street and Rafiz stopped in front of a pile of cinder blocks. Apparently this was the bus stop; she wondered how you could tell. When the bus came he put out his hand and pointed into the road, and the bus stopped. So that was how you did it. She had stood at a bus stop for an hour once while two buses went past her, and she'd wondered if they hadn't stopped because they could tell she was a tourist. The new information pleased her, made her feel like an experienced traveler. If only Rafiz would stop insisting on his ridiculous superstitions everything would be perfect.

Even with all the windows open, the heat inside the bus was stifling. Casey sat next to an old woman with long gray hair and earrings made out of silver coins. Between her feet she held a crumpled brown shopping bag on which Casey could read "Macy's San Francisco." She grinned. The bag moved suddenly and two chickens bobbed their heads out of it and then retreated.

Rafiz moved to a seat farther back and started talking to the man sitting next to him. After fifteen minutes he stood and banged with his fist on the bus's stamped-tin ceiling. The bus stopped. "We are here, Casey," he said, moving forward.

Colonial House looked exactly like the picture on the card, a large white stucco building. A few white clouds floated in the bright sky, like melting ice cream. They paid and went through a hallway lined with dark portraits and into a large, echoing room where chandeliers glittered overhead. A smaller room off to one side had been converted into a souvenir shop, and they joined a group of people milling around the shop waiting for the tour to start. Rafiz was the only native among them. A group of Japanese men and women looked at the jewelry in the shop and took pictures of each other, glancing every so often at a man carrying a small flag on a stick who seemed to be the leader. Two women behind Casey were speaking German.

"It is not a good idea to buy jewelry here," Rafiz said to Casey. "If you wish jewelry, you can get better in the marketplace."

The two German women looked up at Rafiz with interest, and once again Casey felt knowledgeable, experienced.

The tour guide came up to them and began leading them through the cool white rooms. The German women's high heels clattered on the wooden floors. As they walked the guide pointed out the differences in architecture, the layers of Spanish, English and Dutch influence, one layer for each foreign occupation. Ahead of them Casey saw an American family, a mother and father, a boy of about nine and a girl a little younger than herself. The boy was listening raptly to the guide's account of the Revolt of 1860, watching closely as the guide pointed out the bullet holes in the walls. The girl, bored, had pulled a mirror from her purse and was practicing expressions. The mother, who had the glazed, slightly guilty expression of someone who knows she is not enjoying something that is supposed to be good for her, noticed her daughter and pinched her lightly on the arm. "Stop that and pay attention," she said in a carrying whisper. "We didn't bring you all this way to stare at your face."

A current of longing passed through Casey, a desire to be part of that family, to exchange places with the girl. In the evening the family would eat at a real restaurant and discuss all the things they'd seen that day. The boy would eagerly mention the bullet holes, and then Casey would astonish everyone by remembering perfectly everything the guide had said. The mother would say, "I'm so glad we brought the children along—they seem to be getting so much out of the experience." The boy would punch Casey, though not too hard, because she'd seen more than he had, and she would punch him back, and then when one of the parents told them to stop they would talk about the ruins they'd seen by moonlight last week. The fantasy was so real that when Casey looked up she saw they were in another room entirely and the guide was pointing out Victorian furniture.

As they circled back to the large room they'd started from Casey heard what sounded like cannon fire. The boy, who had been making loud squeaking noises by jamming his tennis shoes against the smooth wooden floor, looked up. The guide stopped a moment, confused. "A thundershower," he said finally. "Very unusual, especially for this time of year."

As if the thunder were a signal, everyone started talking at once. Rafiz, who had started to lag behind when the guide had pointed out the cramped servants' quarters, moved through the group toward Casey. "A thundershower," he said. "Very unusual."

"It's a coincidence," Casey said.

"Very well," he said. "A coincidence." He pronounced the word so badly Casey wondered if he knew what it meant. "But it is good that we made no plans for the rest of the day, yes?"

The group moved back into the main room. The guide described the ballroom during the English rule, the men and women sweating in fancy dresses meant for a much more temperate climate. Casey shrugged. "I guess so," she said. "It's probably time to go home anyway."

The tour guide moved over to the next group of tourists. The Japanese man with the flag led his party over to the souvenir shop. Casey and Rafiz went out onto the porch, where the overhang shielded them from the rain. Lightning cracked in the distance, and the spires and domes on the hills jumped out at them briefly. "What shall we do next time?" Rafiz asked. "Gaudi Park, would you like that? Or the marketplace, for jewelry? Or shall we let the cards choose once again?"

"Whatever you want," Casey said. "Is there a bus that can take me back to the university? I can walk home from there."

"Of course," Rafiz said. "I will show you." He seemed a little disappointed, probably because Casey didn't sound enthusiastic about her next visit. She didn't care. The improbable rainstorm Rafiz had predicted had disoriented her. But the whole day had been strange, starting with the discovery of her picture on a card played by gamblers in a dilapidated bar. And although she firmly believed that the rainstorm and the card were coincidences, the number of coincidences in one day had left her feeling a little strange, as though she were coming down with the flu or had smoked too much dope. She wondered if she would come back and visit Rafiz after all, if the feeling of unreality was somehow tied to him and his weird superstitions. Now that Rafiz had shown her how to take the buses maybe she could explore on her own.

They walked down the steps to the bus stop. Rain pelted her hair and drenched the flimsy shirt she had picked out that morning. The bus came and Casey pointed out into the street as she had seen Rafiz do. "Good-bye," Rafiz said, standing on the curb. He looked even wetter than she was.

"Good-bye," she said.

Twenty-fifth November Street: 2

Ten years ago Sotano had had the shop on the other side of Mama. Then his wife died, and he closed the store and went into mourning. For over a year no one saw him except when he left the store for food, once or twice a week.

One day Mama noticed that Sotano's shop was open again, and she went inside. Everything was the same as it had been before his wife had died: the piles of old magazines on the floor, the mannequin leaning against one of the walls, the long high counter down the center of the shop behind which Sotano stood, adding and subtracting columns of numbers on a large piece of yellow paper, just as he always had. "So," Mama said, not quite knowing what to say, "life goes on, eh?"

"Life goes on," Sotano said, looking up from his yellow paper for just a moment.

"Good luck," Mama said, and turned to go. Like everyone else on the block she had an almost photographic memory when it came to stock, her own or her neighbors', and she was a little surprised that Sotano had not changed the contents of his shop at all since his wife died, had not gotten a single new piece or sold an old one in over a year. But as she was leaving she saw, on the high counter next to Sotano's ashtray, a small piece of what looked like bone. "Anything new, Sotano?" she couldn't resist asking.

"No, nothing new," he said, not even looking up.

The rumor that spread quickly up and down the street was that Sotano had kept a piece of his dead wife's finger, the bone between the first and second joint. (Opinions on which finger it was varied from person to person, and from day to day.) Suddenly Sotano was busy from morning to evening, besieged by shopkeepers who stopped by "just to talk." But he managed to ignore all their hints about the piece of bone, and when they asked him outright he evaded the question. When the man across the street offered to buy it Sotano told him it was not for sale.

A few weeks after he reopened Sotano took on an assistant, a young man studying at the university, "to help me out with a few things the wife used to do," he explained. The young man was questioned, was invited into every house for sweet sticky bread and cups of thick cinnamon coffee. But he knew even less than the shopkeepers, and the invitations soon stopped.

Finally one day the young man had news. An American tourist had asked about the bone, and Sotano had told him it was a replica of the finger bone of a saint—the patron saint of Amaz, Sotano had said. The young man couldn't remember what name Sotano had used for the saint. Now at last it was clear what Sotano was doing, something they had all done at one time or another. He was having a laugh at the expense of the tourists. The patron saint of Amaz, the shopkeepers said to each other, and chuckled, and started home.

"Wait," the young man, Sotano's assistant, said. He stood in the middle of the street, gesturing, attracting more and more people. "There's more. Sotano made up this long story about the saint and how he was martyred and everything, and the American said he wanted to buy the bone. And Sotano said that that was his bone, that it brought him luck, but he'd have more next week. And the American said he'd be back."

The shopkeepers looked at each other and shrugged. Who knew what the crazy Americans would want to buy? Well, that was what kept them in business. Thank God for the Americans.

By next week Sotano had replicas of the bone, crudely carved wooden copies, in a chipped china bowl on the counter. The American didn't seem to notice how badly made the copies were. He bought three.

By the end of the week Sotano had sold all his copies. He went away for the weekend, and when he came back he had much better versions, made of ivory or, it was hinted, human bones. Blue Rose was sure Sotano had robbed a graveyard.

The invitations to the young assistant began again, and this time he had much more to tell. Sotano made up a new story for every customer. The bone was the finger of the man who had started the turbanned cult and had been killed by the Jewel King. It had belonged to a revolutionary, shot down by the British. A young woman who had been promised to an old tyrannical king had cut off her finger rather than wear his wedding ring. The story of the young woman was the favorite of nearly everyone on the street, including Mama.

Those days nine years ago, when Sotano sold the finger bones, were good times for the shopkeepers on the street. Never before and never again would they be so united on nearly every subject, never before and never again would almost all their differences be put aside. There was even talk of forming an organization, The Associated Antique Dealers of Amaz, but nothing ever came of it. The only feud on the street was that between Blue Rose and Mama, who hadn't spoken to each other for eight years, but everyone said that that would be resolved soon. It was winter and the evenings were cool, and people would build huge bonfires out in the street and talk and drink rum and coffee, and repeat to each other Sotano's latest story on the bone.

Mama's six children would run up and down the street, from fire to fire. Every so often Sotano would come out for an evening walk, and the shopkeepers would yell at him, "A revolutionary, eh, Sotano? Keep it up!" and he would smile and wave and keep walking.

And a steady stream of Americans came to Twenty-fifth November Street to visit Sotano's shop. Everyone saw Sotano staying up late into the night, smoking and adding long columns of numbers on his yellow pieces of paper. The finger bones, the young assistant reported, were now being made of plastic, and every weekend Sotano would leave the street and return with a large bag of them, sometimes two bags. Finally Sotano bought a car to carry the bags in. He was the first person on the street to own a car, and the shopkeepers had something new to talk about. "It won't last," they said to one another, sitting around the bonfires after a day's work. "Now he's getting ahead of himself." When Mama saw the license plates on the car she shook her head, but she said nothing.

With Sotano's new car, envy came to the street. A few of the shopkeepers tried to sell their own replicas of the finger bone, but for some reason the Americans only bought them at Sotano's store. And these Americans didn't wander up and down the street looking into other shops, maybe buying a few postcards, the way normal tourists did. They bought their bones and got back into their cabs and drove away.

A year later the assistant came to the bonfires with the most astounding news of all. Sotano was going to sell all his stock and move away. At first no one could believe it. It was only the poor shopkeepers, the failures, who left Twenty-fifth November Street. The successful ones stayed on, especially the ones who had such a good spot on the afternoon side of the street. But when Sotano put a sign in his window that said, "All Stock, 50% Off," they knew it was true. They fought over his mannequin, his counter, his piles of aging magazines. Several people approached him privately and asked, in whispers, if he had more of the finger bones, but he shrugged and said they were all sold. His shop was broken into one night and ransacked, but nothing was taken. Two shopkeepers claimed the cracked china bowl the bones had been displayed in, each believing it would bring her luck, and finally one of them managed to break it.

Sotano sold the shards. Jockeying started for his location, one of the prime spots on the street. When he drove off in his new car, no one said good-bye. The good mood of the street was broken entirely, like the bowl.

Rumors started again, slowly at first and then faster as each shopkeeper added his or her embellishments. Sotano had been seen coming out of a marble house in the hills, walking an ocelot. He had moved to the tourist city in the north. He had moved to America. He had given the assistant a new car in exchange for his help. He and the assistant had become lovers.

Seven years later Sotano came back to the street. His pants were torn and stained with oil, and his shoes came from two different pairs. He would tell no one where he'd been. He wanted to open a new shop on the street, but because he had lost his seniority the only place he could get was on the morning side at the very end. While he waited for the previous shopkeepers to move he walked up and down the street, playing with what looked like the old finger bones, though smaller, darker and more worn. A new rumor started, the last one ever to be told about him. In the excitement of selling the bones seven or eight years ago, people said, he had forgotten which one had belonged to his wife, and that had brought about his downfall. Some people even swore they had seen her haunting him, late at night. Whatever the truth was, they saw him on the street nearly every day, looking closely at one or the other of the bones and then shrugging, almost in despair. And he never tried to sell the bones again.

Satl, Mama's fourth child and second daughter, was the quiet one. Mama always thought that Satl was so quiet because she had been conceived in absolute silence. She remembered Satl's father better than most of the other fathers. He was a tall, thin, intense man who once said to her grandly, as though he were giving her an expensive present, "I should like to marry you someday. Even though you already have three children." He looked so hurt when she laughed in his face.

But he took her to visit his parents, something none of the others had done. She had to call in favors up and down the street to get people to watch her children for the three days she would be gone.

His parents lived high in the mountains, in a large cool white house surrounded by palm trees and gardenia and hibiscus flowers. His mother gave them rooms at opposite ends of the house, but on the first night, as she lay stiffly in the huge brass bed and worried about her children, she heard the creak of the wooden floor inlaid with green marble and knew that he was coming to visit her.

Satl was conceived on that night. She remembered moving slowly so as not to shake the brass bed, remembered holding her breath during her orgasm so that his parents would not hear her. When she told him later that she was pregnant he looked at her horrified, as though she had some sort of contagious disease, and she never saw him again. Some of them stayed through the pregnancy and some of them didn't. One had even tried to get the child away from her.

Now Mama looked at Satl as she played quietly in the street. Where had they all gone, all the men, none of them ever staying to father more than one child before moving on? The first one she thought she would marry, and the second one she thought she might marry, and by the third one she realized she didn't need to marry them at all. One of them had gone on to become a cabinet minister; she heard about him or saw his face among the cards every so often. Rafiz was another, but he had never acted as though he knew it, never made any claims on his child, and Mama was glad. That was the way she preferred it. The children were what she wanted, after all.

Rafiz came slowly across the street toward where she sat in the old leather chair. "Listen," he said, squatting beside the chair. "That child who came here to visit me, you remember her?"

For a moment Mama, still half in reverie, thought that he meant his own child. Then she nodded.

"She's very important," Rafiz said. "To this street, maybe to Amaz. Please, next time she comes, if she comes, don't be so rude to her."

"I wasn't rude to her," Mama said. "She speaks English, that's all. You heard her."

Rafiz sighed. He knew he could not talk Mama out of her feelings for English-speaking tourists any more than she could talk him into seeing colors. "Please," he said. "Try. She's very important—"

"—to the street, yes, you said," Mama said. "And I agree with you. I've seen her face in the cards, as the Traveler. But I can't. You know how I feel. Anyway she hasn't come back for weeks now. I heard that you and she didn't get along, that she had an argument with you and ran off shouting. The missionaries used to say, 'Let him who is without sin cast the first stone,' though they cast too many stones themselves for me to quite believe them."

"Who told you that?" Rafiz said. "We didn't have an argument. It's just—she didn't understand a lot of things." He pointed his chin at Sotano, coming toward them from his shop far down the street. The hand that held the bones waggled a little as though keeping time to music. "Like Sotano. He came into the Sun and Stars, and she didn't want to leave. She didn't understand that he's unlucky."

Mama leaned over and spat on the street, disgusted. "Of course he's unlucky," she said. "Look at him. If only we'd set up that organization when we had the chance. We could have kept him from opening a shop here again."

"If you hadn't been fighting with Blue Rose we could have done it," Rafiz said. "She refused to join if you did."

"That's her problem," Mama said. "Not mine."

"It's both your problem," Rafiz said. "You know what they're saying about you? They're saying that you stole her tattoos."

"I had nothing to do with that," Mama said. "Anyway, she stole my son."

"They're calling her Blue Glove now," Rafiz said.

From somewhere inside Mama's fat body a short deep chuckle sounded. "Blue Glove," she said. "That's good."

"Don't you think it's time to stop this stupid bickering?" Rafiz said. "I'll bet both of you have forgotten what the fight was about."

"What's the girl's name, anyway?" Mama said.

"Casey," Rafiz said, annoyed that she'd changed the subject.

"Ca–sey." Mama lingered over the foreign syllables. "Well, I can't promise anything, but I'll have the children talk to her if she comes back. How's that?"

"She says she's trying to learn Lurqazi," Rafiz said.

"Huh," Mama said. Sotano shuffled past, the bones in his hand clacking. Mama nodded to him.

"How many tourists have you ever heard of that spoke Lurqazi?" she asked Rafiz.

"This one's different," Rafiz said. "I told you. And the cards say so too."

Mama nodded and closed her eyes against the sun. It was a dismissal. Rafiz stood up slowly, hoping his legs would hold him. That was the best he'd ever get from Mama, he knew. And maybe Casey wouldn't even come back. He frowned, then headed back to the shade of Blue Rose's shop to read the cards. A new deck had come that morning.

The Jewel King's Palace

Claire hailed a cab and said, "Super Shop, please." The driver nodded emphatically and she got in.

But when the driver stopped a few minutes later she saw nothing that she recognized, not the burned-out neighborhood or the shiny new building rising from the wreckage, incongruous as a diamond. "No," she said, leaning forward from the back seat. "The Super Shop. Groceries."

"Yes," the driver said. "We are here. Bookstore."

Startled, Claire looked out the window again. "Joe's Bookstore and Car Repair," the meticulously painted sign over the small shop said, and in smaller letters, "English Language Books Sold Here."

Claire nodded in understanding. The liquor store would have to wait. She couldn't pass up a chance like this. "Thanks," she said, paying the driver and getting out of the car.

From the outside, except for its astonishing sign, the store looked like nearly every other shop in the city—small, dusty, neglected. But when she got inside Claire saw a clean store, trim head-high rows of white bookshelves against the walls and down the center, the books neatly arranged. The store was bigger than it looked from the outside, and the lights were brighter. Behind a counter at the front sat a young man—Joe?—reading a book. "Hello," he said as she closed the door behind her.

Claire nodded. She was already caught in the enchanted net of the bookshelves. She walked down rows of books about history, science, cooking, a large section devoted to car repair. Her feet on the linoleum floor, and the young man turning pages, made the only sounds in the store. It's like drinking, Claire thought, delighted, running her fingers over the spines. Worse, because the spell lasts longer. If you read, don't drive. She found the fiction section and the new Stephen King and the new Philip Roth—books that hadn't even been out when she'd left the States—and took them to the counter. The young man set down his book.

"Do you really repair cars?" she asked.

"You bet," he said, ringing up her purchases on the cash register. "Says so on the sign, doesn't it?"

"Where are you from?" she asked. "You're American, aren't you?"

"Des Moines," he said.

"How on earth did you end up here?"

He put her books in a white plastic bag with the name of the store printed on it. For a moment she was back in the United States, in the chain store in the shopping mall where she bought all her books. "There's some of us the city likes to keep," he said. "I don't know why. Maybe because all the tourists come here. It must think it's only fair to take one or two of us."

She took her books outside, stopped another cab, and went on to the Super Shop, where she bought much less than the last time. In the cab home she settled back against the seat, surrounded by her purchases, feeling pleasantly worn out. There's some of us the city likes to keep, Joe had said. She didn't feel as though the city wanted to keep her, but she did wonder if it had singled her out for something. She felt sheltered, muffled, cushioned in the city's soft embrace like a piece of jewelry nestling in cotton inside a cardboard box. She had noticed Angie had stopped going outside, that she and Casey looked a little sickly, and she wondered what the city had done to them, why it had picked her as the sole recipient of its bounty. But these things, like so many other things in life, were not to be studied too closely. The cab slowed at the university, and, feeling like a seasoned traveler, she directed it the rest of the way home.

Casey went into the kitchen, got out cereal and milk and made herself breakfast. Mitchell had already left for the day. She sat at the table across from her mother, who was reading from what looked like a new hardcover. More books were piled by her elbow, with a thin brown pamphlet at the top of the stack. Casey reached over for the pamphlet. *A Few Proverbs of Amaz*, by Percy Swafford-Brown, the cover said. It was badly smudged.

She opened the book, looking for something Rafiz had said to her: "Only a fool argues with the cards." "Big things walk, small things roll," she read. "Time is divided by two."

"Hey, Mom," Casey said. "Where did you get this?"

Claire looked up slowly from her book, a finger marking her place. "Bookstore," she said.

"An English-language bookstore?" Casey said. "I never saw one."

"Oh well," Claire said. "You have to know where to look, I guess." She smiled, the look of the mischievous child that Casey had seen more and more since they'd come to Amaz.

"What do you think this one means?" Casey said, reading from the book. "'Jagged and curved things can never marry.'"

"I don't know," Claire said. She closed the book and seemed to make an effort to concentrate. "Maybe your father knows."

"I don't think that's his field," Casey said.

"Are you going to go out today?" Claire asked.

"I don't know," Casey said. "I guess not."

"What happened?" Claire said. "Didn't you have a friend out there, a pen pal or something?"

"Yeah, well, it's a long story," Casey said. Then, in a rush, she said, "Things have causes that can be seen and understood, right? I mean, don't you think so?"

"I used to, I guess," Claire said. "Now I'm not so sure. I've seen things happen..." She drifted back to her book and started to read.

Casey stood and began to wash her breakfast dishes. I should have known better than to ask her, she thought. She put the dishes away and went back to her room, taking the pamphlet with her.

In her room she sat cross-legged on the bed, looking through her Lurqazi phrase book. She seemed to have forgotten everything she ever knew about the language. And she would probably never have occasion to say "Please park my car in the garage" or "This wine is not suitable. Could you bring us another bottle?"

In fact, she would probably never have occasion to speak Lurqazi again. Her day with Rafiz had shaken her more than she'd known at the time. How had her picture come to be on a playing card? How had Rafiz known about the thunderstorm that had taken the tourists by surprise? As she'd said to her mother, things had causes that could be seen and understood. Things did not happen because a playing card said they would.

She put down the phrase book and looked through the book of proverbs. Did people really say these things? Even more important, did they understand them?

Of course she could go out on her own, without Rafiz. But there were crazy cabdrivers out there, and women who wanted to sell babies to her. It was not enough, she was beginning to think, to understand the language. A few days ago she had seen a woman stand in front of a storefront and yell at another woman walking away from her down the block; the first woman had shaken her forearms after the second woman's retreating back. What did that mean? Was she cursing her, blessing her, saying good-bye, saying she would never speak to her again? And what about the graffiti that covered every vacant storefront and burned-out house, the strange calligraphy of sharp and rounded letters? Even if you lived here for years you would never really know the place in a way the natives did.

And she was starting to feel homesick, too, just like the tourists she looked down upon. She missed pizza and ice cream, missed living in a place where everyone spoke English and it wasn't a struggle just to make yourself understood. Everything seemed difficult, a strain. In some ways it would be easier to stay inside until school started.

But if she stayed indoors all the time she would become like poor, pale Angie, she would not have taken full advantage of her year in another country. Angie. Her mother hadn't wanted to talk to her, but maybe Angie would. She could visit Angie's bedroom, see how she was getting on. And then tomorrow she could go out into the city.

She got up and went into the hallway. Her father had wanted to put her and Angie in the two bedrooms next to each other, but she had pointed out how much better it would be if she and her parents took the two adjoining bedrooms and Angie took the room across the hall. That way Angie would be out of the way, and everyone else could get some quiet.

Angie sat inside her room with her head bent over a black notebook, her hair coming down over her face like a shining veil. "Hi," Casey said, coming in without knocking.

Angie looked up. "Oh, hi," she said.

Casey sat on the bed next to her. "Want to go out into the city with me tomorrow?" she said.

"No, why?" Angie said. "I'm busy here."

"Oh," Casey said.

"You're losing the war, you know," Angie said.

"Yes, I rather thought I would be," Casey said.

"It's not funny," Angie said. "If you think it's funny you can just get the hell out of my room."

"I don't think it's funny," Casey said.

Angie wrote in her notebook for a few seconds. "I need a word for soldier," she said.

"*Mafirq,*" Casey said, giving her the Lurqazi word.

"Thanks," Angie said, writing some more.

Casey felt a powerful pull of nostalgia, as if they had somehow been moved back two or three years to when they had played the game of the Two Kingdoms nearly every day. To fight it she said, "You sure you don't want to go outside with me? I can show you around, show you Colonial House, it's real interesting—"

"No," Angie said, not looking up.

She had to do something to take Angie away from her notebooks, even if it meant making a sacrifice. "Listen," she said. "I'll take you to Twenty-fifth November Street, introduce you to my friend Rafiz. You'd like him. And he can show us both around, he's lived in the city all his life—"

"I just don't have time," Angie said.

"Sure you do," Casey said. "You can still work on the kingdoms and go out every so often. You used to like to go out with me. Remember the time I showed you how to use the gym rings at school?"

Every recess in grade school Casey had seen Angie hanging from two of the circle of rings without any idea of how to move on to the next ring. Finally, unable to stand it any more, Casey had stayed after school with her and shown her the secret, shown her that if she moved in toward the center of the rings the momentum would carry her back outward and on to the next ring. After that Angie had spent every recess on the rings, moving gracefully around the circle, and by the end of the year her palms had thickened with calluses.

To Casey's surprise Angie looked up from the notebook and smiled. "Yeah, I remember," she said. She rubbed her palms together as though the calluses were still there. "You know what I used to think after that? I thought that everything in the world had a secret, and that all you had to do was to learn the secret. Algebra had a secret, and so did how to make friends, and how to be a good cook like Mom. I spent hours trying to figure these things out. And then I realized that the world was more complicated than I thought." She laughed softly.

"And that's when you started your kingdom?" Casey said. "When you noticed that things weren't as simple as you thought they were?"

"Don't try to psychoanalyze me, Casey," Angie said, not angrily. "The kingdoms aren't simple—they're more complicated than lots of things. I added a lot to them after you stopped."

"Yeah, but you still control everything that happens," Casey said. "It's much easier than real life."

"So what?" Angie said. "What's so great about real life anyway?"

"It's unexpected," Casey said. "You don't know everything that's going to happen."

"So what?" Angie said again.

"I give up," Casey said, standing up. "Look, you want to come with me to Twenty-fifth November Street you let me know. And if you want to stay here and rot that's okay with me too."

"I want to stay here and rot," Angie said. "I just read an interesting statistic."

"Oh?" Casey said. "So you read other things besides your notebooks?"

"Sometimes," Angie said. "Anyway, this statistic said that most car accidents occur within a one-mile radius of your house. You know what that means, don't you?"

"I'm afraid I don't," Casey said. "Enlighten me."

"That means it's much safer to stay inside," Angie said. "Never leave your house and you'll never get into an accident."

"Maybe it means you should never go home," Casey said.

"Well, I'm not going anywhere," Angie said. "I've got to stay here and make sure you lose this war."

"If you control the whole thing I don't see how I could possibly win," Casey said.

"Oh, Casey," Angie said. She bent back to her notebook. "You used to be able to understand."

Mitchell squinted at the distant hills, the towers, spires and domes jumbled together like white and gold chess pieces at the end of a game. Casey had asked about them, he remembered, after he'd picked the family up from the airport. He'd never found out who lived there. Maybe by now Casey had.

He turned to Jara, feeling, as he always felt next to the small dapper man, too large, out of scale, Oliver Hardy to the man's Stan Laurel. But the whole damn country was the size of Jara, a country of Laurels. "Well," he said, "should we get started?"

"Yes," Jara said eagerly. He studied a neatly typed sheet of paper he held in his hand. The other hand held a briefcase. "That way."

The two men walked in silence for a while. As always when he was with Jara Mitchell's thoughts began the familiar litany: How much can you trust this man? Who did he tell about the manuscript? Does he know who broke into the house that night? He stopped himself. Why would Jara have had anything to do with the break-in? He'd had the manuscript himself that day.

And yet Jara was acting, Mitchell thought, a little oddly. His department had come back with the opinion that the epic was genuine, and Jara had immediately wanted to follow the trail of clues in the manuscript to find the ancient Jewel King's sword. Nothing wrong with that, Mitchell thought—he'd wanted to check the manuscript himself, to look at present-day sites and see how much of the story was real and how much was myth passed down from generation to generation. But for Jara the search seemed more immediate, nothing to do with scholarship, almost an obsession. Mitchell wondered what Jara would do with the sword if he found it.

Jara looked at his sheet of paper again. His secretary had typed it yesterday, he'd told Mitchell, following his and Mitchell's notes. So that was one more person who knew about the manuscript, who could have told her husband, her next-door neighbor, the man who sold her vegetables. Mitchell had no illusions that this woman would not have understood what she was typing. Everyone in Amaz had grown up with stories about the Jewel King.

"The manuscript mentions the marketplace," Jara said. "Here the Jewel King was reunited with his best knight, who had been forced into banishment. The knight was in hiding, selling leather shoes, but he couldn't resist the glory of the king's sword, and so came out from his tent to touch the sword. And the king, of course, welcomed him back, since he had need of his services."

Mitchell wondered why Jara was going over a story they both knew so well. Well, it was an oral culture after all. Jara, like the secretary, had probably grown up hearing hundreds of variants on the story, though never this one, the only written version outside of twentieth-century folklore texts.

"So," Jara said. "Here is the marketplace, unchanged in location, our archaeologists tell us, for over a thousand years. And probably the beginning of our search."

Mitchell heard the eagerness in Jara's voice again, and it worried him. What did Jara expect from this search? He looked at the market, the noise, the flies, the cattle crowded in unsanitary pens at one end, and tried to imagine the Jewel King coming here with his servants, his knights, maybe even the queen. He couldn't see it. Jara was talking, and as Mitchell turned back to listen he saw a shoemaker's booth, a man in a stained and torn leather apron sitting in front, shoes piled before him like the heads of conquered foes. The best knight in the realm, Mitchell thought. Amused, he started to say something to Jara, then stopped as he noticed two men leaning against the booth, staring at him avidly. One of the men was huge, bigger even than Mitchell, and the other was missing an ear. The smaller man nudged his companion, and they went behind the booth and out of sight.

Now that was strange, Mitchell thought. What on earth could they want?

"Now the manuscript records that next the king and his knights battled the invaders who attacked the marketplace," Jara was saying. Mitchell forced himself to pay attention. "And that the king's best knight acquitted himself so well that the king swore him to allegiance once more after the battle, swore him on the sword. And that they traveled together to the king's house, their friendship newly seamed."

Seamed? Mitchell thought. Maybe sealed.

"But how far did they ride?" Jara said. "And remember that some of the retinue were on foot, and that there were many of them. They arrived at the king's house in time for dinner, for the epic says that the king served his knight a lavish meal, and they were going west, because the sun was in their eyes. So. We must go in that direction—" Jara pointed—"for a few hours, walking slowly." He opened the briefcase and took out a map of the city, so filled with a tracery of lines in different-colored inks that at first it looked like another copy of the manuscript. Mitchell looked on in amazement. When had Jara made that? "My own guess," Jara said, "is the unexcavated wall here, in the Old Quarter." He pointed at a blue spot on the map, then opened the briefcase again, rooted around and brought up a compass. "We must walk in that direction."

Mitchell sighed. His clothes were sticking to his underarms and back, and he was starting to feel hungry. The thought of walking in the noon heat seemed less and less appealing. How had Jara talked him into this, anyway? He dealt with theories, with texts and footnotes and bibliographies, with myths dead hundreds of years, diving deep into books like a dolphin into waves. Not with anything real.

As they were leaving he saw the two men slip around the side of the booth and take nearly the same path out of the marketplace. The men stopped every so often to look at the wares for sale or talk to a merchant sitting in front of his booth, and yet when Mitchell and Jara walked past the cattle pens and left the market the two men were right behind them. Were they following him? Or was he just being paranoid, uncertain in this strange city?

The sky looked bleached to a whitish-blue from the intense heat of the sun. A few cirrus clouds, shaped like ribs, had formed overhead, but they cast no shadows. Mitchell and Jara headed toward the distant marble buildings, cool and impossible as ice. "What are those?" Mitchell asked, pointing at the buildings. "Are they some kind of monument?"

Jara looked up from his compass. "Rich people live there," he said. "And the very poor, they live on the other side of us, in the hills there." He turned to point and the needle in the compass swung wildly. "Rich and poor, they live in the hills. And they leave the city for us, for the middle."

Mitchell doubted that. He'd certainly seen enough poor people since he'd come to the city. And what about Dr. Tamir? Wouldn't he be considered rich, at least by the standards of the city?

They walked in silence for a while. Thoughts of his family intruded like a persistent odor. He wished he were back at his desk in the university, pursuing a fine point in eighth-century Lurqazi linguistics, pinning the meaning of a word like a butterfly. Angie hadn't gone out into the city at all last week, and now Casey was going out less often. And worse, Casey had started asking if they could all go out to the ruins next weekend. He wouldn't mind, but somehow he knew that they weren't the kind of family that did things together. Angie couldn't be pried from her room, and Claire had started drinking again. . . . Well, he thought, maybe Casey and I could go to the ruins together. Though that would just be an admission that there's something wrong with the rest of them. Or, I know—we could go visit the Wileys, and go to the ruins from there. I think they invited us, didn't they? Casey would remember.

Claire might even like that, a vacation from housework and the strange, crazy city. Though Claire was looking better—her cheeks had filled out and her hair looked glossier, not so ratty. Lately he'd been remembering what she'd looked like sixteen years ago, when they had gotten married.

They had both been in college then. He'd dated a series of stupid pretty women on the weekends. During the week, after classes, he would go over to a house shared by a friend of his and five or six other people, and they'd sit and talk philosophy, literature and politics until one or two in the morning.

He'd thought those two aspects of his life were separate, inviolate. The weekends were for physical pleasures, the week for using his mind. He'd been astonished when his friend told him that one of the women in the house was interested in him. In college, away from his small, smug hometown, he'd done a lot of things that would have shocked his younger, staider self. Yet somehow going out with an intelligent woman, introducing her to his weekend life, seemed to him to be breaking the strongest taboo of all.

They rarely went to movies or concerts or museums, all the places he'd taken the other women. (The trips to museums and concerts, he saw now, were intended to demonstrate to those women how much he knew, how cultured he was.) They'd go to restaurants or coffeehouses, begin to talk about something that had happened during the week, and end up staying for two or three hours. Afterward, at her house, they'd try to make it to her bedroom before being stopped by the arguments raging, like small fires, in different rooms of the house. During that time he started to think of intellectual discussions as a kind of foreplay, a prelude to lovemaking.

Sometimes he wondered what had happened between that time and this, would try to find the Mitchell and Claire of those days in his current existence. Where had their torrents of words gone? Claire had dropped out of school when she'd become pregnant with Angie and had given up any thought of returning after she'd had Casey. Had they wanted a family? Had they even discussed it? He couldn't remember. Probably they'd been so busy talking about abstract issues it had never come up.

It wasn't as if he'd never tried to get Claire out of the house. Every semester, when he got the schedule of classes from the university, he'd point out courses Claire could take. Now that Angie and Casey were almost grown, he'd say, she could afford to go out a little. She would nod and even circle a few of the classes, but she would always miss the deadline to register. It was almost as if she'd given up, as if she drank and read novels that were mostly trash to get back at him. But for what? What had he done to her? Nothing that he could remember.

Jara was saying something. Mitchell turned to him, grateful at being forced out of his reverie. "Odd," Jara said. He stopped and rattled the compass like a watch. Mitchell stopped with him.

"What's odd?" Mitchell said.

"We missed the Old Quarter," Jara said. "My grandmother lives in this part of the city, and the Old Quarter is located in that direction, at least three miles to the south. And yet we followed this street here in a straight line, and it should have brought us—"

"You sound like Dr. Tamir," Mitchell said, cheerful now that he could stop thinking about his family. "He said something about the streets moving—"

"Nonsense!" Jara said. He looked truly angry for a moment, as though Mitchell had just insulted his ancestors. "Dr. Tamir is a delightful old man, but in some ways he has changed greatly since he began believing in this Sozrani idiocy."

"In what idiocy?" Mitchell said.

"In this new religion of his," Jara said. "In the last few months before he left he angered all of us in the department. He told us about these delusions of his, his superstitions about the city, but we gave them no belief, and I suggest you do the same. And he implied that he knew something, a secret that we were not worthy to learn." He shook the map out in front of him as though trying to rearrange its lines and angles, and bent to study it.

Mitchell noticed with amusement that the angrier Jara got the more British his accent became, until finally he sounded like an old-fashioned boy's adventure book. He wondered if Jara was so impatient to find the sword because he wanted to establish it as a real thing, lift it out of the category of superstitious nonsense. He turned to ask him, but at that moment he saw two men, one much bigger than the other, hurry around the corner of a building. They were too far away for him to see if one of them was missing an ear, but his amusement vanished and he felt almost cold. "Do you think," he said slowly, trying to phrase his question so that Jara wouldn't think he was an ignorant foreigner, "we're being followed?"

"Followed?" Jara said sharply, looking up from his map. "By whom? Why should we be followed?"

"Well, because we're looking for what would be the most valuable artifact in Amaz, if it exists," Mitchell said.

"Yes, but I see no evidence we are being followed," Jara said. "Who else knows about it but us?"

"That's what I'd like to know," Mitchell said. "Look, first my house was broken into, and then at the marketplace I saw these two guys watching us, and right here, right over there, I saw them again, or two men who look a lot like them. Who else did you tell? The people in your department who checked the manuscript, your secretary, who else?"

"What are you implying?" Jara said coldly. "That in my department is a group of thieves, including my secretary?"

"No, no, not at all," Mitchell said, trying to sound placating. "I'm not implying anything. I'm just saying that my house was broken into—"

"Yes, and nothing was stolen," Jara said.

"Because the manuscript was at the university, don't you see?" Mitchell said. "They didn't take anything because they were after the manuscript."

"Well but if, as you say, my department was responsible," Jara said, "then why would my department break into your house, if they knew that the manuscript was at the university?"

Mitchell tried not to think of an entire anthropology department breaking into his house. "Yes, but did they know that you had the manuscript?" he asked. "Did you tell everyone?"

Jara threw up his hands, one of them still holding the map. "How can you possibly expect me to remember?" he asked, his cold manner replaced by another climate entirely, hot and volatile. "All right, very well, I will now suspect all my department, including the chairman, who will retire some time this year because he is going blind, including Dr. Otaq, who is so obese he could barely fit through your door, let alone one of your windows. Would you like that? Would that comfort you, that my entire department has been set against itself?"

"All I'm saying," Mitchell said, "is that my house was broken into. And that I think I saw two men following us. And that I'd like to know how many people knew about the manuscript, that maybe—*maybe*—someone you know told someone, who told someone else, who told someone who might, just might, be interested in the Jewel King's sword. That's all."

"Where are these two men following us?" Jara said. "Show them to me."

"They went around that building there," Mitchell said, pointing to a car-upholstery shop. "They probably heard us arguing and ran away."

"Come," Jara said. "Let us see if we can find these two men of yours."

Mitchell sighed and followed Jara. He knew what he would find before they reached the building, and of course once they got to the back of the shop they saw no sign of the two men, just an empty field covered with brown weeds. "Maybe these men are part of your imagination, eh?" Jara said. "Maybe there never were any men, eh?"

Mitchell shrugged. "Like I said, they probably heard us," he said. "What about the burglary? Was that my imagination too?"

"You are a rich American," Jara said. "There is no mystery to why you were burglarized."

"Look," Mitchell said. "I don't want to argue. I don't want to follow this wild-goose chase any longer, either. You can keep going, look for your palace, but be careful. Those men were real, and they're probably still around here somewhere. I'm going back to the university."

"Fine," Jara said. "And when the sword is found there will be only one man who will get the credit. There will be only one name on the card when the sword is displayed in the national museum. You go back to the university. I will continue to chase wild geese, is that right?"

Mitchell opened his mouth to say that there was no national museum in Amaz. Then he saw the low wall halfway across the field, almost hidden by the weeds. The wall shone like a mirror in the sun.

Was it marble? Hardly daring to guess, Mitchell walked through the weeds, thistles catching on his pants, until he put his hand on the wall. Graffiti and dirt covered it, but it was definitely marble. "You are going in the wrong direction!" Jara said, and now Mitchell realized that Jara had been shouting at him for quite a while.

"Forget it!" Mitchell said, shouting back. "Come over here and look at this!"

Jara seemed to understand. He hurried across the field and touched the wall exactly as Mitchell had. "Marble," he said.

"Do you think—?" Mitchell said. A man came out of the back door of the upholstery shop and started toward them, shouting. "Look," Mitchell said. "You can almost see a floor plan. And I think there's another wall across the field. And look at this," he said, excited. A patch of an old mosaic ran along the base of the wall, faded blue and red and green tiles that spelled out something in jagged letters. Farther on along the wall the letters looked as though they had been pried up, and another mosaic, of newer, more rounded letters, had been put in their place. Now what did that remind him of? Something. . . . He couldn't remember.

"There will have to be tests made, an excavation," Jara said. "It is obviously too early to tell. But if it is, then what a find—"

"Why are you here?" the man from the upholstery shop said angrily, coming up to them. "You should not be here. This is—"

"We think we've found something," Mitchell said. "This wall, we think this wall might be—"

"It is the house of the Jewel King," the man said, saying "Jewel King" in perfect eighth-century Lurqazi. "Everyone around here knows that."

Jara and Mitchell looked at each other and started laughing.

Later, over sweet sticky bread and cinnamon coffee, Jara said, "Of course if we investigated every wall that someone says is the palace of the Jewel King we would be at it for a hundred years. Even the ruins of the walls of the city are thought by the ignorant to be the palace, and they are made of nothing but ordinary stone. But this one is a very good candidate, just the right distance from the marketplace, in just the right direction. . . . And of course the fact that there is a legend around it does not hurt our case at all."

"Can the archaeology department at the university handle it?" Mitchell asked, tearing off a piece of bread. They had looked for a place to eat lunch but had only been able to find this crowded coffee-and-pastry shop. It looked as though everyone in the shop had been sitting there for hours, maybe days, getting refills on their coffee, gossiping and arguing politics and making business deals. Mitchell had not had any breakfast, and the sugar in the bread and coffee hit his bloodstream hard, making him manic. "I know the chairman of the department back in the States, he'd be only too happy to get in at the beginning of this. . . ."

Jara held up his hand. "Let us see if we can do this ourselves, without outsiders," he said. "After all, this is a matter of national pride. If what we have found is the palace . . ."

"Of course," Mitchell said, sorry he'd brought it up. He shouldn't be talking so much.

"But think what this will mean to us," Jara said. "No longer will they be able to call the stories of the Jewel King ignorant superstitions. He lived, he existed, he united the kingdom some time around the ninth century. . . . This could be the beginning of a new nationalistic movement, a resurgence of our pride. Everyone will want to come see the site, the actual site of the Jewel King's palace."

"It'd make a good tourist attraction." Mitchell said.

Jara looked at him oddly, and for a moment he feared he'd said the wrong thing again. Then Jara laughed. "You Americans," he said. "That is all you think about, your tourist attractions. You are the great spectators. The other countries of the world put on their shows for you, display their ruins, their pottery, their dances and religions. And you watch. You watch because your country has no past of its own. Is that right?"

Mitchell shrugged. He had never really given it much thought.

"But you are right," Jara said. "It would make a good tourist attraction. That would be one way we could finance the excavation."

Ah ha, Mitchell thought. You laugh at the Americans, but when you need money for something we're the first people you think of. Still, he was glad to see Jara in such a good mood, his anger spent. If they hadn't found that wall he and Jara would probably not have spoken to each other for the rest of his time in Amaz.

"You will be here tomorrow?" Jara asked. "I will tell the archaeology department about the wall and we will continue our research."

"Sure," Mitchell said.

"And maybe tomorrow we will find the sword," Jara said.

The waitress Casey liked was taking orders behind the counter at McDonald's. "Good evening," Casey said in careful Lurqazi, and told her what she wanted.

The waitress giggled. When Casey had first met the waitress, she had thought the giggles must mean that she, Casey, was making terrible mistakes in Lurqazi. After a few tries she realized that the waitress giggled at everything, that she found the idea of an American learning Lurqazi almost unbearably funny. She read the order back to Casey in English.

"Very good," Casey said in Lurqazi.

"Do you think I am ready for the United States?" the waitress asked.

"Oh, yes," Casey said. "Your English is very good. When are you going?"

The waitress sighed. Somehow she managed to convey that she found even the idea of sighing funny. "When I can get someone to take me," she said. "I am looking for an American to marry me and take me back with him. What about your family? You must need someone to help cook for you."

"We can't—" Casey said. Defeated, she fell back on English. "We can't afford a cook. Otherwise we'd love to take you back with us."

"Of course you can afford me," the waitress said. "All Americans are rich, aren't they?"

Casey laughed. The waitress laughed with her, though Casey wasn't sure the waitress had been making a joke. "Some of them are," Casey said, and added, "Good luck," in Lurqazi.

They took their trays to a table. Before they could sit down Mitchell said, "I think we found the Jewel King's palace today."

Claire took a sip of wine. "Really?" she said, brushing a wisp of hair from her eyes.

"Yeah," Mitchell said. Casey couldn't remember seeing him so expansive, so willing to talk. "My colleague, Dr. Jara, he made up these charts and maps and things. I thought he was crazy, but we followed the directions in the epic and we ended up finding an old ruined wall just where we thought it would be. There's even a legend around it that says it's the Jewel King's palace."

"So you think you're working with an authentic manuscript?" Claire asked.

Casey saw her father frown. He had told them the epic was probably genuine weeks ago. She knew he wouldn't want to remind Claire of that. "Well, yes," he said. "Dr. Jara thinks it's the Book of Stones, since most of it takes place at the Battle of Stones, the king's last defeat. And I'm coming to agree with him."

"I think it's great, Dad," Casey said. "Where's the palace?" She looked at Angie, hoping her sister would want to say something too. But Angie was busy taking her hamburger apart and dividing it into separate sections, pickles in one, lettuce in another, tomato in a third. Casey watched as Angie started to eat the pile of lettuce. Angie had a system for everything.

"I couldn't really tell you," Mitchell said. He laughed. "Jara gave me a map so I could find my way back. The wall's somewhere near the Old Quarter, I think."

"What does it look like?" Casey asked.

"Well, it's not very impressive," Mitchell said. "It's just an old marble wall covered with graffiti. But there's a mosaic at the base of it which we think is rather promising." His free hand traced an intricate pattern on the surface of the table. Was that the mosaic, Casey wondered, or the graffiti?

"Are you going to start excavating?" she asked.

"Well, the university is," Mitchell said. "We're going to keep following the directions in the epic. Jara has this—well, I think it's an obsession about finding the Jewel King's sword. But you know, I wonder if the university can handle all the work. It's not the first time I've seen these sorts of colleges take on these projects that are too big for them. Maybe I'll write to the States, line up someone to step in when it gets too tough."

Claire sipped at her drink. "But you know what the weird thing was?" Mitchell said. He was looking at Casey now, as if he realized she was the only one paying attention and had given up on the others. "All the time we were out there I got this definite feeling we were being followed. I saw these two men at the marketplace, and then I think I saw them again right before we found the wall. But Jara refuses to discuss it. He thinks I'm accusing his entire department, when all I'm saying is that someone there might have told someone who was interested in the sword. I mean, who else knew about the manuscript?"

Casey took a bite of her hamburger to cover her confusion. Someone else knew, someone her father couldn't possibly be aware of. She had told Rafiz in one of her letters to him. Dammit, that had been stupid. Why hadn't she seen that the discovery of the manuscript might be important to more than just her father and other academics? Now she'd have to go back to Twenty-fifth November Street and confront Rafiz. That'd be embarrassing, after the way she'd ignored him for so long. And depending on what she found out she might have to tell her father what she'd done, and that would be even worse.

Her father had stopped talking and was looking at her as if he expected an answer. No one else said anything, all of them caught in their old awkward silences. Casey bent her head to her plate and continued eating. Tomorrow, she thought. She'd have to go see Rafiz tomorrow.

When she got up the next day Casey noticed that all her dirty clothes had been washed. She shook her head, a little bemused. Now where had her mother found a laundromat? Even more puzzling, how had her mother gotten up the courage to go out into the hot smoggy city? But she'd been bringing home groceries and books for a long time, ever since the dinner with the Wileys.

Casey felt, and was surprised to feel, a little jealous. She had lost her edge, she was no longer the one the rest of the family turned to whenever they had a question about the language or customs of Amaz. All her reading, all her studying before she came here, and her mother had somehow effortlessly become the seasoned traveler Casey had dreamed of being.

It meant rethinking all her assumptions about her mother, Casey thought, as she put on her jeans and the embroidered blouse she had bought in the marketplace. As a kid she had read everything anyone left lying around the house, anything from magazines to junk mail from funeral homes, and she'd gone to her mother, sitting in the kitchen drinking and reading her own book or magazine, for an explanation whenever she ran across a word she didn't understand. She had been astonished by the number of things her mother didn't know. She didn't know, for instance, the difference between a bicep and a tricep, or what it meant when upholstery was described as "chintz," or what tapioca pudding was made out of. And this vagueness extended to every part of her life, so that, for example, whenever she saw a movie, she never recognized people she'd seen in other movies, thinking, perhaps, that directors hired an original cast of unknown actors for each new movie, actors who faded back into the general population after the movie was over. Once, Casey remembered, her father had delivered a series of guest lectures at the university in Berkeley, and they'd driven over to Berkeley on the Bay Bridge from their motel in San Francisco every day for a week. And at the end of the week Casey realized from something her mother said that she thought there were two bridges crossing the bay, one to Berkeley and one to San Francisco, that she hadn't realized they'd taken the same two-tiered bridge to go and come back. Casey couldn't believe it. "Didn't you see that there wasn't any other bridge going from San Francisco to Berkeley?" she asked, almost angrily. "Oh well," her mother said, lifting her hands vaguely, as though she'd forgotten where she was going to put them. "I never really looked."

How on earth had her mother found a laundromat? Casey thought as she ran her brush once through her hair. How had she found the liquor store, or the English-language bookstore where the fat new hardcovers piled on the kitchen table came from? Had she—Casey paused, staring at the bathroom mirror but not really seeing herself —had she underestimated her mother all these years?

She went outside and hailed a cab. On Twenty-fifth November Street she nodded to the fat woman in the chair, and to her surprise the woman nodded back, though a little grudgingly, Casey thought. Then she went into the shop next door. "Do you know where Rafiz is, please?" she asked carefully in Lurqazi.

The woman with the blue gloves said something Casey didn't catch and Rafiz came out from behind the curtain. "Hello, Casey," he said, sounding pleased.

"Hello," Casey said. Now that it came to it she didn't know what to say to him. Maybe he would be offended, would think she was accusing him, just as Jara had. "I've got something I want to ask you."

"Then let us go outside," he said. They went out and sat at the curb, their feet stretched out into the street.

"You remember I wrote to you about my father finding that manuscript," she said. Rafiz nodded. "Did you ever tell anyone else about it?"

"No," Rafiz said slowly. "But I think someone is reading my mail. I think, in fact, that Blue Rose is reading my mail."

"Blue Rose?"

"The woman I am staying with," Rafiz said. "Once she had blue roses tattooed on the palms of her hands—"

"Why would she want to read your mail?" Casey asked, interrupting him before he could get started on another story. Storytelling seemed to be the big form of entertainment here, like football in America.

Rafiz shrugged. "I do not know," he said. "But maybe she read one letter out of curiosity and found out about your father's manuscript. Maybe she wants it to sell."

"Maybe," Casey said. "Or maybe she's looking for the sword, the Jewel King's sword, the one my father's looking for. I bet that would be worth a lot of money."

"Yes, that could be," Rafiz said. "I know she was disappointed once, very disappointed, a long time ago when she had something valuable and then lost it. But why do you ask me if I told anyone else about the manuscript?"

"Because my father thinks someone's following him," Casey said, and she told him about the Jewel King's palace.

"Ah," Rafiz said. "These men following your father. Is one of them missing an ear?"

"I don't know," Casey said. "Why?"

"Because I have seen Blue Rose talk sometimes to a man named

Zem, a man who would follow someone for a price," Rafiz said. "And Zem is missing an ear."

"I'll ask my father," Casey said. A cab drove down the street and Casey and Rafiz moved their feet out of the way. The cab stopped in front of the fat woman's store and two American tourists got out. "But what can he do about it? Can he go to the police?"

"It is not a good idea to go to the police," Rafiz said. "Though if you are a rich American, perhaps— But I do not think the police will do anything unless there has been a crime."

"Well, then, what can we do?" Casey asked. "You mean this man can follow my father and there's nothing we can do about it unless he commits a crime?"

"Yes, that is what I mean," Rafiz said. "But I will talk to Blue Rose about this man and try to find out what she is playing at. And in the meantime you can tell your father to be careful. Maybe he can pay a man to help, how would you call that?"

"A bodyguard?" Casey asked, feeling worse. With one unthinking gesture she had put her father in danger, maybe threatened his life. This was terrible.

"Perhaps," Rafiz said. "Perhaps it is not so bad. Perhaps the men are only following him, nothing more."

"Maybe," Casey said. She sighed. "I don't know—it seems so strange. The whole thing. I just can't believe that something I did caused all this. That the man following my father comes from this street."

"This street," Rafiz said, "is at the center. It is the dry river that runs through the dry city. Everything comes from this street and soaks through the rest of the city, becoming weaker and weaker as it gets further from the center. We stand," he said, gesturing broadly, "at the very heart."

Casey looked at him, trying not to show her amazement. She had never heard him speak so poetically.

"Would you—may I show you around today?" he said. "We could see the marketplace, would you like that?"

After his outburst of eloquence he sounded almost shy. And Casey felt sorry that she had ignored him for so long. She felt ashamed that she had come back only because she had wanted something from him, and that he had been so eager to help despite the way she had acted toward him. So what if he believed in those silly superstitions? That was his problem, not hers. "Sure," she said.

"Wonderful!" he said, standing up quicker than she thought he'd be able to.

Twenty-fifth November Street: 3

The tourists brought the paper money of Amaz to Twenty-fifth November Street but the shopkeepers had a different currency. In the evenings, after the stores had closed and the tourists had gone away, they would visit each other and sip coffee and rum and exchange stories. Something that could be expanded to epic size happened nearly every week on the street, and if it didn't someone always made something up.

When Zem the One-eared showed up on the street five versions of how he had lost his ear appeared within the week. No one knew the true story, but to the inhabitants of Twenty-fifth November Street that didn't matter. What mattered was how the stories grew and were embellished, like silver filigree, in the hands of the master story-tellers. Blue Rose thought that a jealous girlfriend had cut the ear off. Someone else was sure that Zem had been marked by one or another of the criminal groups in the city for failing to do something for them.

Zem worked as a handyman. He didn't live on the street as Rafiz did, but in the month after he arrived he got more jobs than he could handle, even taking over some of Rafiz's. But he never told anyone how he lost the ear, and he was nowhere near as meticulous as Rafiz, and after a while the odd jobs stopped and he drifted away again. He came back three months later, made some money and left again, and came back at odd intervals after that, establishing an eccentric rhythm, a kind of counterpoint to Rafiz's stately reliable pattern. After a while interest in how he lost the ear dwindled to the point where if you asked people on the street to describe him, the missing ear might be one of the last things they would mention.

The truth was that Zem never told the story to anyone because he didn't understand it himself. He was born during the years of dream-lessness, and while his mother never suffered from the strange sickness Zem as a child didn't dream until he was six or seven. His mother came from the country, where the sickness was not as severe as in the city, and she never recognized the symptoms of the disease in Zem—the glazed eyes, the inattentiveness, the long periods of sleep, sometimes as much as twenty hours a day. She worked long hours as a housecleaner, leaving Zem alone in their own house, and she had no one to tell her that other children didn't sleep so much, other children weren't so quiet. Zem's father had left her before Zem was born.

When Zem began finally to dream he didn't understand what the dreams were. He thought that they were another kind of life, a night life; that everyone had seen the tigers walk down the center of the street and that the crack that broke down the side of the house during the night had been quickly repaired before day.

Then the terrifying dreams of childhood began. He woke night after night, hoarse with screaming and covered with sweat, from dreams where snakes had crawled out from under his mattress or his mother had changed into an unrecognizable monster. His mother couldn't understand why her child should suddenly have such bad dreams. He tried to keep himself awake every night, but every night he lost the battle and fell into what he was starting to think of as the pit.

One night he had a dream worse than any of the others. He had been warned not to go in the crawl space underneath the house, but somehow he was there, and strange night animals walked or crawled or flew in a circle around him. They thought he was protected, but he wasn't, and he knew that when they found out he would be killed. Already the circle was spiraling inward. He tried to keep his eyes on one animal, a giant leathery bird that spit poison, but it kept disappearing and then appearing again in front of him.

"We know a secret," a snake said, starting to move close to him.

"What?" he said, stepping backward.

"Ahhh," the snake said. "We can't tell you."

"Why—why not?" he said.

"Why should we tell you?" the snake said. "Have you ever done anything for us?"

The leather bird swooped in front of him, and when he looked back at the snake he saw that a giant spider had come within inches of his foot. He jerked back again. "I will!" he said loudly. "What do you want me to do? I'll do anything. Tell me the secret."

"Ahhh," the snake said. "You can give us a gift."

"Anything," he said. "Anything you want. What's the secret?"

"The secret is," the snake said, coming closer, close enough so that its tongue licked at his ear, "we aren't real. We're inside your head. But now, what can you give us? You have nothing."

He looked around and saw that it was true. Even his clothes were gone, and he stood naked, cringing, in front of the animals. "Nothing!" the bird said, and the other animals took it up as a chant, hissing or barking or cawing. "Nothing! Nothing! Nothing!"

"This ear is very nice," the snake said, coming even closer. "Yes, very nice. We will take this ear in exchange for our secret." All the animals moved nearer, hemming him in. He felt a terrible pain, and then a sharp throbbing where the ear had been, and he woke up screaming.

He lay still for a moment, listening to his mother getting up in the next room. The snake wasn't real. All the animals and everyone in the night life weren't real. That explained why no one else ever saw the snakes under the bed or the tigers in the street. It was all inside his head, he thought, relieved.

He put his hand to his ear and felt the startling absence just as his mother came into the room.

He never had nightmares again. The snakes, the leather bird and the other night monsters never returned. His mother blamed herself for the missing ear, thought that he had injured himself somehow while she was away cleaning houses. He couldn't ask her, couldn't ask anyone, didn't know the words to ask. But he thought about that night for the rest of his life, sometimes believing one thing, sometimes another. Had the snake been telling the truth or not? And if it had, what had happened to his ear?

Since then he found it difficult to distinguish between dreams and reality, and when Blue Rose asked him to break into the house of the American tourist he agreed immediately. Tourists definitely belonged to the night life, the dream world. They spoke a dream language, wore dream clothes, had more money than anyone Zem knew in the waking world. There could be nothing wrong with robbing a dream person.

He didn't find the manuscript Blue Rose was looking for, but his work must have been acceptable to her because she hired him on for another job. This time he was to follow the tourist and his friend. He hesitated only enough to wonder if he should ask her how much the job would pay or wait for her to tell him. The only problem with the dream people, Zem thought, would be if they disappeared while he was following them.

Blue Rose told him how much she would pay. It was agreeable, enough so that he could leave the street again and go back to the gambling district. Money was another thing Zem was pretty sure belonged to the dream world: it came and went of its own volition, had nothing to do with him. He could never understand why people told him to stop gambling.

A few evenings later Zem visited Blue Rose and was invited upstairs for coffee. Zem told her about following the American tourist through the marketplace and across the city. He mentioned that he had gotten a friend to help him in case the tourist and the smaller man split up, hoping Blue Rose would suggest a raise in pay. She said nothing. He went on, telling her about the man's strange behavior by the wall. "They were talking that weird tourist language so I couldn't really understand them," Zem said. "But they seemed to be happy about something, happy about finding the wall, I guess, though as far as I could tell it was just another ruin. It seemed silly to me. Why should they care about a bunch of old rocks?"

He had hoped to phrase the question more subtly, but it didn't sound too bad now that it was out. Why was Blue Rose interested in this man, and why was the man wandering around the city looking at old ruins, instead of spending his time like all the other tourists at the far more impressive ruins to the north, or at the beaches? Even more important, was there money in it for him? He knew Blue Rose was a real person who had a real existence in the waking world, so he couldn't cheat her. Maybe they could come to some sort of deal, not bribery exactly, just a sort of arrangement. But Blue Rose said nothing.

"And that's it," Zem said. "They went to a pastry shop and sat and talked, and then they went home."

"What did they talk about?" Blue Rose asked.

Zem shrugged. "I told you, I don't speak their language," he said. In fact he had not dared to follow them inside, worried that the tourist might have spotted him earlier. But he couldn't tell Blue Rose that.

"Did they seem happy in the pastry shop too?" Blue Rose asked.

"Oh, yeah," Zem said. "Very happy."

"Good," Blue Rose said. She thought a moment and then said, "I want you to keep following this man. He'll probably go back to the wall and start out from there, so if you lose him you can pick him up again at the wall. But don't lose him."

Zem nodded. She dismissed him and he went downstairs into the shadowed shop, wondering how he could find out more about this man.

The Jewel King's Tomb

*T*he spy from Borol saluted the king's guards and walked uncontested into the king's chambers. The king of Marol lay on the canopied bed, asleep. The spy brushed aside his long robe and touched the jeweled hilt of his curved dagger. He unsheathed the dagger and—

Angie sat back, her pen still poised over her notebook. If the king of Marol died, then of course the war was over. And then what? The army of Borol would come marching in, and some in Marol would be executed and some promoted, and that would be the end. There were long weeks to go before school started, and what would she do until then? The war was supposed to have taken her through September, at least.

She wished Casey were here. Casey would know what to do next. Well, suppose the spy couldn't get to the king. Suppose he killed someone else, someone like— She gasped.

Both she and Casey had taken on the roles of some of the people in the Two Kingdoms. Angie was Andara, the king of Borol's daughter. She saw a spy from Marol salute the king's daughter's guards, saw him stand over her as she lay asleep on the canopied bed, saw him finger the dagger's hilt. A thrill went through her like a wave.

Last week they had been walking home from the McDonald's when a car had sped around the corner, overshot the street and came up on the curb. Her father had reached over and pulled her out of the way, and her first thought, after she saw that the car had gone and she was in no danger, had been, Too bad it didn't hit me.

Something had gone wrong with the configurations of her family, with the way they interacted. Even she, spending most of her time dreaming over the histories of Borol and Marol, could see that. They were tied in a terrible four-way knot now, and none of them could break away without tearing one or more of the others loose. They could only chafe against each other, living so close that the wounds they caused never healed.

But if she died, that might change. If she were gone the knot would weaken, might slip apart entirely. Maybe they'd even miss her. She saw Casey open the black notebooks of Borol and Marol, take up the history where she left off. The picture was irresistible; Angie held it in front of her for a long time, feeling a strange combination of pleasure and pain, before coming back to the idea of her death as a way to heal her family.

She felt death open up within her like a new, undiscovered country. And yet the impulse had been with her for a long time. Once, a long time ago, even before she and Casey had invented the lands of Borol and Marol, she had stood by the road at midnight and tried to hitch a ride. A neighbor had found her and brought her home. Her parents had been more puzzled than angry. "What on earth were you thinking of?" her mother had asked. I wanted to make you notice me, she'd thought then. Now she realized that that had been her first hesitant answer to the question of death.

She wrote in the notebook, and Andara lay still on the canopied bed, her red blood painting a new pattern on the embroidered sheets.

As Mitchell's cab dropped him off at the ruined marble wall he saw that Jara had gotten there first and was walking back and forth in his impatience. "Come," Jara said to him. "I have marked where we must go today. Today we will look for the tomb."

Mitchell nodded. He felt tired even before he began.

"The tomb is described as being of marble and gold," Jara said. "From this tomb it is said that the Jewel King will come again when Amaz has need of him. He was buried in his gold-and-purple robes of state, and with his sword in his right hand so that he could go into battle immediately. Of course, all the gold on the tomb will probably have been stolen."

At least Jara, who seemed to become more certain of extravagant finds every day, did not expect to find the tomb whole and unplundered.

"So," Jara said, taking his map and compass from his briefcase. "The epic says that the knights bore their dead king secretly and at night from the palace after his defeat in battle there, and that they went westward. It was dawn when they buried him and marked the spot so that they could come back and build the tomb. So we must go in that direction," Jara said, pointing, "and we must walk all day."

They walked nearly an hour without speaking, following a spidery line on Jara's map. Once Mitchell thought he saw at least one man, and possibly two, following them. Finally he said, "You know, this story about the Jewel King returning to help his people—it's a lot like the story of King Arthur."

"Yes, and the myths of other peoples, too," Jara said. "I wrote my thesis about that."

"Well, what I mean is," Mitchell said, "this tomb might not exist. People have a need to believe that their great heroes will come again. So they invent—"

"What do you mean?" Jara asked. "We found the palace, yes?"

"Yes, but this tomb—it sounds like something tacked on to the end of a more-or-less historical account," Mitchell said. "After the

Jewel King died and the people wanted him to come back. I mean, look—how could the knights build an elaborate tomb like the epic says they did if the whole country had been conquered? Wouldn't they be running for their lives instead?"

"They built the tomb later," Jara said. "Much later."

"They'd be a bunch of old men by then," Mitchell said.

"Yes," Jara said. "They would."

Mitchell walked silently for a while. Everyone in this country seems to win arguments by agreeing with you, he thought. It must be a rhetorical trick the rest of the world hasn't discovered yet. "They haven't found Avalon," he said, trying again.

"They think that Glastonbury—"

"Avalon was an island."

"They think that Glastonbury was an island at one time," Jara said.

"How could Glastonbury have been an island?" Mitchell asked, feeling a little uncertain now. This wasn't his field. He sifted through recorded folk tales and old manuscripts. What the hell was he doing out in the hot midday sun looking for a tomb he was pretty sure didn't exist?

"Waters shift," Jara said. "The land changes."

A truck painted in camouflage jungle colors took the corner in front of them too fast and went up on two wheels. Mitchell watched it push through the congested traffic, saved by its presence from having to come up with an answer. As it passed them Mitchell thought he saw a soldier aim a rifle down the street out of one of the rear windows of the truck.

Jara saw him staring after it. "Soldiers," he said.

"Where are they going?" Mitchell asked. "You're not at war, are you?"

"The communists," Jara said. "Up in the mountains. People say they are going to invade again."

"Communists?" Mitchell said, feeling slow and stupid. No one had mentioned communists when the university had invited him to Amaz. Had he brought his family into danger? But Jara didn't seem too concerned. Mitchell took one last look back at the truck, thinking that the jungle colors were not going to be much use in this desert country, and then followed Jara.

Several hours later they stopped at a pastry shop for sweet bread and coffee. "What's curious," Jara said, "is the way the epic places emphasis on the sword. It is almost as if the manuscript's sole purpose is to give us directions. We are being led somewhere. We are being told to be on a specific street at a specific time of day. It is almost as if the story itself is secondary."

Mitchell looked around him, thinking that this pastry shop could be the same one they ate at the last time. People sat at small round tables or on cushions on the floor, talking, gesturing, showing no sign that they would ever move that day or maybe even the day after. Next to Mitchell sat a man in wide trousers and an old-fashioned ribbed shirt, adding numbers on a solar calculator, talking to a man in a turban across the table from him. That's the first person in a turban I've seen outside of our street, he thought. I wonder if Jara knows who they are. But what had Jara been saying? "Well, I thought it was directions when I found it," Mitchell said. "I told you that."

"Yes, but more than directions," Jara said. "There is a purpose to our being here, on this street at this time, even if we are going away from the sword. Maybe if we were not here at this time we would never find it. Do you feel that?"

"No," Mitchell said. Now Jara was starting to sound like Tamir, attributing mysterious qualities to perfectly ordinary things like maps, streets, directions, though he would be outraged to hear Mitchell say it. What was it about Amaz that turned everyone into a mystic, that encouraged nonlinear thinking? "Not really."

"Ah, well," Jara said. "We are nearing the end of our quest. I can feel it. Maybe when we hold in our hands the sword you will understand what I mean."

"Maybe," Mitchell said.

"I hope so," Jara said.

The sun was falling before them when they started out again, sinking through the hot layer of smog covering the city and staining the west the color of red wine. Outside of the one glimpse he'd had at the beginning of their walk Mitchell hadn't seen the men who had followed them last time. He thought of Jara's odd little speech, thought about maps and signs and directions. A strong, irrational feeling came over him, a feeling that the two men he'd seen last time were plotting their own course through the city, following their own map, writing their own signature, were even now one street or two streets over, gliding past twilit stores and houses on some incomprehensible errand of their own. Why not? It seemed to be the way things worked here in Amaz. Everything seemed to run somehow parallel to him, and he ended up only finding out what things meant much later, if at all. The young student who meets you at the airport turns out to be your co-worker. The house where you live turns out to be a church. Perhaps Jara was right. Perhaps there was a reason for them to be on this street at this time, and if so perhaps there was a reason for the other two men to be on other streets at the same time.

Mitchell shook his head. It was getting late; the same strain of mysticism he had seen in Dr. Tamir was beginning to infect him. The streets grew darker and a few of the cars turned on their lights. He stopped and looked at his watch. "It's almost night," he said. "I've got to get home for dinner."

"Good," Jara said. "We will meet here again tomorrow."

"Meet where?" Mitchell said. "Where the hell are we?"

"I think," Jara said, looking around, "we are near Gaudi Park. Yes. The park is two blocks in that direction."

"I don't know where that is," Mitchell said.

Jara took a pen and a piece of paper out of his briefcase, sat down with the briefcase in his lap and wrote out long and elaborate instructions. "Tomorrow, then," he said.

Mitchell nodded wearily and hailed a cab.

He let himself into Dr. Tamir's house feeling discouraged and tired and very hungry. No one said anything as they went out for dinner, not even Casey, who was usually the most talkative. When they got back Angie went to her room and Claire to the kitchen, and Mitchell sat on one of the hard wooden benches in the living room and paged through a Xerox copy Jara had made of the manuscript. "Dad," Casey said. "I have to tell you something."

Mitchell looked up. Casey pulled one of the benches over and sat on it facing him. "Sure," he said, feeling absurdly pleased. "What have you been up to? How was your day?" He sounded inane to himself, and probably to Casey too.

"Well," she said, "you know I have this pen pal. Rafiz. And—"

"Hey!" Angie said, running into the living room.

"And I went to see him today, because—"

"Look outside!" Angie said. Her voice sounded different, more alert somehow. They went to the heavy wooden door and pushed it open. Across the street, in front of a bonfire, the men and women who stared at the house were moving, swaying slowly first to one side and then the other, their arms raised as if they were reaching for something. The blue and red skirts of the women rippled as though moved by a breeze.

"Well, look at that," Mitchell said. "I wonder what that is."

"Maybe it's a holiday today," Casey said.

"Maybe," Mitchell said. "Jara didn't say anything about it."

Claire came out of the kitchen and joined them at the door. The movements of the dancers became slower, the dancers' arms dropped gracefully, and the dance stopped. "Well, isn't that interesting," Mitchell said. The bonfire guttered low. The dancers walked into the fire, stomping it out energetically, the women lifting their skirts above their knees. "I'll have to ask Jara about it tomorrow."

He closed the door. Behind him he heard Angie and Claire leave the living room and go back to whatever it was they had been doing. When he turned around he saw that Casey had gone too. Hadn't she wanted to tell him something? He shrugged and went back to the manuscript.

A few hours later, stopped by a word he didn't understand and that wasn't in his dictionary, he remembered Casey again. He walked down the corridor to her room and opened the door. Light from the corridor fell on his daughter, asleep in bed with half the blankets off. He felt the same welling of love he'd felt at seeing her at the airport, even stronger this time. It's easy to love your kids when they're asleep, he thought.

Casey opened her eyes. "Come on in, Dad," she said. "I'm awake."

He went inside carefully, picking his way through the room by the dim light from the corridor. In the dark he couldn't find a chair, and he sat on the edge of the bed the way he used to do when she was much younger. She's really too old for this, he thought, but he didn't get up.

"Do you think people will ever be immortal?" she asked.

"I don't know," he said. "Someday, I guess. Maybe."

"Yeah, but soon?" She rolled over and sat up, leaning against the wall, blinking sleepily. She wrapped the blanket around her. "I mean, in my lifetime? See, if there's a chance I could live forever I'd be able to arrange my life differently. I could study everything I want to study, not just one or two things. I wouldn't have to go into physics immediately, the way I'm planning to do now. But if I'm going to live a finite amount of time I'd better start with physics right away, because there's a lot I have to learn. What do you think?"

"I don't know," Mitchell said again. "It's not my field."

"See, I'd like to do some writing, too," she said. "Maybe fiction, maybe nonfiction, I'm not sure yet. And I was considering astrophysics instead of the field I wanted to go into, which was—"

Mitchell laughed.

"What's funny about that?" Casey said. He thought she sounded a little hurt.

"Nothing," Mitchell said quickly. "I was just thinking—the word 'consider'—it means 'to know the stars' in Latin."

"Really?" Casey said. "Oh, of course. Like sidereal. But what do you think? There's lots of new stuff going on in astronomy. I mean, it's a good field to get into right now, isn't it?"

Mitchell almost said "I don't know" again. She wanted something, though, or she wouldn't have asked nearly the same question twice. "You really don't have to decide all of that now," Mitchell said. "There's enough time for that when you grow up."

She didn't move, and Mitchell knew that that wasn't the answer she wanted. It was odd how everyone in the family used gestures, silences, as a kind of shorthand to express the things they couldn't say aloud. Like a Chinese character, he thought, one symbol standing for a whole complex issue. "I'm sure you'll do fine whatever you decide," he said. "I know I don't have to worry about you."

She stirred slightly. New patterns of light and shadow formed on the blanket, a map Mitchell couldn't read. "You never worry about me, Dad, do you?"

"No, why should I?" Mitchell said. "You've always been able to take care of yourself."

"What about Angie? Do you think she's able to take care of herself?"

"Well," Mitchell said. "She's going through a stage right now. You went through it too, remember? All that writing in all those notebooks. You outgrew it."

"Yeah, but I'm younger than she is."

"I think she'll be okay," he said. "We just have to be patient with her. What are you saying—that there's something wrong with her? Do you think we should try another psychologist?"

"No, not a psychologist," Casey said. She hesitated, and he thought, Now. Now she's coming to it. Everything up to this point, all her talk about immortality, astronomy, her future and Angie's, had been leading up to this, to something she wanted to say about her sister. But she would never criticize directly, because that was not the way the family worked. If they started criticizing they would never have time for anything else. A can of worms, he thought, and then wondered where that expression came from. It had to be fairly recent. How long had cans been around? But Casey was saying something. "But she's been acting weird lately, weirder than usual. She doesn't go outside, not ever."

"Well, this is a foreign country, after all. You have to remember it's very different from what she's used to, the language, the customs. She might be afraid to go out."

"Mom goes outside."

"Well, your mother's more adventurous than Angie."

"Is she?" Casey said. "She never was at home."

Another can of worms, another issue skirted. Claire had stayed indoors so much that when Mitchell had run across an article about agoraphobia in one of her women's magazines he had immediately thought of her. Surreptitiously he had filled out the accompanying test for her and discovered that she had five out of the ten symptoms listed. One of his reasons for bringing his family to Amaz had been to get Claire out of the house. At least that had worked out, he thought. "Well," he said. "People change."

"And you think Angie will change too?" Casey said. "I saw that article you were looking at at home, the one on agoraphobia. Maybe Mom's not agoraphobic, but do you think Angie is?"

Did she read his mind? She was a spooky kid in some ways. "Angie will be all right," he said. "Listen—didn't you have something you wanted to tell me?"

"Oh, yeah," Casey said. "Right." She hesitated again, but this time Mitchell thought it was unplanned, that she might be out of her depth. "The man you thought was following you. Was he missing an ear?"

"Yes," Mitchell said, surprised. Of all the things he'd thought she'd say he had never imagined this. And how could she possibly know? Spooky. "Yes, he was. How do you know?"

"Well," she said. Another pause. "Well, you know my pen pal, Rafiz. I wrote him, I stupidly wrote him about the manuscript you found, and about the Jewel King, and all that."

"You mean Rafiz is following me?" he asked. He had never given any thought to Casey's pen pal, and now he wondered why he hadn't. Didn't other fathers worry about their daughters going off with unsuitable men? How were you supposed to know all this stuff? There weren't any books you could read. Suddenly he remembered the camouflage truck and the communists he'd seen that afternoon. It seemed there were dangers besetting his daughter from all sides. He wanted to tell her to be careful, to stop her adventures in the city, at least until he found out more, but he knew he couldn't say anything. One of the things he had always admired about his daughter was her independence.

"Not Rafiz," she said. "He thinks someone opened his mail, a woman he works for named Blue Rose. And she's been talking to this man with one ear."

"But what do they want?" he asked. "Why would they want to follow me?"

"We think they might want the manuscript," she said. "Or maybe the sword. To sell. Blue Rose—she owns a kind of antique shop."

"Great," he said. As if he didn't have enough problems. He thought of the break-in, of his accusations to Jara, and realized he would have to make his apologies to him tomorrow. "Well, what do I do? You don't have any proof, do you? I can't go to the police without proof."

"Rafiz is going to talk to Blue Rose," Casey said. "And he said you might want to hire a—a bodyguard. I'm sorry."

She hates being wrong, Mitchell thought. He had never realized that before. It must be rough having everyone think you know all the answers. "It's all right," he said. "It's not your fault. You couldn't know someone was going to read this guy's mail." He shook his head. A bodyguard. What next? "Well, tell me what happens," he said.

A Trip to the Ruins

*M*itchell shifted noisily into first gear, and Casey, watching him from the back seat, wondered how long it had been since he'd driven a stick shift. All the family cars she could remember had been automatics, but the rental place only had uneven rows of identical dusty Volkswagen Rabbits.

The family was silent as Mitchell drove the car out of the lot and into traffic. A car honked loudly behind them. It was probably a victory, Casey thought, that they were going on this trip at all, but she couldn't help contrasting her family with the picture of an ideal family she had picked up somewhere. They were supposed to have packed a picnic lunch, for one thing, and they should be singing silly songs. Her mother held the open map on her lap, which was proper behavior for the mother of the ideal family, but she hadn't referred to it once. Though at least she was looking out the window. Angie hadn't looked up from the floor since the trip began.

They headed through the congested traffic toward the mountains. The houses grew smaller, shabbier, older. At the foot of the mountains they barely looked like houses at all but like some kind of weird mechanical growth made of scraps of corrugated iron, mangled car bodies and large cardboard boxes. A green scar, where water had once flowed and might flow again when the rains came, divided the sad village. People sat in the little shade of the houses, their faces as solid and unreadable as a blank piece of paper. A goat stood on a rock, not moving.

Casey looked out at the village with amazement and horror, wondering what it would be like to have grown up here. No school, no medical care, not enough food, probably no hope for the future. They passed a ravine filled with garbage—rusted bedsprings, beer cans and wads of old paper—and then headed down, away from the village. Now they could see only burnt scrub and small dirt trails leading away on either side of them.

Mitchell reached for the dashboard, and for a moment Casey thought he was going to turn on the radio. Instead the air-conditioner came on laboriously. They rolled up all the windows but the car seemed hotter, if anything. "The hell with it," Mitchell said, opening his window.

The road leveled out. Finally they rounded a bend and saw the ocean, turquoise near the shore and darker blue farther out. They passed one hotel, then a small group of them, then a solid row of taller hotels standing like teeth near the water's edge. "What hotel are we staying at?" Mitchell asked.

Claire said nothing. "The Americana," Casey said.

"Did we pass it?" Mitchell asked.

"I don't think so," Casey said. "No, there it is, up ahead." Mitchell pulled into the hotel's parking lot.

It seemed strange to step into the hotel's clean, air-conditioned lobby, as though they had somehow been transported back to the United States. The lobby was completely deserted, with the unreal quiet of a library. They got their room key and took the elevator to their floor. Casey almost laughed out loud when she heard the Muzak in the elevator, "Raindrops Keep Falling on My Head."

In the room they changed into swimsuits and went down to the beach. Casey saw the Wileys first, stretched out side by side on a large fluffy white towel. As they came closer Mrs. Wiley rolled over and sat up. She was wearing a gold one-piece bathing suit cut high on her thighs.

"I'm so glad you could make it," she said. "Especially since we're going home in three days."

Casey and her family spread their motley assortment of towels. Claire hung back, making sure that at least one other person stood between her and the Wileys. Of course, Casey thought. She hasn't had her drink yet. She's nervous. Mitchell looked back at Claire as if waiting for her to answer, and Casey realized how much he depended on his wife to carry on conversations, to smooth over any social awkwardness. How much he depended on her to become the person she was after a few drinks. Funny how families worked, she thought.

"I hadn't realized you were leaving so soon," Mitchell said finally.

"Not soon enough for me," Mrs. Wiley said. "What with the communists just waiting up in the mountains."

"The communists?" Mitchell said. "Do you really think they're a threat?"

"Oh, yes, very much so," she said. "Don't you listen to the radio?"

Mitchell laughed a little. "Not enough, apparently," he said. "But in the city no one takes them seriously."

"Well, they sure as hell take them seriously here," she said. "Our hotel is almost deserted. And one or two of them down the beach have had to close, I hear."

"Really, Mitchell." Mr. Wiley sat up next to his wife. He had a long scar an inch wide running down his breastbone—a heart operation, Casey thought. "If I were you I'd take your family and go home. This man, Commander Cumaq, he's serious. He's ready to invade any day, they say."

"I'll think about it," Mitchell said. "I'd hate to have to leave now, just when my work is going so well. But I'll listen to the radio more, I promise you."

"Do more than think about it," Mr. Wiley said. "Remember, you're in a country that has no formal ties to the United States to begin with."

Mrs. Wiley stood up. "Want to go into the water?" she said.

"I have to go to the bathroom," Claire said. She got up and went back toward the hotel. Mitchell and Casey watched the Wileys, tanned and athletic, walk out to the ocean, careful not to look back at Claire, careful not to acknowledge that they knew what she really wanted at the hotel. They had both seen the bar just off the lobby.

The Wileys walked without hesitation into the water. What a strange juxtaposition, Casey thought. The communists up in the mountains and the luxurious white hotels down here along the ocean. But then it was all strange, and nothing was stranger than the sight of her family, pale and unexercised, lying on a beach among the carefully maintained bodies of the American tourists. The only one among them with a good body was Angie, and she had hidden it away in a bulky black swimsuit. All in all they looked like a illustration out of one of those kid's books: What Is Wrong with This Picture?

Claire came back from the hotel at the same time the Wileys returned from their swim and began to talk to them animatedly. Disgusted, Casey went down the beach to the water.

In the late afternoon Casey and her family went back to their room to change and then downstairs to meet the Wileys in the lobby. The Wileys had promised to show them the best restaurant on the beach.

The family waited silently in the lobby. Casey had tried to get Angie to put on suntan lotion but she hadn't listened, and as a result her nose and arms had turned the color of bubble gum. Claire walked a little loosely; she had made a number of trips back to the hotel during the day. She greeted the Wileys enthusiastically when they stepped out of the elevator, and the two families went outside.

The restaurant turned out to be in another hotel farther up the street. Inside the restaurant, on a small stage to one side, a woman backed by a six-piece band sang songs in Lurqazi and English. She wore the bright colors of the women of Amaz, but she had raised the hemline of the skirt and added a slit down the side and lowered the neckline of the blouse. A spotlight followed her as she walked back and forth.

Claire ordered a glass of wine as soon as she sat down. "What are you going to do when you get back to the United States?" she asked Mrs. Wiley.

"Oh, I don't know," Mrs. Wiley said. "Probably nothing for a while, just lie back and listen to people speak English. We have some relatives in New Orleans, we might go visit them."

The waiter came with Claire's wine and she drank half of it in one swallow. "It must be nice," she said. "Having a husband who's retired. So you can do anything you want." She looked at Mitchell almost slyly out of the corner of her eyes, but Mitchell, busy studying the menu, didn't see her. Casey saw her, though, and suddenly she wished she could be anywhere else but in the restaurant with her family. She had seen that look before and knew what it meant: that her mother had reached a point where she might say anything.

"Oh, it is," Mrs. Wiley said.

"Not that I'd want Mitchell to retire, of course," Claire said. "God knows what I'd do with him hanging around the house all day. It's bad enough when he's there on the weekends."

"Are we going to see the ruins tomorrow?" Casey said.

"Sure," Mitchell said, looking up from his menu, puzzled. He never sees these things coming until they're right on top of him, Casey thought. "I said we would this morning."

"He works a lot of evenings," Claire said. "Did your husband work in the evenings before he retired, Betty?"

Mrs. Wiley shrugged. "No, not that much," she said.

"Or at least that's what he says he's doing," Claire said. "I don't know, it's all a mystery to me."

"Do you know what you want to order, Claire?" Mitchell said. He's got it, Casey thought. Finally.

"Did you know I used to be a physicist?" Claire asked Mrs. Wiley. "Well, I was studying physics, anyway. I couldn't do any work because I got married and started having babies." She looked vaguely at Casey and Angie, as if unable to connect them with the babies she remembered.

Angie was doodling on a napkin in front of her. "Help me," Casey said to Angie in Bordoril. "Stop her." Angie looked up briefly and then went back to her doodles.

"So I wouldn't exactly say that it was Mitchell who put a stop to my career," Claire said. "He was the one who wanted to get married, though. And then we had the kids. I told him once, I said, you know, Mitchell, I feel my whole life just went nowhere. If I hadn't gotten married during college I could have done something with my life, worked on something important. And you know what he said to me?" Her voice had gotten louder. People at the neighboring tables were turning to stare. "He said maybe I should see some kind of counselor. As though the whole thing wasn't his fault. As though he could make a mess and then go away and have someone else clean it up for him. But that's the story of his life. I mean, he did the same thing with his kids. Look at Angie over there. Angie's never going to say one word to us her entire life. Are you, Angie?" She went on without waiting for an answer. "And whose fault is that? I mean, who's responsible for that?"

"Hush, Claire," Mitchell said. "Claire, please be quiet."

Claire finished her drink and stared at the empty glass. When she started speaking again, it was in a voice so quiet Casey could barely hear her. "Did your husband make you give up your career when you got married, Betty?" she asked. "Did he make you start having kids?"

"We decided not to have any kids," Mrs. Wiley said. "It's Al's second marriage. He's already got a family."

"Second marriage," Claire said. Her eyes closed. "Must be nice." She put her head down on the table, barely missing the empty wineglass. "God, I'm sleepy."

"Why don't I take you back to the hotel, Claire?" Mitchell said. "You can go to sleep there."

"I can sleep here," Claire said. "Oh, this is nice."

"Come on," Mitchell said. He pulled her to her feet and put his arm around her. "Let's go," he said as he led her out of the room. Someone laughed loudly after they had gone.

Casey looked at the menu for a long time, pretending she was not at the restaurant with her sister and two people she barely knew but out with Rafiz. Finally Mrs. Wiley broke the silence. "So," she said, "what grade are you in?"

"I'll be going to the university next year when we get back," Casey said.

From the look Mrs. Wiley gave her it was clear that she didn't believe her and was insulted at having been lied to. Casey returned to her menu and no one said another word in the long minutes it took Mitchell to get back.

Claire had a headache the next morning and declined to go to the ruins, and Angie said loudly that if Claire wasn't going she didn't see why she had to. So it was only Casey and Mitchell who signed up for the hotel's tour and waited in the lobby with four other guests until the bus pulled up.

The man who had signed them up escorted them out to the air-conditioned bus. "Only six?" Casey heard the driver say to him in Lurqazi.

The other man answered him, shrugged and went back into the hotel. Obviously they had expected more people. Were tourists really staying away because of the communists? Casey had discounted everything Mrs. Wiley had said just because it had been Mrs. Wiley who had said it, but now, looking around, she wondered if the shallow woman could have been right. She went down the aisle and took a seat next to Mitchell.

The bus drove past the row of hotels, turned away from the water and headed out into the desert. After a few minutes she felt as if the air-conditioning had shut down, but the windows looked permanently sealed. The desert stretched away on all sides and drummed with heat.

She scowled and tried to get comfortable in the hot vinyl seat. It was all ridiculous anyway, trying to pretend that she had a normal family like everyone else. If the family were normal then her mother and Angie would be here, and everyone would be looking out the windows and pointing and laughing. Even the emptiness of the bus seemed somehow her family's fault, a reproach. They could never manage to get anything right.

"There it is," Mitchell said, pointing out the window.

A wall of marble, white as sea-foam, rose before them out of the desert. The driver pulled into the parking lot and opened the door. "The temple of Marmaz," he said. "I leave in one hour. One hour."

Casey and Mitchell got off the bus. A small group of natives who had been smoking cigarettes in the meager shade of the wall got up and headed toward them across the parking lot. "Silver?" one of them said, dangling a chain. "Cards?" said another. Casey thought they sounded as if their hearts weren't really in it. What would happen to these people when the tourists stopped coming?

"See that part, the portico?" Mitchell said, pointing to the ruins. "That was added three hundred years later. If you get up close you can see that the marble's a different color. By the time they added it they'd forgotten where the original builders had gotten the marble."

Casey walked on ahead, impatiently. In her ideal family Mitchell would have explained all about the temple to her and her mother and Angie, and the other tourists would have gathered around, amazed and delighted that they had an expert in their midst. Now that it was just her, though, she found she didn't want to listen to anything her father had to say. Damn her mother, anyway.

She went inside the cool marble building without looking to see if her father had followed. She wandered from room to room, looking at fragments of tapestries and mosaics, at the fountains and towers and red-and-green-tiled patterned floors, at the cracked domed ceiling open to the sky like an observatory. In one large white room she heard a guide's explanation of the dining hall echo off the far walls.

The guide looked at her, stumbled for a second and continued on with his speech. Then he herded his small group of tourists expertly through a crumbling doorway: "Careful, please, as you go through here. In the next room..." and Casey thought she must have imagined his hesitation. But as he followed the group through the doorway he motioned almost infinitesimally with his head, beckoning her to follow him. Annoyed—with him, with everything—she went in the opposite direction, back the way she had come.

She went through a room filled with statues, another room where every square inch of the marble walls had been carved, and then found herself back in the parking lot. She couldn't see her father anywhere. So that was the famous temple of Marmaz, the one she had begged her father to take them to every day for a week. Of course she might have enjoyed it more if her mother hadn't made that disgusting scene at the restaurant last night. That's the last time she gets away with something like that, Casey thought. She stood for a moment, enjoying her foul mood and the oppression of the heavy sun, until she became aware that someone was making his way toward her across the parking lot, shimmering with heat haze. The guide from the temple.

He reached her before she could make up her mind whether or not to walk away. "Hello," he said. "I saw you at the temple, do you remember? I have wondered if you have seen the last printing of the cards?"

"Yeah," Casey said, looking across the parking lot for her father.

"I do not wish to sell you anything," the guide said quickly. "But I wish to show you—to tell you that your picture is in this deck. And to ask you if you knew that. That the cards have mentioned you, that they say you are about to do something important."

"I've seen it," she said. "There's a picture of someone who looks like me."

"Look," the guide said, as if he hadn't heard her. He reached into his pants pocket and pulled out a deck held together by a rubber band. "See, here is the Traveler—" He shuffled through the cards. "And there is another strange thing, and that is that the Sun and Stars is missing. The card of good luck. It has not been missing for ten years. No, for longer than that. The last time we did not find it in the deck we had the big earthquake and then the fires."

"So what are you saying?" Casey said. "That we're going to have an earthquake because you can't find a card in the deck?"

"Maybe it is not an earthquake," he said. "But something big, some kind of change. And you are part of it. I have seen your picture in almost every deck for the past two months. Do you feel it? The change that is coming?"

"No," she said. "I'm sorry. I don't believe in stuff like cards."

"Ah," the guide said. "But the cards believe in you." He held up the Traveler as though it were the successful conclusion to a magic trick. Abruptly Casey realized that the card had changed since the last time she'd seen it, the last printing, that the girl in the picture was now wearing a blouse similar to one she had bought in the market a week ago. And someone stood behind her in the card, someone blonde—but it couldn't be Angie. Even if you believed in the cards it would take a leap of the imagination to think that Angie would ever do anything important. The guide turned the card over and slipped it into the deck. The strange pattern of lines on the back seemed to writhe like snakes.

"There's my father," Casey said. "I've got to go now."

"Be careful," the guide said, calling after her as she walked across the parking lot.

Casey and her father got on the bus. The other four tourists followed them, one of them putting his camera away in an expensive-looking leather box after he sat down. The bus backed up noisily and headed toward the hotel.

Without discussing it the family ordered dinner from room service that evening. The next morning they left the hotel without eating breakfast and without saying good-bye to the Wileys. As the car started up the mountains Mitchell turned the radio on and fiddled with the tuning knob. They heard flutes and bells playing in a minor key, a burst of static, a play in what sounded like Chinese and finally a news broadcast in English. "Some observers report as many as ten thousand troops camped in the mountains above the city," the announcer said in a British accent. "Among them is said to be the Russian-backed communist army, led by Commander Cumaq."

Mitchell snapped the radio off. "That's it," he said, taking his eyes off the road to look in the rearview mirror at Casey and Angie. "I don't want either one of you going outside when I'm not at home. We'll just have to wait until this thing blows over. And if it doesn't blow over we're going back to the United States. Do you hear me?"

Casey nodded. Angie said nothing, and Mitchell seemed to take her silence for assent. "Parenting," Casey whispered to Angie after he had turned his attention back to the road, their old word for those moments when Mitchell seemed to feel it was necessary to assert his authority. Angie didn't smile. And after a few minutes Casey began to feel depressed. Cooped up in the house all day with Claire and Angie, unable to go outside—what kind of a vacation would that be, anyway? Who knew how long something like this would last? And what if they had to go home?

A Trip into the Mountains

Claire was sitting at the kitchen table as though nothing had happened when Casey came in for breakfast the next day. A fat new hardcover book lay open to the first page in front of her. The radio played what sounded to Casey like an old English folk song. Claire looked up, nodded and went back to her book.

Casey got out milk and some of the sweet bread Claire had bought and sat at the table. A dysfunctional family, she thought, a term she had picked up from a psychology book. Claire took a sip of her drink. "Good morning," Casey said loudly to her mother.

Claire looked up briefly from her book again. "Too bad you

couldn't have come with us to the ruins," Casey said, feeling maliciousness rise within her like a black cloud.

Finally Claire put the book down. "Were they interesting?" she said.

"Oh, yeah," Casey said. "Very interesting. Lots of families there, taking the tours," she said, knowing she was lying, knowing her mother would never find out.

Claire smiled softly.

"Normal families," Casey said. Her blood beat against her skin as if it wanted to break through. She wanted to stop but something pushed her on. If only she could go outside, visit Rafiz, wander aimlessly through the city.

Claire went back to her book.

"Families where the mother doesn't embarrass her children every chance she gets," Casey said. All around her barriers were breaking down, the rules she'd lived with ever since she was a small child. A part of her stood aside and watched with amazement, wondering how far she was going to go. "Where the mother wants her kids. Happy families."

Claire felt for her drink without looking up. Casey moved the glass out of her reach. "Families where the mother doesn't drink so much," Casey said. "Or any of this other shit you do."

Claire looked up, her eyes and mouth vague. "What are you talking about, Casey?" she said evenly.

"You know what I'm talking about," Casey said. "The way you embarrassed all of us at the dinner with the Wileys. All those things you said, about how me and Angie ruined your life."

"Oh, come on," Claire said. Only her fingers, tapping on the tabletop, betrayed her nervousness. Casey moved her mother's drink farther away. "You're exaggerating. I didn't say anything about you and Angie."

"Oh, come on," Casey said, a vicious imitation of her mother. "How the hell do you know what you said?"

"Casey," Claire said, trying to sound stern. "I want you to stop talking like this. I won't have it, do you understand? I'll tell your father when he gets home. Whatever you have against me we can settle it then, reasonably, without you spreading all these lies about me."

"They're not lies and you know it," Casey said. "You don't remember the dinner at all, do you? All you remember is waking up the next day with a hangover."

"The subject is closed," Claire said. She reached for her drink again, unaware that Casey had moved it to her side of the table. Her fingers jumped like grasshoppers. She looked down at her book. Casey would have bet anything she wasn't reading.

"The subject is not closed!" Casey said, almost yelling. She heard Angie scream something from her bedroom, what sounded like the Bordoril word for "stop." "You drink too much and you know it! If you want to wait till Dad gets home, fine, we'll wait. He'll just say the same thing. What do you think, that he hasn't noticed?"

Claire did not look up from her book. The hand not holding the book open clenched and unclenched.

"It would be fine if it was just you, if you were only ruining your own life," Casey said. "But it's everyone, all of us. You said Dad ruined Angie's life, but I think it was you. You were the one who didn't pay attention to her. To any of us. You're the selfish one."

Claire turned a page. Casey stood, shaking. She ran into the living room and out the front door, slamming the heavy wooden door hard on her way out.

Claire took a sip from her glass thoughtfully. That had been strange, she thought. She had never seen Casey so angry. Of course it hurt when your own daughter made accusations about you. But it wasn't true that she drank too much. If she drank too much she wouldn't be able to keep the house as clean as she did, or to buy groceries for four people, or to navigate her way to the English-language bookstore every so often. Mitchell would say the same thing. Just a few days ago, before they'd gone to the beach, she'd bought a delicate silver bracelet inlaid with stones for her sister. The bracelet had cost her about four dollars in American money. She'd like to see Casey find something that good. Would Casey have known precisely where to go among all the beggars and street merchants and marketplaces in the city?

The difference between me and Casey, she thought, feeling peace settle over her again, is the difference between the native and the tourist. Casey wants to see all the sights, the beaches, the ruins, but it's as if I live here. She's interested in the surface, but I go beneath that. So I didn't have to see the ruins with her and Mitchell, because that's for the tourists. That's just a show they put on. Even as a child, I wanted to know how the insides of watches worked, to see the backs of things. I was always running off into the Employees Only section of stores, or taking vacuum cleaners apart to see how they worked. And when I got interested in physics—but no, it's probably better not to think of that.

She smiled, thinking of all the places she had gotten into that she was not supposed to have seen: the back room at the post office, the employees' lunchroom at the amusement park. The surprised looks on the faces of salespeople and security guards. I haven't done that in a long time, she thought. What does the stockroom of the Super Shop look like? Where does Joe repair his cars? Well, but you get tired, you don't have as much energy as you used to. And raising two daughters—they've settled down now, but I had to watch them all the time when they were younger, especially Casey. It just gets easier to sit down, to conserve your strength. And after a few drinks you forget this need you have, this urgency to see the reality behind everything.

Casey. Claire closed the book and rubbed between her eyes. There had really been no reason for her to get mad like that. You never knew what might set people off. All of a sudden you found yourself blundering off into an area you never even realized was there. I know my way around this city better than I know my own daughter's mind, Claire thought, getting up to pour herself another drink. We're all tourists in each others' lives. We all have monuments and ruins, places of strange beauty and forbidden sites chained off and locked securely so that no visitor can get in. And none of us has the guidebook to anyone else, or even the list of most commonly used phrases. We just have to get along the best we can.

She went back to her book. When the announcer broke into the music for a news bulletin she was already on page sixty. "In a broadcast in London this morning the BBC announced that the army camped up in the mountains has started to move. Some observers report as many as ten thousand troops converging on the capital, among them the Russian-backed army led by Commander Cumaq. The government has denied the BBC story, calling it an unfounded rumor."

Oh my God, Claire thought, alarm breaking briefly through the haze surrounding her. Casey's out there. And shit, didn't Mitchell say something about her staying inside? What's he going to say when he gets back?

The haze returned, a soft golden web wrapping her close. She'll be okay, Claire thought. She's always been able to take care of herself. Claire took another sip of her drink and went back to her book.

The streets were less crowded than Casey had ever seen them. Even the group of men and women standing across the street seemed smaller. Casey remembered the Wileys' warning at the beach and thought about going back to Dr. Tamir's house. But she couldn't face her mother after the things she'd said. Everything would be different when she got back.

Now she noticed radios on all around her, in cars and taxis driving by, near groups of men and women squatting on the sidewalk, held close to their ears by people hurrying past. A family sat around a cooking fire, oblivious of the heat, a radio next to a pile of freshly caught fish. Even the turbanned people had a radio. She couldn't remember ever hearing a news broadcast in Lurqazi before; Rafiz had said that people in Amaz got their news from the cards. The entire street seemed to be holding its breath. Slowly, fighting the inertia she felt on every side of her, she went to the bus stop and waited for a bus.

A bus that she knew went to Twenty-fifth November Street came around the corner, and it was only then that she realized she was going to visit Rafiz. She motioned for it to stop and got on. Someone ran toward the bus, panting, and as Casey turned to look at him she realized that one of his ears was missing. The bus pulled away from the curb before the man reached it. Casey looked out the window and saw him run a little after the bus and then stop, looking disgusted.

The bus driver said something to her in Lurqazi. "What?" Casey said, first in English and then in Lurqazi. "One," the driver said, and she realized that he was asking her for her fare. She took a one with its disturbing picture of a fat coiled snake out of her purse and handed it to him. A boom box next to his seat was on but the announcer spoke too fast for her to understand him.

She walked down the aisle of the nearly empty bus and sat in front of a man wearing a startlingly white turban. Was Zem now following her instead of her father? What did he want? Or maybe that was someone else, just a poor guy running for the bus. There had to be more than one man missing an ear in Amaz. Still, Casey thought she would feel better if she could talk to Rafiz.

The radio crackled with static. Casey heard the word "Cumaq," the name of the commander of the communists up in the mountains.

The bus seemed to snake through every part of the city. They passed streets of burned-out rickety wooden houses and streets of houses fronted with marble and brass and screened from the road by fantastic cactus gardens. A long time later they came to Twenty-fifth November Street and Casey banged on the roof to be let off.

Twenty-fifth November Street was as empty as the rest of the city. All the junk that had grown like mechanical lawns in front of every shop had been taken inside. The tourists whose cameras and loud conversations in English and German and Japanese Casey had encountered everywhere in the city had disappeared from the street. She opened the door to Blue Rose's dim shop and stepped inside.

Blue Rose had a radio on too. "Excuse me," Casey said, speaking over the announcer and trying to see through the gloom.

Blue Rose looked up quickly. "Hello," she said. Casey thought she looked a little surprised to see her, but any visitor on a day like this would probably be unusual.

"Is Rafiz here?" Casey asked.

Blue Rose looked quickly at the curtain that led to the back of the store. "No, he's not here right now," she said. "Why don't you sit down and wait for him? He'll be back in a few minutes."

"Uh, no, thanks," Casey said. Zem and this woman worked together, she remembered, and Blue Rose seemed a little too eager to keep her there. Was Blue Rose waiting for Zem to return? Or was she just being paranoid? "I'll come back later. Tell him I stopped by, okay?"

"I wouldn't go home by myself if I were you," Blue Rose said as Casey backed toward the door. "Haven't you heard the news? We're about to be invaded from the mountains at any moment. I'm surprised your parents let you go out today."

They didn't, Casey thought. "I'll be okay," she said. "I got here all right."

"I'd feel much better if you'd wait for Rafiz to take you home," Blue Rose said. Her pale-blue gloves rubbed and twisted together, and, unbidden, a picture of her hands inside the gloves came to Casey, dry and white as chalk. "Or my assistant—he had to run a few errands, but he'll be back in a minute—I'm sure Zem wouldn't mind taking you home."

At the mention of Zem's name Casey knew she didn't want to wait in Blue Rose's shop. How long would it take Zem to get another bus? What if he decided to take a cab? "No, thanks," Casey said. "I'll be fine. Really." She opened the door and nearly ran to the bus stop. A few minutes later a cab drove by and she waved at it. The driver, she saw with surprise, was a short fat woman with gold coin earrings. Casey gave her the directions to Dr. Tamir's house and got inside.

Fifteen minutes later the cab stopped opposite the house. The heat felt oppressive, as if a thunderstorm were about to break at any minute. Casey stepped out of the cab. A man on the porch of Dr. Tamir's house stood up and she saw with horror that it was the same man who had run for the bus that morning. So he hadn't gone back to Blue Rose after all. She got back inside the cab. "Drive," she said in Lurqazi.

"Where?" the driver said, and then more words in Lurqazi she couldn't understand.

"I don't know," Casey said. The phrase book didn't cover this situation. She saw Zem hail a cab and get in it, pointing at her. "Please. Fast."

Zem's cab made a U-turn in the nearly empty street and ended up three cars behind her own. Her driver seemed to understand. She pulled away from the curb without looking, made a left and then two rights in quick succession. Zem's cab followed, a block behind them and then dropping back little by little. Her driver turned left and drove up onto the curb and through a part of the block burned out by fire. Casey looked back. Zem's cab followed them up the curb, a little closer now. Her cabdriver said something that sounded like a long string of curse words and sped up.

They took a corner on two wheels and Casey grabbed for the dashboard. The driver turned to her and said something in Lurqazi, grinning. "I don't understand," she said. She wished the driver would look back at the road. Zem's cab came around the corner. It had dropped back again.

They came up on Colonial House. A small group of people stood outside near the front porch. Tourists? Casey thought. Today? The cab swerved to avoid them and narrowly missed a horse-drawn cart coming toward them in the opposite lane. Someone outside Colonial House yelled after the cab and a few people raised banners. Protesters, Casey thought. The banners were in the old style of writing, like her father's manuscript.

Zem's cab headed straight for the protesters and they scattered. The cab came close enough for her to see Zem turn to the driver, to see the emptiness where his ear should have been. Then her driver stepped hard on the gas and they pulled ahead again.

They made a right turn between two houses and Casey saw that what had looked like a driveway widened out to become a dirt road. All the houses on this street had burned down in the fire, and Casey saw tents made of blankets and coats on either side of them. The street became smaller again, looped like string back and forth and finally seemed to turn in on itself. The driver held the wheel tightly, a look of hard determination on her face as they lurched over the rough streets. For the first time Casey couldn't see Zem's cab anywhere behind them.

They turned a corner and Casey saw Colonial House again. "He's gone, yes?" the driver said, grinning again.

Casey looked back again to make sure. "He's gone," she said.

Still speeding, as though the emergency had given her the right to drive as fast as she wanted, the driver took Casey back to Dr. Tamir's house and pulled up next to the group of people across the street. "A thousand thanks," Casey said politely. She gave the driver all the money she had in her purse and got out of the cab.

The cab turned the corner, driving fast. Casey watched it go and then looked around her. Zem's cab came toward her from the opposite direction. Oh shit, she thought. Now what? And at the same time a logical voice inside of her said, Well, of course. He knows where you live.

She pushed blindly through the group of men and women on the street. To her surprise they parted to make a path for her and then closed up behind her. She heard them murmur something over the voice of the announcer on the radio, one word passed from one to the other like a coin. A man unwrapped his turban and quickly wrapped it again around her head. Two or three people pressed against her, not unpleasantly, shielding her from the street.

She could see a little through the crowd, and she watched Zem get out of the cab and stand in the street, looking around him. After a while he walked over to Dr. Tamir's house and sat on the steps.

The group swayed a little, moving Casey with them. They smelled of cinnamon and some kind of incense she couldn't identify. He couldn't wait there all day, could he? He would have to give up some time and go home. And in the meantime she was probably as safe here as anywhere in the city, surrounded by people on all sides.

She turned to the man who had given her the turban. "Excuse me, please," she said. The man motioned her to be quiet. Did they observe some kind of rule of silence? She couldn't remember hearing any of them talk, even when they had performed that strange dance. She wondered what time it was. Had any of them brought some food, or did they fast all day?

A cab pulled up in front of Dr. Tamir's house and a very large man got out. The man walked up to Zem and talked with him for a moment. Then Zem got into the cab and the man sat down on the porch, motionless, as if waiting for something.

Damn, Casey thought. He's got reinforcements. Now what? If she could get to a phone she could call the police, or call her parents. She pushed against the wall of flesh surrounding her but everyone moved closer, hemming her in. Were they trying to tell her it would be dangerous to leave the group? She sank back. There was nothing to do but wait until her father came home and discovered a strange man sitting on the porch in front of his house. The crowd around her swayed again.

Time passed. Casey heard the announcer on the radio and the rustle of clothing as the crowd rocked back and forth together, but otherwise the street was silent, deserted. The man waited on the stoop, alert and unmoving, his feet stretched out in front of him. It was only fifty feet to their front door but the door was as unreachable to her as the moon. She wondered if her mother had missed her yet. Probably not. She felt hungry and thirsty, and her hair under the turban itched.

A bus stopped in the street in front of them. At first Casey thought everyone had started to sway again, but then she realized that the group was moving together toward the bus. She started to giggle. Well, they had to travel somehow.

Women in colorful skirts and men in turbans got off the bus. The two groups made muffled conversation as they passed, and then Casey's group started to board the bus. One person walked on either side of her, one in the back and one in the front, as if by accident. She tried to break away and join the new group but the press of people around her did not let up. Against her will she was moved up the steps of the bus and down the aisle. When she tried to take a seat someone held her back, not unkindly, and sat in the window seat. They were still shielding her from the man on the porch.

By looking past the man who had gotten in the window seat she was able to see the man on the porch. He was watching the two groups intently, almost as if he knew where she was. No, Casey thought. If he suspected something he'd be over here this minute. He's just watching us because we're the only interesting thing on the street right now.

Casey followed his gaze to the new group arranging itself on the sidewalk. In all the time she'd lived in Dr. Tamir's house she had never seen this changing of the guard. Makes sense, she thought. After all, they can't stand there forever.

The bus started up. I guess when we get where we're going I'll call my father, or the police, she thought. Unless I'm a prisoner. They weren't too gentle hustling me into the bus. But why would they want me? Probably they were just trying to protect me from Zem's friend. But why?

"Excuse me, please," she said to the man next to her. "Where are we going?"

She didn't understand his answer and shook her head. "Mountains," the man said slowly. She liked the way he looked immediately, with his medium-length white hair and neat bushy white beard, his small silver-framed glasses. "We are Sozranis."

She looked in her purse for her dictionary and discovered with relief that she had brought it along, though she didn't have the phrase book or the guide book. The word he had used—Sozrani—wasn't in the dictionary. "Why am I here?" she asked.

"You are *motmot*," the man said, using the word she had heard muttered back and forth when she'd joined the group.

She didn't expect to find *motmot* in the dictionary either, but it was there, with the longest entry on the page. "A person, place or thing not holy in itself that becomes holy through association with a holy or sacred person, place or thing."

She looked up the Lurqazi word for "holy" in the dictionary and then turned to the man again. "Is the house holy?" she asked.

The man swayed back and forth in his seat. "Of course the house is holy," he said.

"Why?"

The man looked at her carefully over his glasses and she wished she could take back the question. Maybe she couldn't be *motmot* if she didn't know why the house was holy. "Because of the holy Sozran," the man said.

"The holy Sozran lived in the house?" she said.

"Of course," the man said.

Of course, she thought. Well, no one ever told *me*.

The bus started climbing into the mountains. She watched the houses closely, looking for landmarks she could use to get back. The man swayed against her again and she noticed that everyone on the bus had started to move back and forth like a field of brightly colored wheat. Outside the window she saw another group of people standing and swaying in front of a nondescript house. Had Sozran lived there too? Maybe he moved around a lot. Or maybe someone else just as holy had lived in that house.

"When did the holy Sozran live?" she asked the man next to her.

"The year One," the man said.

That was no help. "How—how long—" she asked.

"Twelve hundred years ago," he said.

She nodded. "Before the Jewel King," she said, wanting to let him know she was not totally ignorant of his history.

To her surprise he turned away from her and spat out the window. "The Jewel King," he said, sounding disgusted. He spat again.

Okay, I won't say that again, she thought. She wondered what the Sozranis had against the Jewel King, and if her father knew. Maybe I can tell him when I get back. Maybe the information'll give him a whole new perspective on his manuscript. I might even get an acknowledgment.

If I get back, she thought, as the bus took the winding roads farther up the mountain. They passed houses of white and green and red marble, some of them set so far from the road she could barely see them. One house trimmed with copper and brass sat at the other side of a dark-green lawn that must have cost a small fortune to keep up in the harsh climate of Amaz. What do these people want with me?

The bus stopped and everyone stood up. Outside Casey saw what looked like the largest house of all, made of white marble and topped with golden spires and thin poles flying flags she didn't recognize. These Sozranis aren't as poor as they look, she thought. As she walked down the aisle, hands reached out to pull her turban off. "Not holy," the man with the silver glasses said. She guessed he meant that it would be sacrilegious for a woman to wear a turban.

She followed the Sozranis out of the bus and down a wide path lined on either side with rosebushes. Beyond the path stretched the lushest lawn she had seen so far. On one side a box hedge separated the lawn from a neighboring house. To the other side she could see the street and then another imposing house past that. Apparently only two houses shared this one block. A fountain scattered drops like pearls over the lawn, a flagrant waste of water.

They went up a wide marble stairway, waited until someone unlocked the front door, and were ushered into a large, echoing room. On either side of the room stood rust-red marble columns which reached to the ceiling. The floor was tiled in the same color, and to Casey it looked at first sight as though a lot of blood had been spilled a long time ago. Men and women walked back and forth, coming and going from unguessable errands, their sandals hushed on the marble floor. Echoing over and around their soft noises she heard the booming voice of the radio announcer. Now she remembered that the radio had been on in the bus on the way over too.

"Please, do you have a telephone?" she asked the man who had sat next to her.

The man turned to her, about to say something. The sound of gunshots came into the room, loud, insistent, terrifying. Most of the people stopped what they were doing and some threw themselves face down on the floor. Someone screamed. The man next to her looked startled for a moment and then started to smile. What's so funny? Casey thought, looking around desperately for a place to hide. Maybe one of the pillars. "The radio," the man said, and then said it again, loudly, so that the whole room could hear. Someone said something else in Lurqazi that Casey couldn't follow.

Oh, she thought, feeling stupid. The shots are from the radio.

A new announcer came on, speaking harsher and faster than the last one. Casey heard the word "Cumaq" but could not understand anything else. "Please, what is happening?" she asked the man next to her. The man motioned her to be quiet. All around her people were standing still and listening intently.

After about ten minutes the voice on the radio stopped. "Soz Mike!" the man next to her called out. It seemed to Casey that even before he spoke a young man detached himself from the others and came over to them. He was tall and thin, with very pink skin and hair so blond it was almost white. His eyes were a watery blue. The other Sozranis had gone back to whatever it was they were doing. "Could you please explain to this woman what is happening? She is *motmot,*" the man next to her said, and something else Casey couldn't follow.

"A thousand thanks," Casey said to the young man.

The young man held up his hand. "Don't worry about it," he said in English. "We don't have to speak Lurqazi if you're more comfortable with English."

"Thank God," Casey said. "Could you tell me what the hell is going on around here?"

"Cumaq's taken over the radio station," the young man—Soz Mike—said. "And other things too—in fact he claims to have taken over the whole city, but I don't know how much of that you can believe. He's declared a curfew, no one outside on the streets tonight, and no foreigners on the streets at all, except on their way to leave the country. I guess that means you," he said.

"Oh, shit," Casey said. "I've got to get home. My parents—they'll be going nuts if I don't get back. Can I—?"

"Sure, you can use the phone," Soz Mike said. "And if you can't get back tonight you can stay here with us. Everyone is welcome. Come—the phone's over this way."

He led her through the room. The radio came on again with an unpleasant squawk of static. Soz Mike stood and listened for a while and then continued on. "He's just saying the same thing over again," he said.

Some of the men and women they passed on their way out of the room carried trays of food, and Casey thought hopefully of dinner. Did "Everyone is welcome" mean she could eat here too? They all seemed so efficient, moving with an unhurried grace and stately precision, almost anticipating everything she wanted before she could ask for it. But something felt wrong, off. Was it that they were *too* efficient, robotlike? No, because they moved like dancers, and each one seemed to be enjoying the dance. She was just paranoid after what had happened earlier. It had been a long day.

They went down an arched hallway and into a small alcove containing nothing but a carved wooden table with a phone and recessed bookshelves covered with glass doors. The titles on the books were in the old script. As she lifted the receiver she noticed that what looked like diamonds were inlaid next to each of the numbers on the touch-tone buttons.

There was no dial tone. She jiggled the receiver button a few times and tried again. "Damn," she said, handing the receiver to Soz Mike.

"Do I have to dial something to get out? I don't hear a dial tone."

Soz Mike held the receiver to his ear and shook his head. "I bet he's cut the lines," he said. "Cumaq. He said something about taking over the phone company."

"Now what?" Casey said. "Can we—go to the police?"

"I wouldn't advise you going out," he said. "And he might have taken over the police stations too. Maybe by tomorrow we can see what's happening, maybe we can disguise you somehow—" He sounded doubtful.

"What about you?" Casey said. "Aren't you American? Don't you have to go back to the United States?"

"I've renounced my citizenship to become a Sozrani," he said. "My name is still Mike, but when I take the initiation I'll be free to change it to a name of Amaz."

"Mike?" she said. "But he called you—"

"Soz Mike," the man said. "The title means that I'm not initiated yet."

"But do you have citizenship here?" she said. "I mean, couldn't it be dangerous?"

"Oh no," Mike said. "I never go outdoors anyway."

At first she thought he meant because of his skin. "You never—"

"Because I'm not initiated," he said. "I don't have a turban. I have to stay inside and work."

"Oh," she said. "Well, when will you be initiated?"

Bells playing a sweet harmony cut off his answer. "Time for dinner," said when they stopped. "This way."

They went farther down the corridor, turned a corner and stepped through an arched doorway into a courtyard surrounded on all four sides by walls of marble. Tables had been set up under trees with pale purple flowers. A monkey climbed hand over hand up a tree as she passed and was gone, hidden in the foliage.

Casey looked around her. "A lot of people in Amaz eat in a court-yard like this," Mike said. "All the restaurants look like this, and some of the bigger houses even have their own courtyards. Because it hardly ever rains, so they can eat outdoors almost every day."

"Not the restaurants I've been in," Casey said, thinking of the Sun and Stars.

"Really?" Mike said. "You should try a restaurant that serves authentic Amaz cuisine some day. It's really very good."

"I have," she said, starting to get annoyed. Did he think she never went out? What about him, sitting and vegetating here behind the walls of his marble fortress? Still, he was being very nice to her. She didn't know what she would have done without him and the rest of the Sozranis. And maybe he did know more about Amaz than she did, unlikely as it seemed.

He led her to a table sparkling with linen and silver and crystal, and they sat down. The bells started up again, ringing a single note twelve times. A man in a long white robe stepped to the center of the courtyard, raised a sword and said something long and sonorous in Lurqazi. She couldn't understand a word of it. It was probably the old speech, before the language had changed in the fifteenth century.

Everyone murmured a response when he had finished, and he sat down. "That sword?" Mike said, pointing to the sword now on the table next to the man in the robe. "When I am initiated I will be able to hold it in my hands. It belonged to the holy Sozran before it was stolen from him by the Jewel King."

"The Jewel King?" Casey said, startled. A man set a silver tray with bread and a bowl of what looked like stew in the center of their table, but she had forgotten her hunger. "That's the Jewel King's sword?"

"You've heard of it?" Mike said, dipping his bread into the bowl.

"My father's writing a book on it," she said. "That's why we came here, because he wanted to find the Jewel King's sword. Wait'll I tell him about this!" She remembered her earlier thought—that she might get an acknowledgment in his book—and she laughed. If he heard about this he'd probably give her part authorship. "How on earth did you guys get it?"

"Through a disciplined use of magic," Mike said. "When I get initiated I'll learn all about it."

She looked at the sword again. It was smaller and straighter than she'd imagined the Jewel King's sword would be. Had her father told her the sword was curved like a scimitar or had she just pictured it that way? And it looked awfully new and shiny for a sword supposedly hundreds of years old. "How do you know it's authentic?" she asked.

"Well, of course it's authentic," Mike said. "It's been passed down for generations. I even heard about it in the United States," he said, as though that proved something. "And when I heard about it I knew I had to find it. Because it confers magic too. Look at us," he said, waving his hand around the courtyard. "That's why we're so prosperous, so successful. Because we have the sword. I dropped out of school in the middle of getting my engineering degree—I'd actually thought that was important, getting that piece of paper—and came all the way down here, just because someone I'd met in a bar one night told me this crazy story about a sword. And I had adventures —wild adventures, some of them, someday I'll write a book—and finally I found it. They didn't want to make it too easy, see, because then I wouldn't value it as much. Someday I'll tell you all about it. You probably haven't heard anything like it, down here with your parents and all, living the easy life. What are you, staying up at the tourist hotels?"

"No, we're in the city," she said. He *was* trying to one-up her. Well, all that meant was that he probably hadn't done much, just run to the Sozranis and shut himself up the minute he'd gotten here. "At a house the holy Sozran lived in, actually."

That was a cheap shot, but at least it got him to look at her with something like respect. "That's right, you're *motmot,*" he said. A man poured wine into his crystal goblet and he took a sip.

"Would you people let my father look at the sword?" she said. "It'd really help him with the book he's writing."

Mike frowned and took some more bread. "Probably not," he said. "We don't want to make it too easy for people trying to find the sword, like I said. Of course he could join us, become initiated, and then he'd get to see the sword."

Sure, Casey thought. Lock himself up in this crazy place. They'd love that back at the university. She tore off a piece of bread and dipped it in the stew. It tasted very good and she took another piece.

A bell rang after everyone had finished eating. People came into the courtyard to clear away trays and dishes. All around her Sozranis were standing up and heading toward the doorway.

Casey stood as well and, trying to look casual, began to walk over to the sword. The hilt was carved and seemed to be made of gold. As she strained to see more a group of people moved toward her, enveloped her and gently pushed her back the other way. Mike led her away from them, looking worried.

"We're going to meditation now," he said. "It'll probably be boring for you, since it's all in Lurqazi, but it can't be helped. We can't let you go outside."

She wanted to tell him angrily that she'd been studying Lurqazi, but that would only drag her down to his level. And it turned out that she could barely understand the meditation, which seemed to be one Sozrani after the other mumbling as fast as he or she could. She sat uncomfortably on a rattan mat in the room of red marble, trying to sit cross-legged, the way everyone around her did so effortlessly, and worrying about her parents. They would probably be frantic.

That night, as she slept on a rattan mat surrounded by softly breathing Sozrani women, she had a dream. She dreamed that she walked through the strange, luxurious house of the Sozranis, and that it was at the same time a house and an exercise in Lurqazi grammar. The first room, the main room, was the noun, and the next room the verb, and various rooms leading out from the first two rooms were adjectives and adverbs, conjunctions and prepositions. And all the while she walked through the maze of the house, through the long and complicated Lurqazi sentence, she knew that she would understand everything when she came to the end, that the end of it would have to be the Jewel King's sword. But when she got to the last room it was bare, with only a tile mosaic of two overlapping calligraphies on the floor.

Twenty-fifth November Street: 4

 $\mathcal{F}$ ive years ago Harhano, on a trip to the country with some friends, met the woman who was to become his wife. He and his friends had started out with plans to visit the Silver Caves, supposedly the place where the Jewel King's son had hidden while in exile, and to do some hiking in the mountains. But by the third day of the trip they were still in the small village ten miles from the caves, sitting in the combined restaurant, bar and hotel and drinking the local beer.

A small woman, wearing an embroidered red shawl despite the heat, her straight shiny black hair pulled back into a bun, walked into the village square opposite them. "See that woman?" Harhano said, gesturing with his beer glass. "I'm going to marry her."

His friends laughed. Harhano was nearly twice the woman's size, big-boned and portly. He needed to have his clothes specially made by a woman on Twenty-fifth November Street, and had to send away for his shoes, which looked like small suitcases. Furthermore, no woman had ever thought that he was handsome; his eyes protruded slightly, like a frog's, and when he smiled, which he did often, his mouth seemed too large.

"Her?" one of his friends said. "You'd crush her the first time you got in bed together!"

Embarrassed, Harhano took another sip of his beer. He didn't really know why he'd said what he had, especially in front of such coarse men as his friends. But now that he thought about it, it didn't seem like such a bad idea. He had never seen anyone as beautiful as the woman standing across from him in the village square, framed by the window of the bar. So what if she was small-boned, like a bird. They would work something out.

When his friends went off to the caves the next day Harhano stayed behind and made inquiries. He learned that her father was unemployed, one of those who had worked in the silver mines until they closed. She, her mother and her two sisters did embroidery work to keep the family going. The second day that he was left alone he worked up the courage to speak to her. By the time his friends came back from the caves he was able to introduce them proudly to his new bride, Arqana.

They had the wedding at Harhano's house on Twenty-fifth November Street and invited everyone on the street. Everyone came, even Mama and Blue Rose, each of whom had sworn never to be in the same room with the other. There was dancing and wine, and in the evening everyone went outside to build a huge bonfire in the middle of the street. Hours later Harhano and Arqana said good night and went back to their house. Everyone called out after them, suggestions that got more ribald and obscene the farther away the newlyweds got. Years later, people who had been there still dated things by whether they had happened before or after the wedding.

Harhano was never quite able to believe his luck. A few months later he moved up to a storefront that had opened up on the afternoon side of the street, and he felt that Arqana was somehow responsible for this change in his fortunes. Then a traveling dream interpreter told him one of his dreams meant Arqana would soon bear twins. His life seemed to be perfect. Once the twins came, he thought, things could not possibly get better.

His new store, unlike most of the stores on Twenty-fifth November Street, had a basement, and one day he went down the stairs to see if the baby carriage he remembered was still there. But after he turned on the light he stopped, hand still on the light switch, so overwhelmed with surprise that he was unable to move. The basement had utterly changed since the last time he'd visited. The accumulation of junk he remembered had been covered with what looked like hundreds of bags and cardboard boxes—bags and boxes that had held the mountains of junk people had brought to the store. He couldn't imagine why anyone would want to save all of them.

Bemused, he went upstairs and called out his wife's name. She came out of the store. "Arqana—" he said again. He found he was unable to stay mad at her once he saw her. "What are all those bags doing in the basement?"

"Oh," she said. "I thought we might need them someday. Maybe if we move?"

"If we move we'll just move farther up the street," he said gently. "We really don't need all that stuff, Arqana. I'll just throw it out, all right?"

"Sure," she said.

When she wasn't working in the store Arqana stayed in the bedroom upstairs and did embroidery, cleverly worked depictions of birds. Harhano, once he saw that she rarely embroidered anything else, wondered if her mother and sisters had had their specialties too, plants maybe, or other animals. Then he noticed that she seemed to have an affinity with birds, that birds would seem to fly near her when she went out walking up and down the street, singing almost in harmony. It was ridiculous, but once or twice he even thought he saw a bird land on her shoulder when she called to it. At first he attributed this delusion to love, to the thought that nothing was impossible for his beloved. But after a while rumors began to fly up and down the street, rumors about his wife, and he realized that other people had wondered about Arqana and her birds too.

On their first anniversary—the twins still hadn't come, but his happiness was undiminished—he bought a dozen rare birds, hoping to surprise her. But when she came into their bedroom and looked around her at the bright neon colors, she began to cry. He hurried over to comfort her. "The—the cages," she said, gasping through her tears. "The cages."

Of course, he thought. What a stupid oaf he was. His friends had been right—he would crush her if he wasn't careful. He opened the cages, opened the bedroom window and let all the birds fly away. He watched them go, feeling little but wonder at their colors like the flags of all the countries he would never visit.

He took the twelve empty cages into the store. They sold slowly at first, but after he'd sold two or three he found that others on the street recommended him whenever anyone asked for a birdcage. Almost against his will he'd acquired a specialty, the way others on the street specialized in rugs or jewelry. He bought more cages, larger, some with elaborate wrought-iron decorations like the tracery of a fantastic spider. Arqana never said anything about it.

Soon after he let the birds go free, he went down to the basement to see if he had an electrical switch a customer wanted. Once again he found the room filled with bags and boxes, filled this time nearly to the ceiling. Once again he talked to Arqana, gently because he didn't want to hurt her, and once again she agreed to let him throw them out.

Six months later he heard noises in the basement and, thinking it was rats, or that one of Mama's kids had broken in, he went down to investigate. He found Arqana trying to lift a load of flattened bags almost as big as she was onto a shelf.

This time he wasn't so gentle, and she cried at the end of his speech. Her tears moved him very much but he knew that he had to be stern, that he couldn't let her get away with her strange behavior again. The bags were a fire hazard, an invitation to termites, who knew what. "Do you understand?" he asked.

She nodded, not meeting his eyes.

Three months later he was in the store, selling an American some baskets made in Taiwan, when another customer asked for a birdcage. "Arqana!" he called. "Arqana, could you come and help me here?"

She didn't come. He got rid of the American by pretending to speak nothing but Lurqazi once the sale was made, sold the other man the birdcage and went upstairs, shouting her name in every room. In the bedroom he noticed that her painted combs were gone, and so was the woven blanket her grandmother had made, and her red shawl covered with embroidered birds. "Arqana!" he called again, refusing to believe the evidence, concocting wild and ridiculous reasons for each of the disappearances. Finally he remembered the basement.

He went downstairs, hoping that he would see her there, struggling with a load of bags and boxes too big for her. She could keep her damn boxes, he didn't care—all he wanted was to take her in his arms and hold her. He turned on the light.

Two birds flew past him, holding a filled bag between them in their beaks. Other than that, there were no bags at all in the basement.

He spent three years wondering what he had done wrong. True, he had given her the caged birds; true, he had sold the cages; but she had started collecting the bags *before* their anniversary. He kept coming back to that. She had been planning to leave before he'd done anything to hurt her. She had been planning to leave all along.

He paid less and less attention to his store. The flair for business that had gotten him to the afternoon side of the street, that had people predicting he would someday even move next door to Mama and Blue Rose, had deserted him. Now, over sweet bread and coffee, people up and down the street said that he would not last out the year at his new location.

One day Zem came into the store. "I don't need anything fixed," Harhano said immediately.

"I'm not here for that," Zem said. He looked around him. There

147

were large gaps in the shelves where Harhano had neglected to fill in more merchandise. Everyone's store was dusty—the people on Twenty-fifth November Street believed that dust added to the ambience of an antique store—but Harhano's piles were thicker than most. "I want to know if you'll help me."

"Help you do what?" Harhano asked suspiciously.

"There's money in it for you," Zem said quickly, misunderstanding. "Blue Rose is paying me—paying me well—to track two people, a tourist and a guy at the university. But I can't do all the work alone. What if they split up, for instance?"

Harhano shrugged. He couldn't say why, but he had never liked Blue Rose. Every six months or so, taking advantage of a time when Mama and Blue Rose weren't around, someone at the Sun and Stars would bring up the feud. It would be passed around from person to person like an old photograph, faded from age and creased with folds, whose details were known to everyone. And he would always side with Mama. When pressed for his reasons he could never give them. He just felt better about Mama, that was all.

"But that isn't the best part," Zem said. "See, Blue Rose wants these guys followed for a reason. Because they have money, or know where they can get money, that's what I think. And so one of these days I'll just follow them on my own. Or maybe get one of the tourist's kids and ask her what's going on. Take her away for a few days, see what kind of ransom I can get. There's a lot of money involved in this, for both of us, if we work this right. I've never known Blue Rose to be so generous."

Harhano remained silent. He had never heard anyone talk so easily of betrayal. Why shouldn't Zem take it into his mind to betray him as well, once they started working together? And if he agreed to work for Zem he would be involved with a sort of betrayal of his own, a switching of allegiances from Mama to Blue Rose. A triple betrayal: of Mama, of the tourists he would be following, ultimately of Blue Rose herself.

He had never thought of himself as a bad person, as a person likely to go along with the kind of scheme Zem was proposing. But Arqana had seen something bad in him, must have, or why had she planned to leave him from the beginning? He might as well start to live up to her expectations of him, then—after all, he had nothing left of her but her expectations. Zem was starting to say something, a guess as to how much money might be involved. Harhano cut him off. "All right," he said. "I'll do it."

The Book of Stones

Mitchell followed Jara through the maze of streets, stopping every so often so Jara could jot down a note or mark a new route on one of his many maps. He barely noticed the emptiness of the city, the few people hurrying by with radios near their ears, the police cars speeding past. Today, he thought. Today when we stop for coffee I'm going to tell him.

Jara stopped, looked at the sun and consulted his compass. "I think we are on the right track," he said. "At last. The streets we were walking last time had not even been built in the time of the Jewel King—that was our error. The streets we want seem to have shifted over the years, and now we are walking approximately where they once were. We are getting closer to the sword. I feel it."

That's what you said last week, Mitchell thought. But how could you argue with someone who thought that streets shifted like rivers?

He followed Jara slowly, feeling sweat drip down his sides and back. And he was not even wearing a coat and tie, hadn't worn them since his second week with Jara. Ahead of him Jara walked as if he barely felt the heat, looking dapper in his brown suit. They're used to the heat, though, Mitchell thought. They've lived with it all their lives. He hurried to catch up.

At last, after Jara had made his last note and folded up his maps, they stopped at a coffeehouse. The place was deserted, without even a waiter to take their orders. From somewhere Mitchell heard the loud voice of a radio announcer. "Jara," Mitchell said.

Jara, in the act of taking out yet another of his maps from his briefcase, stopped and looked up. "Yes?" he said.

"I'm not—I can't go out looking for the sword any more," Mitchell said. "I'm only here for a year, I have to do my research while I can, and write articles, and I don't have the time—and anyway I think finding the palace was enough of an achievement, don't you? That's the kind of thing we can make our reputation on. We don't really have to find the sword."

He had expected Jara to be angry, but Jara just sat there, turning the map over and over in his hands. "Ah," he said finally.

"My article on the palace is almost finished," Mitchell said. "And of course I'll put you down as co-author, let you look it over before I send it out for publication. . . ." He was stating his arguments very badly, he knew. He hadn't felt this awkward since he'd broken up with his girlfriend in high school. If only Jara would say something. "I don't really belong in the field," he said. "My place is more in research. I haven't been in the field since graduate school, really, and I—"

"I wonder when we are going to get service here," Jara said. "Excuse me while I look in the kitchen."

As Jara stood up a man came out of the kitchen and shook his head. "We are not open for business today," the man said. "Go home."

"Your door was open," Jara said.

"Well then, we will close it when you leave," the man said. "You have been listening to the news, yes? You should go home."

"My friend and I would just like—"

"What news?" Mitchell said. "What's going on?"

The man turned to him. "You do not know?" he said. "Commander Cumaq, he is ready to march down from the mountains. Everyone is home, waiting— You truly did not know?"

"No," Mitchell said, standing. The streets *had* been deserted, hadn't they? Why hadn't he realized something was wrong? "Come on, Jara. We've got to go."

"Why do you let this Cumaq frighten you?" Jara said. "He has been in the mountains for as long as anyone can remember. Come, we will find a place that is open, we will have some coffee, and then we will continue to look for the sword."

"No," Mitchell said again. "You look for the sword if you want to. I'm going home." Before Jara could say anything he went out into the street and looked around for a taxi. A cab came fifteen minutes later and he directed it to Dr. Tamir's house.

As he got out and paid the driver he noticed a large man sitting on the porch of his house. Now what? Had something happened to one of his family? He walked faster, but as he got up to the house the man left the porch and hurried away. Mitchell let himself in.

"Claire?" he said. His voice echoed in Tamir's large living room. "Casey?"

Now he could hear the radio playing in the kitchen, and he went toward it. Claire sat at the kitchen table, a drink and a book in front of her. "Claire?" Mitchell said. "Is everything all right?"

Claire looked up sleepily. "Oh sure," she said. "Everything's fine."

"Where are the kids?"

"Angie's in her room," Claire said. "And Casey—I don't know. I think she went out for a bit. She was angry with me for some reason."

"She went out?" Mitchell said. "We're about to be invaded, did you know that? And you let her go out?"

"Well, I didn't let her," Claire said. "She just did it." She laughed a little.

Mitchell stood in the middle of the kitchen, irresolute. He couldn't get mad at Claire, he knew that. It really wasn't her fault. Finally he went down the hallway to check on Angie. He felt a pang of fear when he looked into Casey's empty room, but he forced it away. Then he went back to the kitchen to listen to the radio, and to wait.

At around five in the afternoon they heard the gunfire on the radio, startlingly loud in the small room. The station went dead in midshot. Mitchell turned the knob up and down the dial until he heard a man speaking harshly in Lurqazi. Four or five stations carried the same voice, the same speech. He heard the word "Cumaq." Was this Cumaq speaking, or had Cumaq been overcome in the fighting? And where the hell was Casey?

At six Casey still hadn't returned. Angie came into the kitchen. "I'm hungry," she said. "Aren't we going out to eat?"

"Is that all you can think about?" Mitchell said. For a minute he had thought she was Casey. "We're not going anywhere. You can just forget about going outside until this thing blows over."

"What thing?" Angie said.

"What thing?" Mitchell said. "We're being invaded, that's what. And your sister isn't back yet. Dammit, I'm calling the police."

Angie sat down. If what her father said had scared her she gave no sign of it. Claire poured herself another drink. Mitchell came back from the living room. "The phone's dead," he said. "Where did— Did she say where she was going?"

"No," Claire said.

"Damn," he said. He sat down heavily at the table. "Now what?"

"She can take care of herself," Claire said. "She always has."

"Claire," he said. "We're in a foreign country. We're being invaded. She could be—could be—" He stopped. She was past understanding. And he didn't want to think what might be happening to his daughter. He stood up and walked to the living room, opened the door and came back into the kitchen. "There's no one out there but the turban people," he said. "Maybe nothing's happened after all. We might as well go out to dinner, and if we see a policeman we can ask him what's going on. How does that sound?"

No one said anything. He looked from his wife to his daughter, wondering when they had changed, become unrecognizable to him. Had it happened gradually or all at once? Or did they just act differently when Casey wasn't around, when one loose strand unraveled the entire pattern of the family? They stood up and followed him outside.

They saw nobody on the streets on the way to the McDonald's, no cars, no tourists, none of the frantically hurrying pedestrians. Once inside Mitchell saw that the nice waitress, the one that Casey talked to, was on duty. At last, he thought, letting himself feel a little relief. Someone I can talk to. He went toward her, then stopped when he noticed what she was wearing, slung behind her so he hadn't seen it at first. A machine gun.

"Excuse me," he said. "Do you know—?"

The waitress said something in Lurqazi.

"I'm sorry," he said, trying to smile. Surely she remembered that they only spoke English? "We don't speak Lurqazi."

"Why not?" the waitress said.

"What?"

"Why not? You are in my country now, yes? I am not in yours. Why do you speak your language instead of mine?" She fingered the strap of the machine gun.

"I don't—I didn't learn—"

"But I learned yours, yes?" she said. "You could learn mine just as easy. If you start now, soon it will be second hand to you." Even through his fear and frustration Mitchell realized that she must have meant "second nature." "I am sick of you Americans, thinking that you own the world. But this is one part of the world you will never own again. We have nationalized the restaurant."

Mitchell would have bet she hadn't known the word "nationalized" yesterday. "So then Commander Cumaq—"

"Long live Commander Cumaq," the waitress said. "Long live the revolution. All foreigners must leave the country."

"We—we can't leave the country," Mitchell said. "I don't know where my daughter—you remember Casey? She was trying to learn Lurqazi."

"All foreigners must leave the country," the waitress said. "All foreigners must be off the streets."

"But my daughter," Mitchell said. "Is there anyone who can help, one of Cumaq's men maybe? As soon as we find her we'll go, but we can't just leave her here."

The waitress shrugged. The machine gun followed her motion. "I do not know," she said. "May I take your order please?"

Mitchell blinked. Had he heard her correctly? But she was standing at the counter attentively, fingers poised over the keys of the cash register. "My order?" he said.

"Yes," she said. "We are still a restaurant."

"But I thought you said we had to be off the streets," he said.

"As long as you are here I may as well serve you," she said. "After all—" her shoulders lifted with pride—"I *own* this restaurant now."

They ate in silence and walked back to Dr. Tamir's house. The streets had grown darker; the road ahead of them ran black as ink. It was a darkness that seemed suddenly more menacing, that could be hiding anything—snipers, jungle animals, a convoy of tanks. From somewhere Mitchell heard the stutter of a European-style siren, the kind that always made him think of World War Two movies.

Even the turbanned people had gone, and the statue holding the egg stood alone, looking taller and somehow out of place. The family went inside the house and Mitchell tried the phone again, but it was still dead. He paced back and forth, let himself outside and stood staring out over the mad city. A fire was burning out of control in the mountains, and he heard machine-gun fire from somewhere to his left, though whether it was fifty yards or fifty miles away he couldn't tell. Casey was out there somewhere. He looked hard at the darkened street, hoping for a taxi that could take him to the police, where he could—could what? The police would probably just order him out of the country, and he'd never see Casey again. He went back into the house, feeling a weight he was not prepared to handle.

Angie lay awake on her bed, her eyes wide open. I know where she is, she thought. A dozen times during dinner she had started to tell them, but something had always held her back. She hadn't said anything of importance to her parents in so long that she wasn't sure she could start now.

But I know where she is, Angie thought. She's out there, and I know where. Twenty-fifth November Street, the same place she wanted to take me to that one time. Should I tell them? Or—why don't I just go there myself?

She shivered in the darkness. No foreigners were allowed on the streets—she had heard the waitress say so at dinner. It was dangerous out there. If she left now she would almost certainly be killed. Even if she waited until morning— All right, she thought. I'll get up early, get out of the house and go to Twenty-fifth November Street. Either I die or I bring her back. Either way it would end. She closed her eyes. A siren in the distance was the last thing she heard before she drifted off to sleep.

She woke the next morning in darkness, dressed quickly and went outside. The sun was coming up and she could feel the promise of heat.

The streets were still deserted. Well, that didn't matter. She could walk aimlessly until she found a taxi, and the driver would know how to get there. She walked along the main street, past the statue, thinking that something looked strange, different. Right. The turbanned people weren't there any more.

Once she noticed that she began to notice other things. She had never heard anything like the song of the birds that seemed to come from all around her, two long notes and then a shorter one, like an afterthought. A horse and rider came toward her, the man wearing a yellow shirt and green pants. Strange, she thought. Those were the colors of the mounted guard of Borol. And the fountain in the park up ahead—Casey had invented a fountain just like it for a park in Marol, the water going in toward the center and then shooting up in a straight line. In fact—

It seemed as if a door had opened, somewhere in her mind. In fact, she was in the Two Kingdoms right now. The daughter of the king of Marol had disappeared, and she was sent for to find her. Only she understood the mind of the king's daughter, only she knew where to look for her. Around her people were starting to come out of their houses and gardens, speaking in Bordoril, which she understood perfectly: comments about the weather, the king's health, the costumes in the tournament last week.

A cab pulled up alongside her. For a moment everything was su-

perimposed, Borol and Marol on one hand and this strange country
—she had forgotten its name—on the other. Then she got into the
cab. "Twenty-fifth November Street," she said, and sat back.

A few minutes later the cab stopped at a shabby-looking street.
"Here it is, miss," the driver said. "Twenty-fifth November Street."
She paid him and got out.

Was this the place Casey had wanted to show her? There was
nothing here but badly painted houses and a bunch of junk. The only
person up was a fat old woman sitting in a cracking leather chair,
surrounded by things no one would want to buy in a million years.
What on earth had Casey found to interest her here?

Then the Two Kingdoms took over, and she stood not in the middle of a crumbling street but in the bazaar of Borol, looking for the
king's daughter who had run away and hidden here. Protected from
all harm because she was on the king's business she walked up to the
woman in the chair and said, "Excuse me. Do you know someone
named Rafiz?"

The woman stirred. For a minute she looked as if she were about
to pull herself up out of the chair and walk away. Then she waved her
hand, the hanging flesh under her arm quivering. She could have
been dismissing Angie or shooing off a fly. Or she could have been
pointing to the store next door.

What a rude woman, Angie thought. Maybe a spy for someone.
She went to the store the fat woman had indicated and knocked on
the door. A woman called out something in Lurqazi. Angie pushed
open the door and went inside.

It took a moment for her eyes to adjust to the dim light. Junk was
piled all around her, on the floor, on rickety tables, on shelves lining
the walls, and dust covered everything. The only light seemed to
come from the electronic numbers on the cash register, which
glowed an eerie blue in the darkness.

"Excuse me," Angie said. "Is Rafiz here?"

"Rafiz?" the woman said. "Yeah, just a second." She started toward the back and then stopped and turned back toward Angie. Now
Angie could see that the woman's hands were covered with pale-blue
gloves. "What do you want him for?"

"I think he knows where my sister Casey is," Angie said. "She didn't come home last night, and we're worried."

The woman pushed aside a curtain at the back of the store and called out a long sentence in Lurqazi. A man came through the curtain. "Hi," Angie said uncertainly. "Are you Rafiz?" The man was missing an ear.

"No, not Rafiz," the man said. He pulled a knife out of a leather sheath at his belt and came closer to her. Angie tried to back away but the man grabbed her wrist and pulled her roughly toward him. She cried out a little in panic.

"I'm afraid you're going to stay with us for a while," the woman with the gloves said. "At least until your father agrees to pay your ransom."

Mitchell woke early the next morning. A night's sleep had done nothing to diminish his feeling of dread. He dressed and shaved, avoiding the kitchen for no clear reason he could give himself. When he opened the front door he saw that the sun was already shining, and he started to feel a little hope. Maybe today was the day he would find someone to help him.

A man wearing a turban came toward him. Mitchell nodded at him and brushed past. He was eager to get started. Maybe he could get directions to the police station and walk there, if it wasn't too far. . . .

"Excuse me, please," the man said.

"Yes?" Mitchell said, stopping.

"Excuse me," the man said again. "But we have your daughter."

"You do?" Mitchell said. "Oh thank God. Where is she? Is she safe?"

"We have your daughter," the man said. "And we will give her to you—"

"Yes?" Mitchell said.

"—if you give us the sword."

"What?"

"If you give us the sword," the man said. Now Mitchell noticed that there was something wrong with the way the man spoke, as if he didn't speak English and had memorized the phrases he had to say.

"What sword?" Mitchell said. "Look, I—"

"The Jewel King's sword," the man said.

"I don't have the sword," Mitchell said. "What is this, some kind of ransom demand? Look, I don't even have— If you don't take me to my daughter right now I'm calling the police."

The word "police" seemed to set the man off again, to call forth more memorized phrases. "You cannot go to the police," he said. "You are a foreigner. We will give her to you if you give us the sword."

"But I don't have the sword," Mitchell said. "No sword," he said, speaking slowly and shaking his head. In desperation he repeated it in eighth-century Lurqazi. "I'd give it to you if I had it—you've got to understand that. I'd do anything to get my daughter back. But I just don't have it."

The man seemed to hesitate. Then he said, "We will give her to you if you give us the sword." He turned and walked away toward an empty bus waiting at the corner of the street.

"Wait!" Mitchell said. He looked around for a taxi, but the streets were still deserted. "I have the manuscript—it has directions to the sword—" The bus pulled away from the curb. It had no license plate that Mitchell could see.

He stood on the porch for a while, trying to decide what he should do next. The only person he knew in Amaz was Dr. Jara. Very well, Jara would have to help him. He lived in this damn country, after all. Mitchell locked the door behind him and set out for the university.

Claire finished her breakfast and went outside. At first, looking at the empty streets in front of her, she thought she wouldn't be able to get a taxi. But then she remembered her previous successes, the liquor store and the bookstore, and soon enough a cab came around the corner. She waved at it and got in when it stopped.

"Where to?" the cabdriver asked.

"My daughter Casey," Claire said.

"Excuse?" the driver said.

"My daughter Casey, please," Claire said again.

"I do not understand," the driver said. "I go to Colonial House, to Gaudi Park, to the marketplace, anywhere in the city you want to go. I do not go up to the ruins near the tourist city—too far. Where to?"

"I don't—" Claire said. She had been so sure this would work, so sure she could get behind the facade of the city to wherever it was Casey had gone. "I'm looking for my daughter Casey. She didn't come home last night. I thought that you might—"

"I do not know this Casey," the driver said.

"Oh," Claire said, slumping. The city had deserted her, had barred her from going inside. She had lost the key somehow. She couldn't think of what to do next. "Well, the Super Shop then, I guess."

"Okay," the driver said, and started the car.

She still half hoped that he would take her to Casey, but when he stopped in front of the glass-fronted building, she knew she had to give up. She got out, told him to wait, and went into the liquor store. Once inside she piled her cart to the top, filling it not just with liquor but with meat and bread, eggs and fruit and cheese. It might be dangerous to go back to the McDonald's, especially if the waitress had told someone they were still in the country.

The taxi was still parked at the curb when she finished her shopping. She had thought the driver might have deserted her, along with so much else in Amaz. He got out and helped put her bags in the cab. "Home now, yes?" he asked, looking at her in the rearview mirror.

"Okay," Claire said. The wine waited patiently for her inside the bag. At least the wine wouldn't desert her.

"You are early," Jara said when Mitchell got to his office at the university. "We had arranged to meet at the location on my map, yes?"

"My daughter's been kidnapped," Mitchell said. "They want the sword."

For once it seemed as if Jara had nothing to say. "I am terribly sorry," he said finally. "When did this happen?"

"I don't know," Mitchell said. He stood over Jara's desk, unmoving, unable to move, just as he had that first day when he had brought the manuscript. "She didn't come home last night."

"And they want the sword?" Jara asked. "How do they know that we are looking for it?"

"I don't know," Mitchell said.

"Well then," Jara said. "We will have to find the sword for them. Shall we start now?"

Mitchell stirred. This maniac Jara would probably want to go find his sword in the middle of nuclear war. "I don't want to look for the sword," he said. "I want to go to the police."

"Cumaq has taken over the police," Jara said. "As he has, apparently, taken over everything else. We have received notice that some of his men will meet with us next week to decide the future of the university. And you, of course, should be on your way back to the United States. All foreigners must leave the country. They emptied out the hotels in the tourist city, have you heard? At best you have a week before you are deported, a week to find the sword."

"And if we find the sword, what then?" Mitchell said. "Do we just hand it over to these people? What about your plans for a national museum?"

"Of course we will not hand it to them," Jara said. "We will find the sword and then we will decide what to do with it. Perhaps we can pretend to deal with the kidnappers and then somehow rescue your daughter."

"Without the police?" Mitchell said. "Just us against them? She's been taken by the people who wear those turbans—do you know how many of them there are in the city? There must be hundreds. Thousands."

"Please, do not raise your voice," Jara said. "We will go look for the sword today. And if we must, we will give it to your daughter's kidnappers to get her back." He stood, picked up his briefcase and coat and went to the door. Mitchell followed. Jara was obsessed with the sword, but maybe he was right. Maybe the only way to get Casey back was to give the kidnappers what they wanted. And if they didn't find the sword that day he would think of something else.

The day went by in a blur. Jara, working carefully and precisely, drew lines on his map, aligned his compass, checked his copy of the manuscript, but still it seemed to Mitchell that they were walking in circles. There had to be something else they could be doing. Every so often they passed soldiers dressed in torn and dirty mismatched uniforms, carrying guns, and Mitchell would pray they wouldn't stop him. Jara's words kept coming back to him: "At best you have a week." And what would happen to them after that?

It seemed to Mitchell that they wandered all over the city without finding the sword or any likely place to begin digging for the tomb. He almost wished that they hadn't had such a spectacular early success, that they hadn't found the walls of the palace. Maybe then Jara would have been willing to give up this whole crazy chase, to call it off and go home.

"It's getting late," Mitchell said finally. His voice seemed strange to him in the empty air. "What do you think?"

"Think about what?" Jara said.

"About finding the sword," Mitchell said. "Do you think we're any closer? Or should we just go home and think of some other way to get Casey back?"

"Of course we are closer," Jara said. "We move closer every day. We are now on streets that have existed since the Jewel King's time. Probably we are walking over streets that the Jewel King himself has walked."

"Too bad these streets can't talk," Mitchell said.

Jara stopped and looked at him, amazed. "Yes," he said. "That is very good. Too bad these streets cannot talk. Very good."

Mitchell sighed, too tired to tell Jara he hadn't invented the saying. "I'm ready to go home now," he said.

No traffic moved in the streets except ancient trucks filled with soldiers. They had to walk back to the university and Dr. Tamir's house, Mitchell following Jara and the map, completely lost in the strange, lowering city.

A woman moved out of the shadows of the porch as Mitchell went up the steps, and he backed away a little, startled. "We have your daughter," the woman said.

"Yes, I know," Mitchell said. "I told you this morning, I don't have the damn sword. I'll—"

"This morning?" the woman said.

"Yeah," Mitchell said. What were they playing at? "When your friend with the turban came to tell me you had Casey. I already told him—"

"Casey?" the woman said. Now he noticed that she was wearing pale-blue gloves. Before she could speak again Mitchell knew, if not the exact words, the tenor of what she would say, that something else had gone badly wrong. "Not Casey, the other one," she said. "The blond one. We'll give her back if you give us the sword."

Mitchell said nothing, sagging a little where he stood. He was a researcher, a man who sifted through dictionaries and old manuscripts. Not an adventurer, not someone who was equipped to deal with a strange woman who had kidnapped his daughter in a foreign country. Finally he said, "Angie?"

"Yeah," the woman said. "Angie."

"My other daughter's been kidnapped too," he said wearily. Could he appeal to her sympathy? "We heard about it this morning. They want the sword too. So if I had the sword, which I don't, I don't even know if it exists—"

"It exists," the woman said. "So if you had it you'd have to make a choice, wouldn't you? Which of your daughters would you want back?" She didn't give him a chance to answer. He didn't know what he would have said anyway. "If I were you I'd get to work finding that sword." She went down the porch, to an old rickety car waiting for her at the curb. The car, of course, had no license plates.

Mitchell let himself into the house. He felt infinitely tired. Claire sat in the kitchen, a book and a glass of wine in front of her. "Where's Angie?" he said.

"Angie?" Claire said, looking up from her book. "She's in her room. Isn't she?" Her words slurred together so badly Mitchell knew he would not have understood her if he hadn't had years of practice.

"No, she's not," he said. "She's been kidnapped. So has Casey." Suddenly it seemed absurd, two daughters kidnapped on the same day. He forced himself not to laugh. If he started laughing he might never stop.

"Kidnapped?" Claire said. Alarm showed part way through her vague expression, like the sun trying to come out through clouds. He'd gotten through to her. Finally.

"Yeah," he said. "They want the sword."

"But you don't have the sword," she said.

"No," Mitchell said. "I don't." And that's not the worst of it, he thought, but he didn't think he could burden her with anything more. "Jara took me on another of his wild-goose chases today. Do you know if the phones are working?"

"I didn't check," Claire said.

Of course not, Mitchell thought. He went into the living room and lifted the receiver, but the phones were still dead. Then he walked heavily down the corridor to his daughters' rooms.

"You'd have to make a choice, wouldn't you?" the woman had said. The problem was that it wouldn't be much of a choice. He'd pick Casey over Angie any day, always had. But of course he couldn't think that way. Of course he'd have to do everything in his power to get both of them back. Still, he couldn't rid himself of the guilt the woman's words had stirred up.

Casey's room looked the same as it had the day before. The bed was unmade—they had given up trying to get her to make her bed years before—and piles of clothes and books were scattered around the room. He went closer to read the titles. A physics textbook, *A Few Proverbs of Amaz*, *The English-Lurqazi Phrase Book*, *The Old Curiosity Shop*. Any sane father would secretly prefer Casey to Angie, he told himself. It's nothing to feel ashamed about. But the guilt he felt would not go away, had, if anything, gotten worse.

He went across the corridor to Angie's room. Angie had made her bed, and had placed at least a dozen black notebooks at the foot, arranged in three neatly squared-off stacks. Maybe she had written down wherever it was she had been planning to go. He went over to the bed, sat down and picked up the top notebook on the first stack.

It seemed to be a dictionary of some kind, about ten words to a page, alphabetically arranged. She'd left spaces between the words so more could be added later. He flipped through it quickly. Two or three of the words seemed to be in old Lurqazi, and a few others were in the later demotic form. He closed the book and picked up the next one in the stack.

This one contained nothing but maps. She'd divided the book into two sections, one headed "Borol" and the other "Marol." Imaginary countries? Mitchell thought. Was this what she did in her room all day?

The next book had descriptions of holidays, arranged according to a calendar that, as far as Mitchell knew, had no counterpart in the real world. Suddenly angry—at Angie for wasting her time like this? at himself for prying?—he put the book down and picked up the top one in the last stack.

"And so the best knight in all the realm was ordered from the country, and given from sunrise to sunset to arrange his affairs, as if he were a common criminal who had trespassed against the king...." Astonished, Mitchell turned to another page and read, "They bore the dead king at night from his resting place to the tomb of marble and gold they had built for him...." And later, "The trumpets sounded loudly. The king's son was come to redeem the land, and to clear his father's name."

Mitchell sat on the edge of Angie's bed, the open notebook still in his hand. Everything ran parallel to him, he had thought while out walking with Jara, the day after they had found the wall. Things he didn't understand happened all around him, and he only managed to catch up with them much later, if at all.

As far as he knew the only written version of the Book of Stones was the one he had found at the university, in a box labeled "Arabic Studies." The manuscript had never been translated into English. And yet somehow his daughter, working in ways incomprehensible to him, had managed to translate or reinvent the Book of Stones. Somehow she had done the same work he'd been engaged upon for the past year. Her inner world, the made-up countries of Borol and Marol, had overlapped with the real thing. Was your daughter crazy if her imaginary kingdoms turned out to have an actual counterpart?

And how had it happened? Some slow seepage of magic radiating out along the lines Jara had drawn on his map, out of the colored wheels and arrows of ancient Lurqazi calligraphy? He shook his head slowly. Now he was thinking like Jara, like Tamir. Angie had probably read the notes he was beginning to make on the epic and had fashioned her own story out of them. If he were to read the two versions he'd probably discover that they weren't all that similar. He closed the book and put it back on the stack, relieved to have solved one problem at least. Slowly he returned to the other world, the one where his daughters were missing and the city swirled around him in chaos. He stood heavily, wondering what he could do next.

One Way to Twenty-fifth November Street

Casey woke early, stood up and went to the door, stepping around the sleeping women on their rattan mats. Three woman got up immediately and went to the door to stop her, softly whispering words in Lurqazi. "You can't . . ." they said. "You must . . ." Casey understood enough of it to know that she was not supposed to leave the room.

After about ten minutes a bell rang and all the other women sat up. They went out of the room and down the hall, laughing softly, carrying her along in their midst. They stopped at the large communal bathroom Casey had seen the night before and then, when they had all used the toilets and showers, took her with them to the courtyard.

Breakfast was strong coffee and a sweet pastry, served on bone-white china with a circle of gold inlaid around the rim.

"Where is Soz Mike?" she asked the women sitting at her table. All of them shook their heads and shrugged. She couldn't see him anywhere in the room.

When breakfast ended the women stood and left the room, bowing slightly to the man in the long white robe who had held up the sword the night before. Now what? Casey thought. She tried to follow the women who were at her table but one went to the kitchen, one to the red-pillared room to sweep, one back to the bedroom to pile the rattan mats in a corner. "Can I help?" she asked the woman lifting the mats.

"No, please," the woman said. "You are our—" and then a word that Casey didn't understand, that left her feeling anxious until she looked it up and found, to her relief, that it meant "guest."

She left the room and started to wander through the house. No one came out to stop her, but she didn't believe for a moment that they'd forgotten about her. She passed through a room with a ceiling made of what looked like beaten gold. She walked by an open door, looked inside and saw a room filled with men seated on plain wooden benches, answering questions put to them by an old man in a long dirty white robe. She ended up crossing the courtyard three times, each time coming to it by a different doorway, one tiled, one wooden, and one shaped like a star. Finally she walked down an echoing corridor with walls and floors of checkered white and black marble. The corridor ended in a plain wooden door.

She stood before the door for a while, wondering where she had seen it before. She'd had a strange dream last night. . . . But no, that was ridiculous. The door opened to her touch.

The room beyond the door was empty. Of course, she thought. They wouldn't keep the room the sword was in unguarded, unlocked, open to just anyone. They're making poor Mike go through an initiation ceremony, after all.

The walls were painted an unremarkable off-white, but the floor was covered with a tile mosaic. She went farther into the room to see it better, leaving the door open to catch the light from the hall. The pattern looked like some kind of calligraphy, like the words in her father's manuscript. Some of the words were written in large, rounded letters, and the others, nearly covering the first group, in letters jagged as barbed wire. That definitely reminded her of something, not her stupid dream, but— Of course. Graffiti just like this covered most of the city. But the graffiti she'd seen—she closed her eyes, trying to remember—had been exactly the opposite, the rounded letters nearly covering the jagged ones.

She opened her eyes and went down on her knees to examine the mosaic closer. It looked as if part of it, most of the rounded letters, had been pried up and the jagged letters added later. She ran her fingers over the tiles, feeling the places where the second group of letters did not line up exactly with the original mosaic. There were lots of these places, almost as if—as if whoever had done the second mosaic had wanted people to know they had desecrated the original. She stood up slowly. But why would they have done that, and why hadn't they just taken out all the rounded letters?

"You are not allowed in here," someone said from the open door.

She turned around quickly. The man with the silver-framed glasses, the one who'd sat next to her on the bus, stood there. He didn't look nearly as friendly as he had on the bus, and her first feeling was impatience. Why had he interrupted her before she'd seen everything? "What?" she said slowly, to gain time.

"You are not allowed in here," he said again.

"It's very beautiful," she said. "Very interesting. What is it? How old is it?"

"If you like you may join us here and become initiated," the man said. "Then we will tell you its meaning. Not before."

She had never heard the Lurqazi word for "initiated" but she understood its meaning as soon as the old man said it. "It's different," she said. "The—the letters. In all the others the letters are different, there are more of these letters—"

The man turned away. At first she thought he hadn't understood her, and she cursed herself for not having studied Lurqazi more diligently. Probably she hadn't made any sense at all. Then she heard him spit, very deliberately. "You must not say that again," he said slowly. "It is only because you are *motmot...* " She did not understand the rest of the sentence. "You must leave this room now."

She followed him out the door reluctantly and watched as he closed it to make sure he didn't lock it. Maybe she could get back sometime while everyone was at dinner or at meditation. "Where is Soz Mike?" she asked the man.

"He is busy."

"Well, what do I do?" she said. "Is there something to do?"

"No," the man said. "You must wait until you can go outside again. And you must not go back to that room again."

"When can I go outside?"

"When it is safe," the man said. "When we say you can."

She sighed and walked with him down the checkered hallway. He left her at one of the many turnings of the house and she continued her explorations.

At last she found herself back in the red-floored room. The door to the outside stood across the room, unguarded. Was still locked? All around her Sozranis went back and forth over the red tiles, carrying brooms, mats, candles, books, their sandaled feet making sounds like whispers. She walked purposefully toward the door.

Five feet from the door two turbanned men moved quickly in front of her and began to push her back. "You cannot go outside," one of them said.

"Well, what the hell can I do?" she said, enraged into speaking English.

The two men looked at each other. One of them left the room and came back a few minutes later with the man with the silver glasses and another, younger, man. "This is Tarq," the man with the glasses said. "He will be your companion."

She looked up "companion" in her dictionary and nodded. "All right," she said.

The young man—he was not much older than she was, really—motioned her to follow him. They went out of the red room and he opened a door she hadn't seen in her explorations. Beyond the door lay a flight of stairs. She hadn't even known the house had a second floor. He indicated that she should go up ahead of him.

At the top of the stairs they turned left and walked down a long narrow corridor with identical doors running along one side. He opened one door—how does he know which one?—and they went inside. The room was empty except for shelves standing in one corner. She looked at the floor, half hoping to see looping or jagged calligraphy, but it was covered in ordinary black and white tiles. While she stood in the middle of the room, confused, Tarq went to the shelves and brought back a carved mahogany box.

Tarq sat cross-legged on the floor, opened the box and dumped its contents on the floor. Chess pieces. Now she noticed that the tiles were arranged like chessboards, with larger white tiles separating one board from the next. "You play?" he asked.

"Sure," she said.

After a half-dozen moves she realized that the rules were slightly different from the ones she knew. One knight could only turn clockwise and the other counterclockwise, there was a time limit between moves, and the king could be resurrected under certain conditions. It was this last that made her lose the first game. She protested loudly, in Lurqazi and English, but Tarq kept a look of innocence and at the end said something in rapid Lurqazi that she thought meant, "You said you knew how to play."

She won the next two games, resurrecting her king once, and then realized that if she wanted Tarq as an ally she had better start losing. She lost two games and then, growing bored, ended the third in a draw.

Tarq looked satisfied as he set up the pieces for another game. "Are you initiated?" she asked him.

He looked up, a little surprised, and said, "Of course. I have the turban." He touched the turban with his hand so she would know what he meant.

"The holy Sozran is very interesting," she said. "Can you tell me about him?"

He shook his head. "You must first become initiated," he said.

"I would like to be initiated," she said. "But I am not sure. Maybe if you tell me more..."

"Well, then, I will tell you a little," he said. In fact, he did not finish his story until the bell rang for dinner. She didn't understand a lot of the words, and some of them were not in her dictionary, so she had to stop him and make him explain what they meant. As he talked, the scattered chess pieces in front of him forgotten, his words became lyrical, his gestures broader, his eyes brighter. She had seen the same enthusiasm before—in Rafiz when he talked about Twenty-fifth November Street, in a man who had stopped her to sell her cards. That's what's missing, she thought. Everyone in the city is so passionate about things. Here they're only passionate about their religion. They've lost everything else.

The holy Sozran, she found out, had been king and religious leader of Amaz twelve centuries ago. His rule rested on the sword—"The same sword that shines for us every day, like the sun," Tarq said— and his people were prosperous and content. The man who later became the Jewel King was one of Sozran's men, not a knight, but lower, much lower, a turnkey in the prisons. "His name before he became the Jewel King is not even remembered," Tarq said. "That is because he was not of noble birth."

But the man who became the Jewel King coveted the sword, and finally he put together an army of outcasts and misfits. Because there had not been a war in all of Sozran's reign the king was unprepared, and the Jewel King and his men were able to treacherously overcome him and steal the sword. But the Jewel King's reign, because of his misdeeds, was filled with sorrow, and his enemies were many. At the last battle Sozran made an alliance with the Jewel King's half brother, and both Sozran and the Jewel King were slain. The Jewel King's son—"not even his son but a bastard, fathered on his wife by the best knight in the realm," Tarq said gleefully, as though he personally had been the go-between for the two adulterers—ruled the country for a while, but the kingdom declined and finally crumbled into fragments.

"And the sword was lost," Tarq said. "That is mostly why the kingdom fell apart, because instead of governing, the new king spent his time trying to find the sword. But what he did not know is that Sozran's followers gained the sword and have it to this day. And no one knows it but us."

And me, Casey thought, but she knew she probably shouldn't say so. Instead she said slowly, "The house I live in, the house that is *motmot,* they said that house is three hundred years old. But if the holy Sozran lived twelve hundred years ago, how could he have lived there? How could the house be *motmot?*"

Tarq looked confused for a moment and then, the doubt gone from his face so quickly she wasn't even sure she had seen it, said, "Ah. That is something you will learn when you are initiated."

"The Jewel King," she said, finally understanding something, "did he write like this?" She made large looping motions on the floor with one of the chess pieces. "And did the holy Sozran write like this?" she asked, moving the piece jaggedly back and forth.

This time Tarq did not even bother to hide his astonishment. "How—how did you possibly learn that?" he said.

"It is all over the city," she said. "The writing of Sozran and the Jewel King. But in the city the Jewel King's letters—there are more of them. And here in the room I saw there are more of the holy Sozran's letters."

"You must not tell anyone you know this," Tarq said, almost whispering. "I told you too much. If you tell I will be—"

"I will not tell anyone," she said. Too late she realized that she had nearly done a very stupid thing. If Tarq told his superiors what she knew they would probably keep her here forever. But Tarq had his own reasons for keeping silent. "Okay?"

Tarq grinned, as she knew he would, at the only English word he knew. "Okay," he said. Distantly, on the first floor, the bells rang for dinner.

They put away the chess pieces and went downstairs. After dinner, when Tarq went to meditation, Casey tried the phone again. There was still no dial tone. She wondered if she should try for the front door but she thought she had made enough trouble for one day. Instead she stood as quietly as possible in the red room and listened for noises out in the street. There was nothing—no cars, no sirens, no gunfire. *If everything's gone back to normal why are they keeping me here? Don't they know it'll be harder for me to leave the country the longer I stay here? I'll have to escape,* she thought, and then stopped, a little startled by the word. It hadn't occurred to her before that she was being kept against her will. *All right then,* she thought, *I'll escape tomorrow.* She left the red room and went back to the meditation room to find Tarq.

After meditation the women led her back to their bedroom. A young man sat cross-legged on a mat outside the room, and the women nodded to him and giggled as they went inside. My guard, Casey thought. She started to think of a plan.

She stayed awake for hours after all the other women had dropped off to sleep. She did physics problems in her head. She remembered all the poems she knew and tried to translate them into Lurqazi or Bordoril. She imagined letters she might write to Rafiz, to her parents and Angie, to the kids back at the city college. Finally, when she thought enough time had passed, she got up slowly and went to the door.

The guard lay asleep on his mat. A guttering oil lamp burned beside him. As she had hoped, he had taken off his turban before he'd gone to sleep. She took it and went back into the women's bedroom. The guard stirred slightly as she started to close the door, but he did not wake up.

In the dark of the women's bedroom she stuffed the turban into her purse. Then she lay down on her mat and went to sleep.

Tarq was waiting for her after breakfast. "Would you like to play chess again?" he asked.

"Okay," Casey said.

"Okay," Tarq said, laughing as though the word were a private joke between them. They went back to the room with the chessboards on the floor, and Tarq set up the pieces.

Casey lost three games before she spoke. "Is it warm outside?" she said.

"It is hot," Tarq said, setting up for another game. "Very hot."

Casey sighed. "I would love to go outside," she said. "I am tired of being always inside."

"It is too dangerous," Tarq said. "I am sorry."

"For a minute only," Casey said. "I am sure you will—" She made him wait while she looked up the word in the dictionary and then said, "Protect me."

It was almost too easy. Tarq sat up straighter, hesitated before putting down a piece, and said, "Well—"

"I would be so happy," Casey said. "Just for a minute. Not very far. Okay?"

"Okay," Tarq said. "I will protect you."

They went down the stairs and into the red room. No one stopped them as Tarq took out a key and opened the door. The dark-green lawn stretched out in front of them, smooth as a rug.

Casey went down the marble stairway and stopped at the bottom. Tarq followed closely behind her. "It is so beautiful," she said.

Tarq shrugged. "We should go back inside now," he said.

"Just to the—" Casey said, pointing, not knowing the word.

"Fountain," Tarq said.

"Fountain," Casey said. "It is very beautiful. And then we will go back. Okay?"

"Okay," Tarq said.

The thick lawn felt good beneath her feet. She almost felt sorry for him. She waited until she got the fountain between them and started to run.

"Hey!" Tarq said. "Heyyy!" He came after her. They were too far from the big house for anyone to hear him. His sandals slipped once on the lawn and Casey was gone, through the box hedge and around the back of the neighboring house. She kept running, always picking the streets that led down, but she didn't think he had followed her. He was afraid to leave the safety of the house. They all were.

What they'll probably do, she thought at the foot of the hill, taking out the turban and tying it around her head to cover her hair, is get in their bus and try to follow me. But by that time I'll have found a taxi and gone home. Taxi—I have no money. I gave it all to that woman cabdriver.

She set off down one of the streets, wondering what to do next. Boy, that was stupid, she thought. I'll just have to keep walking until I find something I recognize. Maybe I should have stolen some of the silverware.

The streets were as deserted as they had been two days ago. Is Cumaq still in charge? she thought. What's been happening? She felt sharply visible. She was a walking paradox, a woman in a turban, an American in a city where all the Americans had gone home. And my parents? Did they go home too? They had to have waited for me.

The graffiti on the streets had grown like weeds. They covered everything, every house, every few feet of sidewalk, even some cars —a jagged phrase almost entirely covered by a rounded one. It's a feud that's gone on for twelve hundred years, she thought, wondering. Between the Sozranis and the followers of the Jewel King. And everywhere but in the marble house and a few other parts of the city the Jewel King is winning. I wonder if my father knows.

But she was too worried to concentrate. She passed houses, then an empty burned-out section with a glass-and-chrome supermarket rising incongruously out of the wreckage. "Super Shop," the sign over the glass door said. It looked eerie, standing alone in the deserted city, golden reflections of the sun shining from the glass. She went past it quickly.

At the next corner three streets met and she chose one at random. The day grew hotter. It was probably noon. And what would she do if she was caught out after dark without having found a familiar landmark? What would Cumaq's men do to her if they found her? She wished she knew more about him. She had wanted to listen to the news at home but her mother hadn't liked having the radio on. And anyway she'd been home so seldom.

She passed a park with wavy benches made of orange and red tile, structures of gold and green that looked as if they had melted in the heat. Gaudi Park, she thought. She had been meaning to ask Rafiz to take her here. Someone had defaced one of the benches with graffiti.

Should she rest in the park for a while? No, better to go on. She came to a commercial district, passing stores selling fruit, lamps, brass, wood, furniture. All the stores were closed, and a few of them had signs she couldn't read posted on the doors. She hurried on.

The store ahead of her had sharp gables over the windows and a door shaped like a triangle. The store next to that one was rounder, a scallop design on the roof, circular windows and a large arch over the front door. Did the feud extend even to their architecture? It wasn't that ridiculous an idea. In twelve hundred years the entire city could have been made over into angles and curves. You'd want to know whom you were dealing with when you went into a store, whether the proprietor was a follower of Sozran or of the Jewel King.

Now that she was looking for them, she saw sharp and rounded edges everywhere. Spires and domes in the mountains. Bricks sticking their corners out of a wall, a chimney leaning at a grotesque angle, curving steps, a circular driveway. She'd thought their cars were so old-fashioned because they couldn't afford newer ones, but now she realized that most of the people preferred the rounded lines of the older cars. Newer models like Rabbits were for tourists.

And even the streets, with their sudden jagged turns or long rounded corners, even the streets were part of the feud. No wonder everything in the city was so hard to find. The entire city had probably been knocked down and built up hundreds of times since the war, like a larger version of the mosaic in the house of the Sozranis. And if that was true then she should be taking the rounded corners, because the Sozranis, out of long habit, would be taking the jagged ones.

She turned a long corner, then another one, then another. If you thought the whole thing through it was all pretty amazing. The cab-drivers and the bus drivers who were on the side of the Jewel King would take the rounded corners through the city, and the ones on the side of the Sozranis would take the jagged corners. The feud would control where you lived, who you talked to, what kind of furniture you had, what you wore. And yet there was no hint of any of this in any of the guidebooks. No visitor had ever guessed, starting with the Spanish conquerors hundreds of years ago.

The rounded street corners made her feel as if she was going in circles. But the commercial district gave way to a row of neat little houses, all of them declaring solidly for the Jewel King, and the houses were succeeded by a burned-out area covered with hundreds of tents made of different-colored coats, blankets and cardboard. The street looked familiar. Or did she just imagine that it did, out of desperation?

She turned another corner. Ahead of her on the other side of the street she saw the Sun and Stars. She ran down the street, squeezed between the two houses at the end and looked out at Twenty-fifth November Street.

Casey and Mama

When Angie woke in the dim cluttered room the first thing she saw was an old bamboo tray, and on the tray a loaf of bread and a cup of coffee. She assumed the food was for her. They wouldn't try to starve her, would they?

She sat up and put the tray on her lap. Well, but what if her father couldn't pay the ransom? Was her family rich enough to afford it? She didn't even know. Maybe they wouldn't even bother, maybe once Casey came back they would just go home. She knew they liked Casey better anyway.

But it didn't pay to think of that, and she slipped back into the

Two Kingdoms. As was happening more and more she thought of the history of the kingdoms first, the history she hadn't known until she had come to Amaz. The Jewel King, the best knight in all the realm, the Queen and the son she had conceived with the knight the day her husband fought the War of Stones and began to lose the kingdom . . . they paraded before her in all their finery, the gold bits and stirrups of the horses, the rich tapestries, the shields and swords, and over all the one sword, curved, with a fiery hilt. Where had they come from, these people who had appeared full-grown in her mind when the rest of the kingdom had come to her slowly, piecemeal, with hundreds of revisions and additions? This sudden vision must mean something, but what? That she would come to join the kingdoms of Borol and Marol, that she would fade gradually to the world and finally live only in that other, brighter, realm? That was what she hoped, but she was afraid the vision meant something else, something sinister.

There was a knock at the door. Angie waited, but no one entered. The knock came again. "Come in," Angie said.

The door opened. The light from the corridor hurt her eyes, and now she noticed that light was struggling to pierce the dingy curtain on the far wall. Hours must have passed since she had eaten the bread, but she was used to time passing differently for her while she was in the kingdoms. A man stood in the doorway, his knotted white hair the only thing she could see against the light. Surprisingly, she was no longer afraid. If something terrible happened to her it would be that much worse for her parents if they hadn't come forth with the ransom money. "Are you going to kill me?" she asked.

The man closed the door and sat on a covered stool near the foot of the bed. "No," he said. "Do not be frightened. Blue Rose does not know that I am here."

"Blue Rose?"

"The woman who wears the—the gloves," the old man said. "She is waiting for word from your father. My name is Rafiz. I am a friend of Casey's."

"Oh," Angie said. She couldn't get her mind to focus. Why didn't he go away and leave her with the bright horses, the shining swords?

"We must get you away," Rafiz said. "Blue Rose is waiting for your father to give her the sword, and I fear that if she has it—"

"The—the sword?" Angie said.

"Yes," Rafiz said. "The Jewel King's sword. Your father—"

"Then it's real?" Angie said, disappointed. "The Jewel King's sword really exists?"

"Yes, of course," Rafiz said. "Your father is looking for it. You did not know?"

"No," Angie said. "I thought I made it up. The Jewel King, and the Queen, and the knight, and their son— It's all real?"

"It is all real," Rafiz said. "What do you mean that you made it up? Surely you had learned the legend from your father."

"No," Angie said slowly. "I never talk to my father. I wrote it all down in my notebooks. I never heard any of it before in my life."

"Tell me the story," Rafiz said.

She told him all of it, how the Jewel King had overthrown the corrupt king before him and come to power, how he had gained the sword and used it to unite the realm, but how treachery in his palace and outside the country combined to bring him down. Rafiz listened quietly, his hands resting loosely on his lap. His eyes in the dim light looked impossibly black, like the black coins issued after the death of a king in Borol.

After she had finished he nodded. "Yes," he said. "That is our national epic."

"All of it?" she said.

"Yes," he said. "All of it."

She sat silent a moment. The real world always lay out there waiting, ready to ambush you with something you could not control. The history you'd made up for your own private kingdom turns out to be the national epic of some obscure country. Her disappointment returned. "But how—how could that happen?"

Rafiz shrugged. "There are forces at work that we do not understand," he said. "Forces that brought you here, to Twenty-fifth November Street. Time is divided by two, what we know has happened and what is hidden from us in the future. And I cannot even go to the cards, because for the first time that I can remember the cards have not been printed. But I know that we must get you away from here. Blue Rose must not get the sword."

She didn't want to move. She wanted either to be killed right away or to have her parents ransom her. How much was she worth to them? Thousands? Millions? If Casey had been kidnapped too would they ransom her first? She said nothing.

"I can do nothing now," Rafiz said. "I am only here because Zem thinks I am also working for Blue Rose. He had the sickness of dreamlessness when he was a child, and is slow-witted. But I will come back. You must be ready to leave at once." Angie still said nothing. "Do you understand?" Rafiz said.

"All right," Angie said.

"You are very different from Casey," Rafiz said. "But Blue Rose says you are sisters." He opened the door and went outside.

Angie sat stiffly on the bed after he had gone. She had only talked to him for a few minutes and he was already comparing her with Casey. Her whole life had been like that. Probably Casey, wherever she was, had met up with a better class of kidnapper, probably Angie had somehow failed in that too. She wouldn't mind staying here for a long time, for the rest of her life maybe, as long as they gave her a place to sleep and kept feeding her. She could work on the kingdoms just as easily here as anywhere else. Though it was too bad she couldn't have brought her notebooks.

But the old man—Rafiz—would be back to take her away. Because, he said, Blue Rose must not get the sword. The sword... She saw the Jewel King raise the golden sword high above him, the Queen, dressed all in white and gold, standing at his side. The crowd before him roared as if with one voice.

Claire looked up from her book and saw Mitchell come into the kitchen. She nodded at him and went back to reading.

"It's frustrating," Mitchell said. "I know they're out there somewhere, but there's no one I can talk to. No way to get help." He spread his hands helplessly over the table. "There's just nothing I can do."

Claire put down the book, a little surprised. It had been a long time since he had wanted to talk to her, a long time since the two of them had been alone. They had to have talked when they decided that Angie needed to see a psychologist, but she couldn't remember it. She didn't know how to have a conversation with him that wasn't some kind of furious intellectual argument.

Sometime in the future, she knew, Angie and Casey would move out, go away to college or something, and then it would be just the two of them living alone in the house. But that was in the future, and things were sure to change before then. She wasn't ready for this intimacy yet.

"I don't even know where the damn police station is," Mitchell said. "The phones are dead, so I can't call. And even if I got to the station, who knows what the hell I might find. Cumaq's taken them over too, Jara says. They'd probably just order us to go home."

"Take a cab," Claire said.

Mitchell looked at her and laughed. Now she saw that he hadn't really been talking to her, just using her as a sounding board.

"A cab," he said. "There are no cabs. The streets are deserted."

"I took one," Claire said.

"When?"

"Yesterday," she said. Mitchell looked up at her quickly, and suddenly she felt uncertain. No, it had to be yesterday, she thought, checking back. "Yeah, that's right. Yesterday."

"Where did you go?" Mitchell asked.

"I looked for Casey," she said.

"You looked—where?" he asked.

She brushed her hair away from her face. "In the city," she said.

"Where in the city?" Mitchell said, sounding urgent. "Where did you think she was?"

"Oh, I don't know," Claire said. "Around."

"You got a cab and all you did was drive around?" Mitchell said. "Why didn't you go to a police station? Or a—an embassy or something?"

"Well," she said. "It's hard to explain. See, the first time I got in a cab I asked to be taken to a grocery store. That was when we had the Wileys for dinner, remember?" Mitchell nodded, his eyebrows slightly raised. She went on. "Well, the driver took me to this place called Super Shop. It was a grocery store, but mostly it sold, well, it was a liquor store. As if the driver knew that I hadn't had anything to drink since I got to Amaz."

Mitchell's eyebrows were higher now, the expression on his face one of astonishment. She could see that he wasn't going to believe her. That was the trouble when other people thought you drank too much, they tended not to believe most of what you said.

"So then one time I asked to be taken to the Super Shop," Claire said. "And the driver took me to this bookstore. As if he knew I liked to read. So yesterday when I got in the cab I asked to be taken to Casey. That's all, just Casey. Because they usually know what I want, see, and yesterday all I wanted was to get Casey back."

"And what happened?" Mitchell asked.

"He didn't know what I was talking about," Claire said. She felt a tear leave her eye and move slowly down her cheek. "The city's abandoned me. Something's happened. Something's changed."

"Where did you go?"

"Around the city, like I told you," Claire said.

For a minute she thought he was going to get angry. But he never got angry with her, she knew that. "You weren't abandoned," he said finally. "No one knows where Casey is. It's not your fault."

"Maybe I can get another cab," she said.

Mitchell sighed. "It's all right, Claire," he said.

"No, really," she said. "Do you want to come outside with me? I can try to get a cab, and then you can go to the police station, or wherever."

"The streets are deserted," he said. "There's nothing out there."

"Come on," she said. "Let's go. It's worth a try." She stood up and went into the living room. She could hear Mitchell following behind her. "Maybe I can get on the other side this time," she said, but she said it mostly to herself.

Mitchell looked out at the empty streets in front of him. It was stupid to humor her, he thought. Now she'll just sink further into her depression. There's never any point in showing people the truth behind their fantasies. Probably she hadn't gone anywhere yesterday, probably she'd just stayed at the kitchen table all day.

Something came around the corner. "Look!" Claire said, pointing, and then dropped her arm as the truck came closer. Soldiers called to them from the back as it passed.

"Listen, Claire—" Mitchell said.

"A little more," Claire said. "Just a little more time. Maybe the city will help me out just once more."

Mitchell said nothing. They stood on the porch looking at the streets, a mirror image of the turbanned people who had once stood looking across the street at them.

Now he saw a small figure walk around the corner and head toward them. The police, he thought, come to take us to the airport, or to jail. We really shouldn't be out here. It's much too exposed.

"Claire," he said. "Let's go inside."

"In a little bit," she said. "Just a little longer."

"Now," he said, trying to sound stern. "There's a man coming this way. Who knows who he is? Could be the police, could be anyone. Let's go." He took one last look at the man and saw that he was wearing a brown suit. Probably not the police, then. Probably worse. The man came closer, a small man, walking rapidly in the heat. Jara.

Mitchell turned back to the house but Jara had already seen him. "Good morning, Dr. Parmenter," Jara called. "I waited for you at the place we agreed to meet, but you did not come."

"I'm not looking for your damn sword any more," Mitchell said as he got closer. "It won't do any good."

"But your daughter—" Jara said, standing at the foot of the porch and looking up.

"My daughters," Mitchell said heavily. "The other one's gone too now. And they want the sword in exchange for her too—some woman came to tell us last night. So unless you can guarantee we'll find two swords, so I can give one to each . . ."

"What will you do?" Jara said.

Mitchell shrugged. "Go to the police, I guess," he said.

"That would do no good," Jara said. "Cumaq controls the police now. They would just arrest you."

"It's my only hope, though," Mitchell said. "I can't think of anything else. The only thing is—I don't know how to get there. Could you give me directions?"

"I will tell you what I will do," Jara said, coming up the porch steps. "I will take you there. And when we are there I will go inside and ask about your daughter—daughters—and see if it is safe for you to come inside too. I will do this if you will come with me to look for the sword."

Mitchell looked at him, surprised. He would never have expected Jara to make an offer like that, to help him so selflessly. Of course it wasn't entirely unselfish, the maniac was still doggedly on the trail of the sword. "Why don't you just go look for the sword yourself?" Mitchell said. "What do you need me for?"

"I do not know," Jara said. "I feel that—I will need you for something before the end. It is not over yet."

"Well, thanks," Mitchell said, sorry for all the times he had belittled the man. "Thanks a lot." He turned to say good-bye to Claire. "Don't go anywhere," he said. "Don't leave the house. Don't even answer the door." She nodded vaguely, closing the door behind her.

Then they set off. Jara led him through the twisting streets, turning corners, doubling back, until Mitchell was completely lost. I never could have done this by myself, he thought. Finally Jara stopped in front of a shabby storefront divided down the middle into two shops, one selling old office machines and the other a shoe-repair store. "Here we are," he said. "The police station."

"This?" Mitchell said. He was very much afraid he had been the victim of an elaborate practical joke. "How can you tell?"

"Upstairs," Jara said, and now Mitchell saw a flight of stairs at the side of the shoe-repair shop. "They do not look like this where you are from?"

"They—no," Mitchell said.

"Wait here," Jara said. "I will go see if it is safe."

Mitchell watched as Jara went up the stairs to the station. As soon as Jara was gone Mitchell felt alone, exposed to anyone who might come along. How do I know I can trust him? he thought. What if he's turning me in right now? What if he doesn't come back? But almost immediately he felt ashamed. Of course I can trust him—hell, if I can't there's no one left in this crazy country who can help me. I'm just being paranoid. Anyone would be, under the circumstances.

Jara came to the head of the stairs and waved to him. Mitchell started up, relieved and apprehensive at the same time. They went into the station together.

Inside it looked a little more like what Mitchell imagined a police station to look like: steel desks and filing cabinets, green walls and gray linoleum floors, a glass door that led to someone's office, another that led down a corridor. A clock on the wall said 4:36.

But if the room lived up to Mitchell's expectations the men in it most definitely did not. They lounged on desks and chairs—there was even one of them up on a filing cabinet—laughing, drinking from paper cups, talking loudly. Almost all of them had the same kind of machine gun as the waitress at the McDonald's, and one man was sighting a pistol carefully at the clock. Another man gleefully tore up the papers on his desk, and when he was finished he looked through the drawers for more. They were dressed in every kind of clothing, jeans, suits, combat fatigues, all torn and stained, all mismatched.

A few of the men stopped talking when Mitchell entered, and one of them came toward him. He wore the charcoal-gray pants of a good tweed suit, a black T-shirt, a green-and-yellow-checked scarf and a beret. "How may I help you?" he said.

"My daughters are missing," Mitchell said. "Kidnapped."

"Ah," the man said. "What is your nationality?"

"I'm an American," Mitchell said.

"North or South American?"

"North—I'm from the United States," Mitchell said.

"Ah," the man said. "The United States. But surely you know that all foreigners must leave the country?"

"Yes," Mitchell said, speaking fast. "Yes, I know that, but my daughter—my daughters—I can't leave without them—"

"I am afraid," the man said, "that we will have to arrest you. Breaking curfew, being in the country when you have been ordered to leave—what else?" He looked around at the other men for inspiration, but none of them was paying attention. He reached into his pants pocket and drew out a pair of handcuffs. "Give me your hands, please."

Mitchell looked wildly at Jara, at the other men in the room, at the door leading down the steps. What would Claire do, alone at the house, if—? Jara was shaking his head emphatically, as if to deny any connection to the man with the handcuffs. Suddenly the man started to laugh. "Funny, yes?" he said, putting the handcuffs back in his pocket. "You truly thought I was about to arrest you, no? That was a good joke, was it not, American?"

Mitchell nodded weakly. Everyone except Jara was laughing. He heard a loud bang and the shattering of glass as one of the other men shot the clock.

"Now," the man with the handcuffs said after the laughter had died down, "you say your daughter is missing."

"Daughters," Mitchell said. "Both of them. They've been kidnapped."

"Ah," the policeman said. "You must be a very rich American indeed. *Two* daughters missing. How much do they want?"

"They don't want money," Mitchell said. "They want—"

"An old manuscript," Jara said, stepping forward. "Dr. Parmenter is a colleague of mine at the university. He discovered an ancient manuscript which various groups are anxious to have for themselves."

"What kind of groups?" the policeman said.

"The people that wear the turbans," Mitchell said. "They've got one of the daughters. And the other one—a woman came to tell us she had her. I never saw the woman before in my life."

"So two different groups want this manuscript," the policeman said. "This strange woman and the Sozranis."

"Who?" Mitchell said.

"The Sozranis," the policeman said. "That is what the people with turbans are called."

"The Sozranis, then," Mitchell said. Where had he heard that word before?

"This manuscript—it must be very important," the policeman said. He looked shrewdly at Jara.

"Yes, it is," Jara said. "It is the story of the Jewel King."

"Ah, the Jewel King," the policeman said. The suspicion which had started to gather in his eyes vanished. "Of course. Of course that would be important."

"So you think you can help us?" Mitchell said.

"Unfortunately I think not," the policeman said. "We have a lot of work to do here, as no doubt you can see for yourself." He gestured at the men talking and drinking and laughing behind him. "What I would suggest is that you go into the mountains to the place where these Sozranis live. Perhaps your daughter is there."

Mitchell started to protest but then realized that he would get nowhere by arguing, that he might even be arrested after all. Defeated, he turned to go. "Oh, and American—" the policeman called after him. He looked back. "You should really be out of the country now." The man laughed, but this time no one joined him.

Mitchell left the station and went down the stairs. He could hear Jara following behind him. Once they got out in the street Jara said, "I am very sorry. I truly thought that they would help."

"So did I," Mitchell said. "It isn't your fault. I guess the only place left now is the embassy."

"What embassy?" Jara said. "You know your country has no ties with Amaz."

Mitchell shrugged. "Well, what embassies are there?"

"I really do not know," Jara said. "We are a small country—no one takes much notice of us. I think there may be a French embassy somewhere."

"Good enough," Mitchell said. "Where is it?"

"I do not know," Jara said again. "I have never needed to go there."

"Well, do you have a phone book?" Mitchell said.

"That would do us no good at all," Jara said. "None of the phones is working."

"I meant for the addresses," Mitchell said, trying not to get impatient. "You have addresses listed with the phone numbers, don't you?" Jara was shaking his head. "No? Well, hell." He sighed heavily. "Well, hell, I just don't know what to do. I can't think. Unless you think we should go into the mountains, to these Sozranis."

"How will we get there?" Jara said. "There is no public transportation. Besides, I am not sure where they live. And once we get there, what will we do? Ask that they give her back to you? I heard that there are many of these Sozranis, thousands of them, all living in luxury up in the mountains."

"That's where I heard that name before!" Mitchell said.

"What?"

"The Sozranis," Mitchell said. "You said something about them once. Remember?"

"Yes," Jara said, for the moment as excited as Mitchell. "Yes, I said that Dr. Tamir was one of them. Or had talked of joining them. I would guess that he never became initiated, since he never wore the turban."

"And he knew that I was looking for the sword," Mitchell said. "Because I stupidly wrote to him and told him, when I was making the arrangements to trade houses. And he must have told one of the Sozranis. So that's why they stood in front of our house like that. They were waiting for the chance to get one of us alone, with no traffic or pedestrians who might notice what they were doing."

"They stand in front of houses all over the city," Jara said. "They stand in front of a house on the same street as my grandmother. They told her it was because the holy Sozran lived in that house."

"Who was the holy Sozran?" Mitchell asked.

"I do not know," Jara said. "All I know is what they told her. She watches them while they watch the house. She is an old woman with very little to do."

"That manuscript I found—" Mitchell said slowly—"it mentions someone named Sozran, very briefly, at the beginning. Remember? He was the corrupt king the Jewel King overthrew."

"Yes, now I remember," Jara said. "But it could not have been the same person. The oral tradition does not give the name of the corrupt king at all. And surely the Sozranis have not been around for twelve centuries."

"Why not?" Mitchell said. "You said they live in luxury. Maybe they've been amassing wealth for twelve hundred years. And another thing—if it is the same person, then he couldn't have possibly lived in Dr. Tamir's house. The house is only about three hundred years old, you told me that yourself. So those Sozranis had to be standing there waiting for us."

"Maybe," Jara said. "But—"

"Well, is there anyone else in history named Sozran?" Mitchell said, sure he was on the right track now. "Is it a common name?"

"No," Jara said. "No one I can think of has that name. I wonder if that was Tamir's secret, that the people in turbans follow the man who was king before the Jewel King."

"It doesn't seem like much of a secret," Mitchell said. "I think it was that he was planning to tell the Sozranis about me—I think that was his secret."

"Maybe," Jara said. "But he is in the United States, and we are here. And we are still no closer to finding out where the Sozranis are or what they have done with your daughter. We know a little more about them, that is all."

"Oh," Mitchell said. He felt his unhappiness return and hem him in, almost a physical thing, like an uncomfortable suit of clothes. "Right. Well, what are we going to do now?"

"There is only one thing we can do," Jara said. "We must find the sword."

"No," Mitchell said. "No, I can't—no, I have to find my daughters."

"You made me a promise," Jara said. "You said that you would help me look for the sword if I took you to the police station. And I have kept my side of the bargain, have I not?"

Mitchell nodded unhappily. "Tomorrow, then, Jara," he said. "I'm not really up to it today. I'm too worried—let's do it tomorrow. All right?"

Jara nodded and reminded him of where they had agreed to meet. "We are very close to finding the sword this time," Jara said. "I can feel it."

Mitchell said nothing. He followed Jara back to Dr. Tamir's house and let himself in. "Did you have any luck?" Claire said when he came into the kitchen.

"No," Mitchell said, sitting heavily at the kitchen table. They said nothing else for the rest of the evening. Claire fixed a light meal and they ate it. It seemed to Mitchell that the slight noises they made echoed all around them in the kitchen and beyond, through Dr. Tamir's cavernous living room and the two empty bedrooms at the back.

• • •

Casey went back to the Sun and Stars and looked inside, hoping to see someone she knew. She could barely see through the murk. And who had she expected, anyway? She didn't know anyone on the street except Rafiz. Disappointed, she turned away. Sotano was coming down the street toward her, shaking his clenched hand angrily in front of him. She was never so glad to see anyone in her life.

"Sotano!" Casey said. He looked up, surprised. "Sotano, please, can you help me?"

He said nothing. Probably he's not used to having people talk to him, she thought. I wonder what the poor bastard did that everyone treats him so badly. "Please, I need your help," she said. "Could you tell Rafiz to come to the Sun and Stars? Only Rafiz. Please?"

Sotano nodded slowly. He said something Casey didn't catch to whatever it was he held in his hand, and then went back the other way.

Casey stood and waited in front of the restaurant. What if he couldn't find Rafiz? What if he said something to Blue Rose or Zem? She was tired of running, of constantly looking behind her, of fear.

Rafiz turned the corner and came toward her slowly. Her relief came and went in the span of a breath. Why isn't he saying anything? Has Blue Rose got him working for her too?

"Casey!" he said finally. "I did not recognize you with the turban. I thought that one of the Sozranis had come for me."

She pulled off the turban and ran the rest of the distance toward him. He put his arms around her when she reached him; she smelled the familiar burnt cinnamon and held onto him gratefully. "The Sozranis wouldn't let me go," she said. "They took me up to their place in the mountains, and I thought they wanted to save me from Zem, who was following me, but they kept me there and wouldn't let me go—"

Rafiz stepped back and held up his hand. "From the beginning," he said. "Please."

She told him about being followed by Zem, about the Sozranis taking her up into the mountains with them, about her escape. It was good to be able to speak English again. "I have to get back to my parents," she said. "They said all foreigners have to leave the country—is that true?" she said, stopped suddenly by the thought that the Sozranis might have been lying to her.

Rafiz nodded.

"So I've got to get back," she said. "They must be frantic. But I don't have any money—I gave it all to the cabdriver—"

"There is another problem as well," Rafiz said. "Blue Rose has Angie."

"Angie?" Casey said. "How on earth did she get here?"

"She wanted to find you," Rafiz said. He shrugged. "She was looking for me, I think."

"Why didn't you tell me?" Casey said. "Why did you let me tell you that stupid story first?"

"We in Amaz love to hear stories," Rafiz said. He shrugged again, palms up.

"What does Blue Rose want with Angie?" Casey said. "Oh. She wants the sword, right?"

Rafiz nodded.

"Oh," Casey said again. "Well shit. We can't leave her here, can we? What do we do?"

"I do not know," Rafiz said.

"Do you know where she's keeping her?"

"At a room on the second floor," Rafiz said. "Zem and Harhano take turns guarding her. I was able to see her once, when it was Zem's turn—he is slow-witted and I told him I was working for Blue Rose. But I was not able to get her out. And both men are very strong, Harhano especially."

"Well," Casey said. "What about a ladder?"

"An excellent idea!" Rafiz said. "We can climb up at the back of the house and take her. But we will have to wait for night. A wonderful idea. I wonder why I did not think of it."

Casey grinned.

"But we must do something about you before night comes," Rafiz said. "You cannot stay out in the street so close to Blue Rose—she is desperate to have the sword. I know—we will take you to Mama."

"To Mama?" Casey said. "Why can't I just go home? Mama doesn't like me."

"Why do you say that?" Rafiz said. "It is true she does not like to speak English, but you will speak Lurqazi to her and she will love you like one of her own children. She is much nicer than you think."

"Are you sure?" Casey said doubtfully. "I'd rather go home."

"Blue Rose might have someone watching your house," Rafiz said. "Or the Sozranis might. Or you might not be able to come back tonight—there are very few taxis running. It is best that we bring you to Mama's. Put the turban back on and we will go."

"What about my parents?" Casey said. "I have to tell them—"

"I will tell them," Rafiz said. "No one will suspect me. Come."

Reluctantly she wrapped the turban around her head. Rafiz looked at her and laughed. "You have not been a Sozrani very long," he said. He took the turban off and wrapped it around again. "This is the way they tie it. It was lucky for you that none of the turbanned people saw you."

Rafiz made sure that no one except Mama was out on Twenty-fifth November Street. Then he led Casey to where Mama sat in her old leather chair and spoke to her briefly. Mama called for one of her children and led Casey and Rafiz into her store. A small girl appeared from nowhere and climbed into Mama's chair.

Inside the store—which was even dimmer and dustier than Blue Rose's—Rafiz explained what had happened to Casey, speaking slowly so that Casey could understand him. Somewhere in the middle of his narrative Mama turned away from him and toward Casey, looking at her shrewdly with eyes as small and dark as raisins. Casey felt as though she were being tested.

"Why didn't the Sozranis want to let you go?" Mama asked her.

"I don't know," Casey said.

Surprisingly, Mama began to laugh, a chuckle that started deep within her body and worked its way outward, like an earthquake. "They want the sword, I bet," she said.

"They had a sword," Casey said.

Mama laughed harder. "A fake," she said. "A fraud. They haven't had the sword for eleven hundred years."

Casey hadn't followed everything Mama said, but she understood the gist of it. "The sword looked new," she said.

"New, yes," Mama said. "And it was straight, yes? Straight?" She pantomimed the word "straight" with her hands. "Not curved?" The movements of her hands changed.

"Straight, yes," Casey said.

"Yes, of course," Mama said. "Jagged and curved things can never marry."

"I have to go," Rafiz said. "I have to tell Casey's parents that she is all right, and that we will try to get the other daughter to them too. I'll leave Casey here with you."

Casey gave him directions to Dr. Tamir's house. When she heard her speak English Mama looked at her sharply, almost as if she hadn't passed her test after all. But after Casey said good-bye to Rafiz Mama put her arm, warm and comfortable as dough, around Casey's shoulders. "We will have a lot to talk about," Mama said. "Would you like some coffee? Some bread?"

"Sure," Casey said, then remembered her manners. "Please."

Mama led her upstairs, into a small kitchen. Through an open door Casey could see a large bedroom with one bed and about a dozen mattresses nearly covering the floor. Mama quickly made sweet coffee and sliced a loaf of sticky bread and put bread and coffee on a lacquered Chinese tray. She led Casey to the tiny kitchen table, sat her down and started talking immediately.

Casey didn't understand a lot of what Mama said, but she thought that if Rafiz had been right and Mama's earlier objection to her had been because she spoke English it would be rude to take out the dictionary. Anyway Mama didn't seem to need any response from her. She was talking about her children, all twelve of whom, according to Mama, had had different fathers. Or had Casey misunderstood something? Mama told her about Jarek, who had stolen something from Blue Rose, and when she told this story she started shaking again, as though she thought Jarek had done something inexpressibly funny. She told her about Satl, the fourth child and second girl, the quiet one. She told the story of the sixth child and fourth boy, who had had two different fathers. But no, Casey had to have misunderstood something there. Even this ignorant woman would know that that was impossible.

In the middle of the story about the twins Mama started calling her *taggi*, which Casey knew from her reading was an endearment used mainly by parents to their children. "When they were born they looked the same," Mama said. "So alike that even I could not tell them apart. I may have even switched them when they were young, started calling one by the other's name. But as they grew older they changed, and are now so different they look like they come from different families. One of them is even older than the other. I asked Rafiz and he says that that can happen, that people can grow older faster or slower. What do you think, *taggi?*"

Casey said nothing, surprised by Mama's easy assumption that Casey was part of the family. And maybe it wouldn't be so bad to be a part of this family after all, living near the warmth of this woman; going to bed surrounded by all your brothers and sisters, like puppies; taking part in the anarchic life of the street. She caught herself, a little surprised. Her own life wasn't that bad that she should envy a poor Third World family growing up in a junk shop.

Mama went on talking as if she hadn't expected an answer. Her bread and coffee still lay untouched on the tray before her, and Casey wondered how she had managed to get so fat. When she finally paused for breath Casey said, "Why does Blue Rose not like you?"

"Would you like some more bread, *taggi?*" Mama said, and started on the story of the twelfth child, who had been born small enough to fit into a coffee pot.

Rafiz walked through the deserted streets, almost not noticing where he was going, taking the curved corners by habit. A few blocks back he had seen a flash of something, something that had to be a color. But which one? It had looked crisp, a bit unfriendly, very self-assured. It had been on a leaf, so he assumed that it was green. But that wasn't how he had expected green to look at all. In spring people always became so excited by green, about the return of color to the trees. So then what was this smug interloper? Maybe it was blue, though he had never heard of blue appearing on a leaf.

Another flash of color, this one startling, almost terrifying. He guessed it was red, though he was by no means sure. He would have to ask someone, but he would have to ask in such a way that people would not suspect what was happening to him. If he could see color, then one day, probably soon, he would be able to see death, and he didn't want anyone to feel sorry for him. For himself he felt he had had a long life, filled like all lives with happiness and sorrow, and he would not be too sad to leave it.

But first he had to find Casey's parents. He reached the university and followed her directions to Dr. Tamir's house. Once there he stopped, amazed. He had not known that Casey's family was so rich, that they could afford such a palace, with what looked like six or seven rooms. It was probably a good thing Casey hadn't told him, he thought, or he would not have been able to treat her with such familiarity. He went slowly up the steps to the porch.

He knocked on the door. knocked again when no one came. Inside he thought he could hear someone moving around, coming hesitantly to the door and then walking away. He waited a long time before going downstairs and back to Twenty-fifth November Street. On the way home he saw a cool, shimmering color, but whether it was blue or yellow he didn't know.

Another Way to Twenty-fifth November Street

By the time Rafiz returned, Casey's eyelids hurt from the strain of keeping them open. Who would have thought the old woman could talk so much? "What did they say?" she asked Rafiz in English.

"Who?"

"Who? My parents, who do you think?" Mama looked from Casey to Rafiz, suspicious, and abruptly left the room.

"No one came to answer the door," Rafiz said.

"No one—" Casey said. "Are they gone? Did they leave the country, do you think? What do I do now?"

"Forgive me," Rafiz said. "I did not mean to give the wrong idea. Someone was in the house, but that person would not answer the door. I could hear him or her moving around inside."

"Well, did you leave a note?" Casey said.

"No," Rafiz said. "I had nothing to leave a note with."

"So they still don't know I'm all right," Casey said. She was angry, and a little frightened too. Maybe someone had taken over Dr. Tamir's house after her parents had gone. Maybe Dr. Tamir had come back. "That's just great. As soon as we get Angie I'm leaving. We've got to get out of the country."

"It might not be safe for you to go back," Rafiz said.

"Well, it sure isn't safe to stay here!" Casey said. "Was anyone watching the house?"

"No," Rafiz said. "Not that I could see."

"What about Zem or Harhano?" she said. "Did you see them?"

"No."

"How about the Sozranis?"

"No," Rafiz said.

He looked so dejected she almost felt ashamed. He didn't deserve this interrogation. Still, if only he'd left a note... "Okay," she said. "It's okay. We'll be leaving soon anyway."

Mama came back into the kitchen to fix dinner. She set a huge pot on the stove and added what looked like all the ingredients she had in the small refrigerator. One by one the children came into the kitchen and ladled out some of the stew. They ate sitting on the floor or one of the mattresses in the other room, on the stairs or in the shop. They talked and laughed all the way through the meal. Casey couldn't understand a word.

After all the children had taken their share Mama motioned to Rafiz and Casey to help themselves. They took their food over to an empty corner of the kitchen and ate standing up. Casey wished she could think of something to say to Rafiz, but she was afraid if she started to talk she'd just end up shouting at him again. She turned away from him and looked at Mama's sink, the tiniest sink she'd ever seen. Of course, she thought. They'd need it small to conserve water. Rafiz broke the silence only once, pointing to her dish and asking, "How do you say the name of this color in English?"

She looked at him, surprised. She'd thought he knew enough English to understand that much, at least. "Blue," she said.

When they'd finished the children took their plates to the sink and one of them, the oldest, ran water over them. Mama went downstairs to close the store. The kids washed and put away the dishes and then moved into the bedroom and closed the door. Casey heard muffled screams and laughter from behind the door, and then, after a long time, nothing but silence. Rafiz and Mama sat at the kitchen table and talked in rapid Lurqazi. Casey joined them but she could barely understand what they were saying. Gossip about the street, about who didn't speak to whom and why, about a woman who had run off with birds. . . . Casey started to feel sleepy. Had they forgotten all about the plan to free Angie?

Finally Rafiz stood. "They should all be asleep by now," he said, still speaking Lurqazi. "It is time to get the ladder."

Casey followed him downstairs. Mama called out something after them, probably wishing them luck. They went out a back door and walked away from Blue Rose's, through the backyards of three or four stores, until they came to the toolshed. She could barely see Rafiz ahead of her in the gloom. He went inside and brought out a ladder.

She followed him back the way they had come, feeling superfluous. He didn't even need help carrying the ladder; for an old man he was surprisingly strong. He set up the ladder so silently that if Casey hadn't known he was there she would not have suspected a thing.

"Are you sure that's the right window?" she asked him, whispering.

"I fixed that window for Blue Rose just last week," he said, turning to her. His eyes were so black they looked as if pieces of the night had been caught in them. "You had better go up. She is your sister, after all."

Casey climbed up the ladder. The window opened easily; Rafiz was probably a good craftsman. The room smelled of wicker and stale food. "Angie?" she said, calling softly through the curtain into the darkened room. "Angie, are you there?"

No answer. "Angie?" she said again. This time she heard a small rustle, as if someone were sitting up. "Angie, it's me. Casey."

"Casey?" Angie said, much too loudly.

"Sssh," Casey said. "We've come to rescue you. There's a ladder here at the window. Can you see me?"

"What if I don't want to be rescued?" Angie said. She was still speaking conversationally, as if she and Casey were sitting in her bedroom in Dr. Tamir's house.

"Quiet," Casey said. "What do you mean, you don't want to be rescued?"

"I like it here," Angie said. "They feed me, they take care of me, and I get left alone to work on the kingdoms. No one ever nags me to do anything else."

"You're nuts," Casey said. She wished she could see her sister's face. "You think they're going to treat you this way forever? If Dad can't pay the ransom they'll probably kill you."

"So?" Angie said.

"What do you mean?" Casey said. The door to the corridor opened.

"Who is here?" someone—Zem?—said in Lurqazi.

Casey said nothing, trying not to move. Her heart hammered against her ears.

"Who is here?" the man said again. "Are you real or a dream?"

"A dream," Casey said, amazed at how calm she sounded. "You are asleep."

"Good," the man said. He went back out into the corridor, closing the door behind him.

"Angie," Casey said, urgently. "Come *on*. That guy will be back."

"What—what did you say to him?" Angie said.

"I'll tell you later," Casey said. "Get out here or I'll come in after you."

Angie said nothing. After a while Casey thought she heard her stand up and come over to the window. Hardly daring to hope, Casey held her breath until she saw her sister fumble with the curtain. She guided Angie to the window and out to the ladder.

Casey had intended to wake up early and go back to Dr. Tamir's house, but she had been up late the last two nights and when she woke it was near noon. Angie lay on the floor of the kitchen next to her. Someone, probably Mama, had covered them with blankets while they slept. Casey sat up as Rafiz came into the room.

"Blue Rose is very angry," Rafiz said. "She is sure we have Angie. She is threatening to bring Zem and Harhano over and break down the door."

"Do you think she'll do it?" Casey said.

"I do not know," Rafiz said. "Mama's friends have said they will protect her. The street is divided between those who support Mama and those who support Blue Rose."

"How come Blue Rose dislikes Mama so much?" Casey said.

Rafiz shrugged. "No one knows," he said. "She has been that way since before I came to the street. Some say they have hated each other for twenty years."

"Mama said one of her kids stole something from Blue Rose, but I didn't catch what it was," Casey said. "Do you—?"

"Her tattoos," Rafiz said.

"What?" Casey said. Was he making fun of her? He had acted strangely ever since he'd come back from Dr. Tamir's house.

"He stole Blue Rose's tattoos," he said. "They were on the palms of her hands. That is why she wears the gloves."

She turned away from him, angry and frustrated. It didn't pay to talk to any of these people—they were all crazy. And the scary thing was that if she stayed another few days she'd probably be just like them, believing all the ridiculous things they believed. "We're going to go home," she said. "As soon as Angie wakes up."

"I would not if I were you," Rafiz said. "Blue Rose is watching the house. And there are soldiers still in the streets. It would not be safe to return to your house."

"And it's safe to stay here?" Casey said, her old impatience with him returning. "Just stay here and let Blue Rose and the rest of them come get us?"

"Mama will not let Blue Rose get you," Rafiz said. "And it is safer here than in the streets. In a few days you can—"

"And what about my parents?" Casey said, loud enough to wake Angie. Maybe she had been right, maybe Rafiz worked for Blue Rose after all. But no—why would he have helped her rescue her sister? "In a few days my parents will probably be gone, and then what'll we do? Stay here for the rest of our lives?"

Rafiz said nothing. She noticed that he was looking intently at what seemed to be empty air, and she began to worry about him. He had been like this ever since yesterday, turning suddenly to stare at something quite ordinary, a chair or a flower or a skirt. But even as she thought to ask him what was wrong, she noticed that the air in front of him had started to sparkle. All of the small kitchen was sparkling gold and silver. She tried to stand, struggling upward against air that seemed to have congealed, to have turned hard as earth. "What—?" she said, frightened.

"Something is happening," Rafiz said.

"What?" she repeated, standing up and leaning against the wall.

"Something . . ." Rafiz said, standing still as if listening.

As Mitchell followed Jara through the streets he noticed that they were about to pass the place where he had rented the car. The lights in the rental office were off, the gate of the fence around the lot locked, and a sign already faded on the gate said "Closed" in five different languages. He looked into the office, hoping for a sign of life, but he could see no one. The rental place had figured in one of his half-baked plans: he would get a car, drive up into the mountains and storm the fortress of the Sozranis. And if he couldn't get Casey back he and Claire would drive to the airport. In a few days the food Claire had bought would run out, and the banks had been closed for several days. They would have to find some way out of the country. It disturbed him that he was already thinking about leaving, as if he had given up.

Maybe he could climb the fence, find the keys to one of the cars. He studied the barbed wire at the top of the fence a little dubiously. How did he come to this, he who had only asked to sit in his study and follow the trail of words as far as it would go? What he'd been thinking of was breaking and entering—and who knew what the punishment for that was here?

And why was he still following Jara on his futile quest? Sure, he'd made a promise, but would he have kept that promise if the police had somehow miraculously managed to get his daughters back? Wouldn't he rather have run to the airport as fast as he could go and booked his family on the next flight out? What did he owe Jara any-way? Wasn't all of Jara's talk of needing him before the end more of the man's strange mysticism?

A truck turned the corner in front of him and his heart seemed to start beating again only when the truck moved out of sight. Every day he and his family stayed here increased the danger. He would have to leave soon, probably tomorrow. He would go back to the United States and contact someone in authority there, someone who could work through the proper channels to get his daughters out of Amaz. He would be like one of those sad men whose pictures he saw sometimes in the newspapers, men who had tried for twenty years to get their children out of Vietnam. You never think of these things happening to you, he thought.

"Look!" Jara said.

Mitchell lifted his head. He had been staring at the sidewalk, which seemed to have been paved with bottle caps. He couldn't see any-thing. "What?" he said. It was an effort to speak.

"An open pastry shop," Jara said. "Over there. Is it too early in the day to eat, do you think?"

"Not for me," Mitchell said, welcoming the idea of sitting down.

They went into the pastry shop. At the table Jara took out a map and several different-colored pens. What do the different colors mean? Mitchell thought, aware of how little the search for the sword had come to mean to him.

A waiter came to take their orders. Now Mitchell noticed that they were the only people in the dim shop. Jara said something to the waiter in Lurqazi. Mitchell turned the map to face him and began drawing on it idly with one of the pens.

"What are you doing?" Jara said.

"I don't know," Mitchell said. "Look, if we follow these streets here we'll be writing the word 'sword' in old Lurqazi."

Jara turned the map toward himself eagerly. "Yes, I see!" he said, excited. "Look, we are here, and if we continue this way, following this route that you drew— But we must draw it like this." He made Mitchell's letters more curved, rounding out the jagged edges.

"Why?" Mitchell said.

"Because this is the way the followers of the Jewel King write," Jara said. "You must have seen the writing on the street, the jagged letters covered by more rounded ones. The letters say 'The King lives,' though probably the people who write them, kids mostly, do not know what they are writing. They only know that they are coming out in support of the Jewel King. And they are covering the same letters written the way they had been written by the corrupt king, the one who reigned before the Jewel King."

"Sozran," Mitchell said. He was starting to get a little excited too. Why hadn't Jara told him the significance of the graffiti before? Surely Jara knew of his interest in the Jewel King. But Jara probably thought nothing of the writing he had seen all his life, writing that had survived eleven centuries.

"What?" Jara said.

"Sozran," Mitchell said. "The corrupt king before the Jewel King. Remember, I found his name in the manuscript—"

"Yes, and the people who write the letters the other way, the way of Sozran, they are probably Sozranis," Jara said. "I have always thought that the jagged letters were written by kids—how do you say it, you have them in the United States—by kids who are delinquents. But if they are written by Sozranis, then that is the secret which Dr. Tamir claimed to have understood—that the King is Sozran, that Sozran lives. And if that is true, then it is possible that the Sozranis have the sword, that they gained it at the last battle and have kept it all these centuries—"

"No, because why would they want the sword to ransom Casey?" Mitchell said. Both men had raised their voices, spurred on by their discoveries.

"No, you are right," Jara said. "They want the sword to win back the country for Sozran, to take back what they consider rightfully theirs. Come—we must go now. If they have discovered the same things we have—"

"Go?" Mitchell said. "Where?"

"We must follow the route you have laid out," Jara said. "It is obvious that this will lead us to the sword."

"I didn't mean—" Mitchell said. "I wasn't saying—"

"Come," Jara said, standing.

The waiter came out of the back of the shop, carrying a silver tray. "What about our food?" Mitchell said.

"No time!" Jara said, calling over his shoulder as he left.

Mitchell hurried to catch up with him, Jara's contagious interest propelling him forward. Now he saw, on almost every house and vacant storefront, the two overlapping calligraphies, rounded and jagged. How could he not have noticed them before, the stylized letters shouting from every corner that "The King lives"? He could feel his own excitement welling up within him. Words drew him on, the words that were his specialty.

But at the same time he knew that they were probably on another wild-goose chase, the last wild-goose chase. How could following a route that said "sword" lead them to the sword itself? Even Mitchell, who loved words, who collected ancient words the way some people collect coins, knew that there was a difference between the word and the thing itself. Still, following Jara gave him something to do, something to think about besides his missing daughters, the empty bedrooms. Tomorrow he would have to admit he'd failed and find some way to the airport. Today he could follow the mad wind raised by Jara and pretend that he was doing something constructive.

Though he wished that Jara would slow down. He wished they'd gotten something to eat at the pastry shop; he was starting to feel almost faint from hunger. Ahead of him he could see tiny sparkles of silver and gold dancing in the air. The heat must be getting to him, the heat and the lack of food.

The sparkles grew brighter. And the air seemed thicker, almost tangible, every step more of an effort. "Hey, Jara!" Mitchell said, wondering if his words would make it through the dense mass separating him from the other man. "Could we rest for a bit? I'm tired."

"No time!" Jara said. Jara had slowed too. He seemed to be struggling against something that blocked his way.

"What's going on?" Mitchell said. "Do you see it too? The—the sparkles?"

"We are—" Jara said. He had to stop, take a deep breath and try again. "We are rearranging the streets of Amaz. The streets we walk now have come into being only because we walk through them.

Before we came here they were sharp, jagged, they declared for Sozran. Now we are forging new streets, rounder streets, streets that declare for the Jewel King."

That's ridiculous, Mitchell wanted to say. But he had to save his breath for the struggle against whatever was holding them back. And maybe it wasn't so ridiculous after all. Something was happening, that was certain. But how did you, as Jara said, forge new streets? What happened to the old streets, to the people living in them? Did they just wake up one day and find that their houses had moved over a few feet to accommodate a new street, a street that now declared for the Jewel King?

He tried to see what was happening around them, straining through the gold and silver. He thought he saw houses jumbled together in front of them, a chimney here, a front door there, a car sticking out of a second-story window. And as they passed the houses re-formed themselves, moved over politely to create new streets.

He turned and looked back. The sparkles stopped a few feet behind him, and he had a clear unobstructed view of the streets they had passed through. Houses sat against the sidewalk, unperturbed, not looking at all as if they'd been picked up and moved like game pieces in the last few minutes. There were even people out on the sidewalk, one person anyway, a man who was—

With a strong feeling of *déjà vu,* Mitchell said, "There's someone following us."

Jara said nothing.

"Did you hear me, Jara?" Mitchell said. He felt as if he were shouting into a strong wind.

"Yes," Jara said. "There's someone following us."

"Shouldn't we—stop? Do something?"

"No time," Jara said.

Mitchell turned back again. The man following them held one hand against the opposite shoulder, holding it as if it pained him. As Mitchell watched, the man stumbled and nearly fell.

"He's hurt," Mitchell said. "Can't we stop and help him out?"

"No time," Jara said again.

"What's so important?" Mitchell said. Every word was an effort now. "Why are we in such a hurry? So what if we find the sword a few minutes later? The man's hurt, Jara."

Jara looked behind him briefly and then continued. Gold and silver sparkles hovered around him. For a minute Mitchell thought Jara carried a sword instead of a map, cutting through the air ahead of them. He blinked to clear his head of the vision. Finally Jara said, "He is a Sozrani."

"What?" Mitchell said. It was difficult to concentrate. The air seemed to make a noise like static.

"He is a Sozrani," Jara said. "The man who is following us."

"How do you know?" Mitchell said. He turned to look at the man again. Oh, he thought. The turban. Jara said nothing, intent on following the directions on his map. As Mitchell watched the Sozrani fell to the pavement and laboriously picked himself up again. "But he's hurt, Jara. The next time he falls down he probably won't make it up again. We can't just leave him there."

"You are talking—" Jara sliced at the thickened air with his sword, no, with his map. "You are talking, as you yourself pointed out, about—" he paused for breath—"about a follower of the corrupt king who lived before the Jewel King. He is following us to gain the sword. We must not let him find the sword before we do. I would fear for my country if that should happen."

"He's not in shape to find anything before we do," Mitchell said.

"We are nearly there," Jara said. "We are almost at the end of the word."

They walked in silence, pushing through the strong, stiff air. Peering through the gold and silver sparkles, Mitchell thought he saw a house straight ahead of them, a house that seemed to move out of their way as they came toward it. The sound of static became louder, until he could no longer tell if it came from inside or outside his head. The man in the turban still came on after them, stumbling every so often and looking, it seemed to Mitchell, beseechingly after them. Despite Jara's last words he felt as if they had walked a long time, as if they would walk through Amaz forever, condemned not to stop until they had written their own long strange story on its streets.

Mitchell looked behind him again. The Sozrani stumbled and fell, one hand still pressed against his shoulder. "Jara," Mitchell said. "He's just lying there. He's hurt."

"He is a Sozrani," Jara said. "Your enemy and mine."

No, Mitchell thought. Not mine. He turned and headed toward the man. The way back was much easier, the haze of the sparkles growing less and finally disappearing altogether. "Hello," Mitchell said, bending over the man, feeling awkward. Blood trickled from the man's fingers holding the shoulder. "Are you okay?"

"Okay," the man said, barely able to get the word out. He grinned, as if at a private joke, but a spasm turned the grin into a grimace of pain. He said something in Lurqazi.

"Dr. Parmenter!" Jara called, an insubstantial figure on the other side of a gold-and-silver mist. "Mitchell! Come! We must hurry!"

"He's hurt!" Mitchell called back to Jara. The wounded man had started to talk again, a torrent of words. "Could you come back here? I can't understand what he's saying."

Mitchell watched with relief as Jara's form came slowly out of the mist, seeming to solidify. For a moment he had thought Jara would leave him there, standing on a street that existed on no map, alone with a wounded man whose only English word was "okay." "You are an idiot," Jara said. "We are so close, we are nearly there—"

"What's he saying?" Mitchell said.

"What's he saying?" Jara said. "He is saying that he is a Sozrani. Can we continue following the map now?"

"No," Mitchell said. "He's saying more than that. Maybe he knows something about Casey."

Jara knelt and listened to the man on the pavement. "He is delirious," Jara said finally. "He is not making very much sense. His name is Tarq. He has been beaten, someone has beaten him, and then they have pierced him with—" Jara's breath caught for a fraction of a second—"with a sword, here, in the shoulder."

Mitchell took Tarq's hand and gently moved it away from the wound. The Sozrani cried out. Mitchell opened Tarq's shirt and wiped the blood away. It was a clean wound, small, one that could very well have been made by a sword. Despite the size of the hole, Tarq had lost a lot of blood.

Mitchell unwrapped the Sozranis' turban and started winding it around the wound. "Okay?" he asked. The Sozrani hissed in pain. "Okay," he said finally.

Jara stood and began to pace back and forth. "Ask him who beat him," Mitchell said. "Was it the Sozranis?"

"We are wasting valuable time," Jara said, coming back to Mitchell and Tarq. "We should be following the map."

"Ask him," Mitchell said.

Jara spoke to the Sozrani and listened to his answer. After a while he nodded. "Yes," he said. "It was the Sozranis. They beat him and pierced him with a sword, and then sent him out to look for us."

"For us?" Mitchell said.

"For whoever it was that was creating the disturbances in the streets of the city," Jara said. "Apparently it was felt throughout the city." Tarq said something else. "The Sozranis think the disturbances occurred because someone, an outsider, had learned too much about their secrets. This person had been staying with them in the mountains and had gone into a forbidden room, a room of—of something, I can't make it out—" Mitchell listened eagerly. "And had escaped—"

"Was it a girl?" Mitchell asked.

Jara translated. Tarq nodded slowly. "Yes, a girl," Jara said. "She escaped while Tarq was guarding her. That is why they punished him, and then gave him the task of finding her." Tarq said something else. "They told him that the girl might lead him to the Jewel King's sword. Tarq says that he is puzzled by this, because he thought that the Sozranis already had the sword, the one that wounded him. He has held it in his initiation."

"So Casey escaped," Mitchell said. "I might have known."

Jara was talking to Tarq now, rapidly, asking him something and pointing to his wound. "He says that the sword of the Sozranis is straight," Jara said. "As it would have to be, to create a wound like this one. But I am certain that the Book of Stones mentions that the sword is curved, as the writing of the Jewel King is curved. Do you remember?"

"What?" Mitchell said. It seemed miraculous that Casey had escaped, that she was alive. Perhaps she had even come home, would be waiting for him when he got back. And they could leave this crazy country, maybe ask the police to give them a ride to the airport— Then he remembered Angie. Well, Angie might turn up too. He refused to let dark thoughts intrude on the first good news he had had in days.

"Is it straight or curved?" Jara said impatiently. "The sword in the Book of Stones. Do you remember?"

"I think it was curved," Mitchell said. "Well, everything having to do with the Jewel King was curved, wasn't it?"

"Yes, but the sword originally belonged to the king before him, and everything having to do with him was jagged," Jara said. "Perhaps it changed shape when it passed from one to the other."

"Maybe," Mitchell said. After what he had seen he certainly couldn't rule out anything as impossible.

"So the sword the Sozranis say they have is a fake, a fraud," Jara said. "That must have been Dr. Tamir's secret, that the Sozranis still had the Jewel King's sword. But if he thought that then he was sadly deluded, like our friend here. And when he passed along to the Sozranis the information that we were looking for the sword, information he must have considered a joke, the Sozranis must have become very interested. Someone in power there knows the true story behind the sword they own." Jara started to pace again. "We must be going," he said. "Now more than ever I am sure we are on the right track."

"Ask Tarq if he'll be okay here until we can come back for him," Mitchell said.

Jara spoke briefly to Tarq. "He said he must go where we go," Jara said. "That is the punishment that was given to him by the Sozranis." Jara laughed. "But I do not think that he will be able to follow us far, in his condition. I do not think he will even be able to stand."

Mitchell put his arm around the Sozrani and helped him up. Tarq leaned heavily against him. "What are you doing?" Jara said.

"I'm helping him come with us," Mitchell said. "I just realized that we can't leave him here."

"Of course we can leave him here," Jara said. "What are you, crazy? You want to take him along with us to find the sword, and when we get there, you want to hand him the sword and say, 'To the

Sozranis, with my compliments'? Do you have any idea what would happen to the country if the Sozranis had the sword?"

"We can't leave him here," Mitchell said again. "The way the streets are shifting we might never be able to find him again. He could die of loss of blood before we get back. And he's in no shape to get the sword away from us, once we find it."

"I have a map," Jara said. "Of course we will able to find him again—"

"Either he comes with us or I stay here with him," Mitchell said. "Remember when you said you'd need me for something?"

"Perhaps your usefulness ended when you marked out our route on the map," Jara said darkly.

"Perhaps," Mitchell said. He was grinning, one arm around Tarq. "Do you really want to take that chance?"

Jara shrugged. "Very well," he said.

They turned and went back the way they came. Jara led, his map carried out in front of him, and Mitchell followed a few paces behind him, held back by Tarq's weight. Almost immediately they ran into the gold and silver sparkles, the heavy pressure of the air. Tarq whispered something to Mitchell in Lurqazi, all harsh guttural consonants and breathy vowels. "Quiet," Mitchell said. "It's okay."

They walked for what seemed like hours but was probably only a few short minutes. Tarq's weight was growing intolerable. Finally the sparkles seemed to become fewer, the air to press a little less heavily. Mitchell could almost make out what was in front of them, burned-out houses and then a building with a section of the roof poised to crash through the intact first floor. But no, he must be seeing only what the mist showed him again. No one could possibly live in a house like that, it was far too dangerous.

The road seemed to end in front of them. Jara walked onward and Mitchell followed, feeling the air lighten, feeling Tarq become almost easy to carry. He wondered if this was what runners felt like when they got their second wind. The road squeezed between two houses and Jara stopped. Mitchell stopped too, and looked over Jara's head at the street in front of them.

"This street is exactly like the street marked on the map," Jara said, his voice hoarse with excitement. "It is the end of the word 'sword.' The sword is here somewhere. I can feel it."

"It's nothing but a bunch of junk shops," Mitchell said without thinking. He shrugged, trying to move Tarq to a more comfortable position along his shoulder.

"Yes," Jara said. "What better place to find an ancient sword?"

Mitchell looked out at the rows of grimy storefronts, the sidewalks littered with what looked like trash. "Where do we start?" he said.

The Jewel King's Sword

"I'm going downstairs," Casey said.

"No," Rafiz said. "Blue Rose—"

"I'll be careful," Casey said. "Besides, I'm sure no one's out there in this—whatever it is." It was an effort to talk.

She pushed herself off the wall and through the gathering thickness in the air. It seemed to take forever just to go down the stairs. Mama stood behind the counter in the shop below, with what looked like most of the kids arranged around her. "Not a good day to go outside," Mama said, breathing heavily. "I knew it when I woke up this morning." Casey could barely see her through the gold and silver sparkles.

"I have to," Casey said, and at that moment the air lightened and she nearly stumbled. "Now what?" she said, almost forgetting and saying it in English.

"Something's happening," Mama said. She stood straighter and seemed to sniff the air.

Casey pushed past her impatiently. Was that all anyone on the street could say? Of course something was happening, that much was obvious. The air had turned nearly transparent again. She opened the door to the street.

Mitchell bent down and carefully settled Tarq on the pavement. "We'll have to come back for you," he said. "Jara, tell him we'll come back for him."

Jara ignored him and stepped into the street. "It is here somewhere," he said. "I know it is."

"It's okay," Mitchell said to Tarq. Tarq looked pale, the palest native of Amaz Mitchell had ever seen, and he was breathing shallowly. Maybe he's unconscious, Mitchell thought. "Jara's an idiot," he said, though who he said it to he didn't know. He hurried after the smaller man.

There was no one at all on the street. Were they all inside because of the coup, or because of what had happened to the air earlier that day? Or maybe no one at all lived on the street, maybe no one had lived there for years. Looking around him at the accumulation of junk piled in front of each of the storefronts Mitchell thought that was possible, even likely.

"Now what?" he said to Jara. "Do we go into every store and ask if they happen to have the Jewel King's sword?"

"Yes," Jara said. The idea seemed to delight him. "Only of course we do not say it like that. We simply ask if they have a sword for sale."

"I think they're all closed," Mitchell said. But even as he said it he saw a door open near the middle of the street, and a small figure step out and look cautiously around.

"There, you see?" Jara said. "There is at least one store that is open today. We will start with that one."

They walked down the street, past the silent storefronts on either side. The slight figure turned toward them and began to walk and then to run in their direction. Casey? Mitchell thought. No, it couldn't be— The young girl ran down the street and embraced him tightly before he could finish the thought.

"Casey?" he said stupidly, moving back a little to see her better. He was not even that surprised to see her, his miracle daughter standing tall and slim as a blade before him. "How did you get here?"

"How did you?" Casey said, laughing. "This is Twenty-fifth November Street—I told you about it, remember? Angie's here too."

"Angie?" Mitchell said. Perhaps Casey had also done her own translation of the Book of Stones and found the Jewel King's tomb while she was gone—he wouldn't put anything past her. "Where? How—?"

"Come on," Casey said, leading them back to the door she had come out of. "We've got to hurry. Blue Rose kidnapped Angie—remember I told you about her, and about Zem? And then we got her back—me and Rafiz—but Blue Rose knows where we took her and will probably try to get her away from us now that whatever's happened to the air has stopped."

"Hold on," Mitchell said. "How did you find out about Angie? And how did you get away from the Sozranis? We heard—"

"There's no time," Casey said. "We've got to get going, get Angie and leave the country." She stopped in front of a storefront that looked no different from any of the others they had passed, maybe a little larger and with a little more junk out in the front. She held the door open for Mitchell and Jara and motioned them inside.

"Just a minute," a woman's voice said behind them. To Mitchell it seemed as if the pile of junk had gained a voice and started to speak. He turned. A thin woman with blue gloves stood among the junk in front of the store, the woman who had come to Dr. Tamir's house with the ransom demand for Angie. On one side of her stood the man with no ear, and on the other a man so huge he made the two others look like dwarves. How had they gotten there so fast? "You have something that belongs to me. I want it back."

"We don't have anything of yours," Mitchell said.

"Oh yes you do," the woman—she must be Blue Rose—said.

"The Jewel King's sword. I had it once, a long time ago, and I sold it, because I didn't know its worth. And the man I sold it to returned it to Mama, instead of to me, and Mama sold it for more money than I'd ever seen. And I want it back."

She's from the United States, Mitchell thought, listening to her talk. It seemed a strange thing to notice in the middle of everything else. "We don't have it," he said.

"But you were looking for it," Blue Rose said. "I know that much about you."

"Sure, we were looking for it," Mitchell said. "But we couldn't find it. I was just about to give up and go home, back to the United States."

"You're lying," Blue Rose said. "You have it, or you know where it is. I haven't set foot in Mama's house or yard for seventeen years, ever since she sold my sword, and I'm not doing it now just to listen to your lies. There are three of you and three of us, but I think you'll find that Zem and Harhano could overpower you easily. And if you don't tell me what I want to know we'll turn you over to the police. All foreigners have to leave the country, you know. You're in violation of curfew."

Claire, Mitchell thought. "We don't have it, but we know—"

"We do not have it," Jara said. "And we do not know where it is. My colleague Dr. Parmenter was telling you the truth."

"All right," Blue Rose said. "Zem, Harhano—" She motioned them forward.

A second-story window opened and Casey looked up. Mama leaned over the sill, nearly filling the entire window. Behind her Casey could make out the faces of a few of the children, their eyes wide.

"Get off my property, Blue Rose," Mama said. "And take those men with you. Zem, Harhano, you should be ashamed of yourselves."

Zem looked confused for a moment. Then he blinked and stared up at Mama, eyes wide and innocent. But Casey thought Harhano looked a little embarrassed.

"What's she saying?" Mitchell said to Jara, whispering.

"Quiet," Jara said.

"I'm not leaving until I get what belongs to me," Blue Rose said. "When that man returned the sword you should have told him to bring it to me. You had no right to take the sword, and no right to sell it again. It was mine."

"Get off my property," Mama said. "I mean it, Blue Rose."

"Or what?" Blue Rose said. "Or you'll call the cops? Just try it and see what happens. And even if the cops came, which is unlikely, you know they'd side with me. It was my property, after all."

Mama ducked back into the room. More children crowded at the window, pointing and talking quietly. "Good," Blue Rose said. "Zem, Harhano—"

Mama reappeared at the window, holding something in her hand. "Casey," she said. "Here. Get rid of her." She threw what looked like a piece of metal toward the group in front of the store. It fell end over end, lazily, so pitted with rust that the sun didn't even glance off it.

Harhano was the first to move, reaching out over Casey's head for the piece of metal. "Hey!" Casey said, running toward him to throw him off balance. His arm brushed the thing, which skittered out of reach of the six of them and came to land on the sidewalk twenty feet away.

As the group stood for a second, watching the rusted metal fall, a small man ran up from the shadows and picked it up. He held it carefully, looking at it with a combination of wonder and distrust. Now they could see that it was curved, and so shot through with rust it looked like lace. But as they watched, it seemed to knit itself together and grow brighter, until they could hardly bear to look at it. The hilt seemed to writhe under the man's grip, the carvings becoming deeper, the gems shining forth. "Tarq!" Casey and Mitchell called out at the same time.

Tarq paid them no attention. "This is—is this it?" he said, holding the thing a little away from him, as though it would blind him if it came too close. "Is this the Jewel King's sword?"

"You thief!" Blue Rose said, shouting up at Mama. "You had it all this time? You had it for seventeen years?"

"Of course," Mama said. "Just because you would have sold it doesn't mean that everyone would."

"Give it back!" Blue Rose said, motioning Zem and Harhano toward Tarq. "It's mine. It belongs to me."

"No," Tarq said. "It belongs to the Sozranis. It was the holy Sozran's before it became the Jewel King's." He looked up at the golden sword as if he weren't holding it, as if it were a thing apart from him. "It was straight then, straight as a bone. I have to give it back to the Sozranis."

"Why would you give it to the Sozranis, Tarq?" Jara said, taking a step toward him. Zem and Harhano didn't seem to notice, and he took another step forward. "What have the Sozranis ever done for you? They beat you and then they stuck a sword into you.... Look at you. You've lost a lot of blood. You might die if you don't get medical attention. And these are the people you want to give the sword to? Give it to us instead. Don't give it to those torturers." He held out his hand.

"Did the Sozranis do that to you, Tarq?" Casey said, nodding at his wound. Jara looked at her in amazement, as if he had never heard a tourist speak Lurqazi before. "He's right. You shouldn't give the sword to people like that. They are not good people."

Tarq looked from Casey to Jara. "Give it to us," Jara said again. "We'll put it in a museum. We'll let everyone come see it, not like those Sozranis, who will lock it away and maybe let you see it once a year. We're with the university. We know what should be done with it."

"They lied to you, didn't they, Tarq?" Casey said. "They told you that they had the sword. But the sword they had was straight, and it was too new. I know, I saw it. They've lied for hundreds of years. Do you really want to give them the sword?"

Tarq sagged a little, still holding the sword high so that it seemed as if it was the only thing keeping him erect. "But what will I do?" he said, so softly they could barely hear him. "Where will I go? The Sozranis were my life. My parents gave me to them when I was twelve years old. I don't know any other way to live."

"You can't live a lie, Tarq," Casey said.

"Give us the sword," Jara said. He took another step forward.

Tarq moved toward Jara, holding the sword out in front of him like a burning brand. Casey heard Zem mutter something, but she didn't want to take her eyes off Tarq, as if by watching him she could help him come closer. "What did you say to him?" Mitchell whispered to her.

They heard a loud crack, and, at what seemed like the same time, saw blood spurt from Tarq's shoulder. Zem hurried toward Tarq, holding the gun in front of him. "The hell with this museum shit," he said. "Give me the sword."

"No," Tarq said, his face twisting with pain. Casey saw that he'd been shot in the other shoulder, so that it looked as if he'd been the victim of some bizarre rite, a ritual that required matching wounds. "No!" Tarq said louder, and reached out with the sword. The hand holding the gun separated from Zem's arm easily, almost as if the two had come apart hundreds of times before. Zem looked at his arm with incomprehension. Then he turned and ran. "Casey!" Tarq said, throwing the sword to her. His eyes rolled up and he fainted.

His aim was off, and once again Casey missed the sword. She heard it clatter behind her and turned and watched it disappear into Mama's store. Someone picked it up, but in the dim light she couldn't tell who it was. One of Mama's kids, probably, she thought with relief. She was completely unprepared for the figure that came out of the darkness of the store, walking into the light as if onto a stage, her blond hair lit by the glow of the sword.

Angie had lain on the floor of Mama's kitchen while the air around her had thickened, pretending to be asleep. She had heard Casey's argument with Rafiz, seen Casey leave to go downstairs, felt the air lighten and return to normal. And still she lay, eyes half-closed, wondering if she should get up or stay on the floor until everything had ended. Whatever was going on, it had nothing to do with her.

She heard Mama come into the room and she opened her eyes and sat up. Rafiz was still there, sitting at the kitchen table. He said something to Mama in Lurqazi as she passed. Mama ignored him, went to an elephant's-foot umbrella stand at the top of the stairs and rummaged through it, discarding canes and umbrellas and parasols and finally coming up with an old rusty piece of metal. Interested, Angie got up and watched as Mama went to the bedroom window and yelled something to Casey in guttural Lurqazi. Then Mama threw the piece of metal down to the street.

Now Angie could hear the clatter of metal against the pavement, hear Mama and Blue Rose raise their voices in argument. Was that strange piece of metal the Jewel King's sword, the thing that Blue Rose had kidnapped her to obtain? Blue Rose's voice pierced the still air. Angie went downstairs, coming into Mama's store just as the sword, a dull blur of gold in the dim light, skittered past her. She bent and put her hand around the hilt. Then, moved only by an impulse to see the sword in daylight, she stepped outside. The sword blazed upward, casting her face in light. She heard someone gasp.

"Angie!" her father said. How had he found her? "Angie, give me the sword."

She felt the hilt, hard and cold under her hand. The sword was heavy, pulling her down. She felt she could sink with it, past this world and into another filled with pageantry and magic. She would see the kingdoms of Borol and Marol with her own eyes, be welcomed into the palace of the king of Borol as his daughter, use the sword to overcome the armies of Marol, take her rightful place on the throne.

"Angie," she heard her father say. "Angie, you have to give us the sword. Quick. It's what Jara and I have been looking for, the Jewel King's sword."

Out of the corner of her eye she saw a large man start to move toward her. She didn't even look at him. The sword, the Jewel King's sword, was real. Her father had said so. It was real as death, and it was in her hand now, this minute. "Angie," Casey said. "Come on, give Dad the sword. Hurry up. Then we can go home."

For the first time Angie looked closely at the sword. The hilt was carved and inlaid with jewels. She could feel one of the jewels press into her palm. The sword was real, but not in the way she had thought. The sword had its own history. She saw its forging twelve hundred years ago. Sozran led his followers to victory only to see, too late, the treachery within his own ranks. The Jewel King won battle after battle, and as the sword passed to him in his final triumph she saw it change shape in some way she did not understand, arcing from straight to curved. It was buried with the Jewel King in his tomb after the Battle of Stones, stolen fifty years later, and passed from hand to hand until its significance was forgotten. She saw a man centuries later look at it closely, trying to decide if the wavy lines in the hilt were carvings or the result of some accident, saw him shake his head and return the sword to his attic. It lay in the attic for hundreds of years, dust settling on the hilt and dulling what was left of the jewels, until a young man found it and took it to Twenty-fifth November Street, hoping to earn enough money to buy food for his family. It passed to a wealthy tourist, and then to Mama, who served as its guardian for seventeen years.

The world shifted around her and she was back in the present. After all its twists, the story of the Jewel King led finally to this small group of people standing in front of Mama's store. Borol and Marol had nothing to do with it. Somehow she had picked up the history of this strange country and had worked it into her own legends. But the history was real, not made up. A real thing.

She would always remember this moment, the sword heavy in her hand, the people—some she knew and some she did not—standing around her in silence, watching her intently. The sun cast light on the sword, hit the things on the lawn, each object with its own shadow, each shadow with its own location predetermined by the sun and physics. She understood clearly the meaning of this tableau, the significance of all the figures, but she would never be able to put it into words. The closest she would ever come to it later on was the sentence "Real is real."

The sword in her hand was real. The sun was real. Casey and Mitchell, the things on the lawn, were real. But Borol and Marol were not real. She was the lost princess, the secret heir, but not in some imaginary kingdom. She was powerful here, now, this moment. She was powerful because in her hand she held the sword.

Everyone watched her, frozen. Blue Rose's mouth was slightly open, as if she wanted to say something but couldn't break the silence. The large man leaned toward her, about to take another step in her direction. Casey had raised her hand, almost in supplication. Her father's eyes, and the eyes of the small man next to him, were wide, nearly terrified.

She had the sword, and so she could do anything. This was what she had played at with the kingdoms, this feeling of power over other lives, but here the feeling was enormous, multiplied a hundred times. She could give the sword to Blue Rose and dash her father's hopes forever. She could turn the sword on herself, dying while they watched with horror. She could even kill Casey, be rid of her forever, and her father couldn't say anything, not if she gave him the sword afterward.

The figures before her hadn't moved. The air had congealed again, thickened by the power of the sword. Everyone looked foolish, caught in the act, even her father, even Casey. The sword felt heavy in her hand.

Real is real, she thought. This was real, the family grouped around her waiting for a decision. She held the knot that bound them all together, and she could cut or loosen it as she desired.

And suddenly she knew what she had to do, the one act around which the rest of her life would turn. She could change the configurations of her family, but the lost princess would have to abdicate. And afterward she could start learning how to live in the world again. Any place that held such marvels as the jewel-encrusted sword couldn't be all bad. She stepped toward the group on the lawn—the sword cut through the air easily—and handed the sword to her father.

He grasped it tightly. The power drained out of the air and everyone sagged forward a little. "Come on," he said. "We've got to get going."

Blue Rose took a step toward Zem's hand, still lying on the pavement and holding the gun. Mitchell turned in her direction and brandished the sword and she stopped, paralyzed. Mama yelled something in Lurqazi from the window, and then called out the only English words she would ever say, "Good-bye! Go! Good-bye!"

"Good-bye, Mama!" Casey said. "Thank you! Good-bye, Rafiz!" Then they were running down Twenty-fifth November Street, following Jara, who was opening his briefcase as he ran and taking out one of his maps. Paper spilled out behind him like a trail, but Angie, looking back, saw that no one came after them.

• • •

Mitchell followed Jara as he ran through the streets of Amaz. What had happened? The patterns of his family had changed, had been rewritten just as the streets of Amaz had been rewritten. Angie—he would never forget how she looked as she stepped toward him and gave him the sword, the way she seemed to shine with a light to rival that of the sword's. She had been smiling, too, the first time he could remember her smiling in years. Had he misjudged her?

He had no time to think of these things, though; he had to use all his strength to keep up with Jara. But although Mitchell was a large man, and although the red sun of Amaz beat down heavily upon them, he did not feel at all winded as he ran through the streets. The sword seemed to give him energy, to call up a reserve of strength he did not know he had. It felt strangely light.

Jara took a rounded corner, then another, his open briefcase flapping against his leg. Mitchell hurried after him, looking back once to make sure that Casey and Angie were still following. When he turned again to Jara he could see the university ahead of them. "We will have to put the sword in the administrative office," Jara said, breathing hard. "There is a safe there."

They stopped in front of the office. Mitchell held the sword out to Jara reluctantly. "Here," he said.

Jara took it from him and the four of them went into the building. The sword caught all the light in the dim corridor and seemed to shape it, twining in into new patterns. The woman behind the desk in a small receptionist's office gasped as Jara came in, holding the sword above him like a conqueror. "We found it," Jara said to her. "As I told you we would." He walked past her into a larger office and headed for the safe set into the wall.

He worked the combination, put the sword inside reverently, and turned toward Mitchell. "I suppose we will not be seeing each other again," he said. "You must go home to your country and I must stay here to await whatever Cumaq's forces have in store for me. I would like to thank you for all your help, for your dedication—"

"What do you mean, whatever Cumaq's forces have in store for you?" Mitchell asked. "What do you think he'll do?"

Jara shrugged. "I do not know. There has been talk of closing the university. I do not know what will happen to us."

"But can't you leave? Can't you come with us?"

"How? I am a citizen of this country. They will not let me leave. But I will write to you as long as I am able, and perhaps we can collaborate on an article or two about the sword and the epic of the Jewel King. Perhaps there will even be enough for a book—"

"Yes, of course. We could write a book, and then if it does well enough, if people start hearing about you, we could start some kind of campaign to bring you to the United States—"

Jara smiled sadly. "Good-bye, my friend," he said. "You must hurry now, you must leave the country quickly. Cumaq's position has grown stronger in the past few days. I'm afraid I may have put you into danger in my urgency to find the sword. You must go to the airport now, quickly. I am sorry."

"I'll write you," Mitchell said. "I'll make notes for the book and send them to you as soon as I can."

"Yes," Jara said. "It is a nice dream, this book." He ushered Mitchell, Casey and Angie out of the room and stood looking at them as they walked past the receptionist. She called out something to them in Lurqazi, some sort of farewell, and Casey answered her.

"Come on," Mitchell said. "We've got to hurry."

"How much was the ransom?" Angie asked as they went quickly past the place where Mitchell had seen the animal market.

"What?" Mitchell asked, surprised.

"How much did they want for me?"

"Never mind that," Mitchell said. "Who told you to leave the house when we'd specifically told you to stay inside? You're lucky I came after you at all."

"I thought I knew where Casey was," Angie said. "I thought she'd go to Twenty-fifth November Street."

"Yeah, well, you should have said something to us instead of running out the way you did," Mitchell said. What was he doing? Who was this man who spoke with the voice of authority, who dared to confront the others in his family?

His hand still felt warm where it had grasped the sword, and he remembered how Angie had given it to him, how she had made a choice. He understood now that he had been granted something of power, that Angie, by her actions, had passed this thing to him.

Many times in the past he had heard Casey and Angie whisper to each other when he tried to assert his authority, "parenting," they had called it, scornfully. But something had changed; in reaching for the sword he had taken on more than he had known.

They turned a corner and a large American car slowed beside them. The driver called out to them in Lurgazi.

Mitchell motioned to Casey to be quiet. "We don't speak Lurqazi," he said to the driver of the car. "I'm sorry. Just English."

"All foreigners must be out of the counry," the driver said. Now Mitchell saw that he was wearing a kind of uniform, and that a rifle stuck up between the two men in the front seat. More of Cumaq's forces, he guessed, though judging from the uniforms they could be with almost anyone. He wondered where they had gotten the car. "You must come with us to the police."

"We're trying to leave the country," Mitchell said. "We can't find a cab to take us to the airport. We've been looking for one for hours."

The driver said something to the man in the passenger seat in Lurqazi. Casey nodded to Mitchell, and he knew it was going to be all right. "We will take you to the airport," the driver said. "Come, we must hurry."

"My wife's still at home," Mitchell said. "Could you take us there first so we can pick her up and get our plane tickets? We don't live far from here."

The driver sighed theatrically. "Do we look like the drivers of taxis? No wife. We must go now."

"We have some money at home too, some Amaz currency. We can't take it out of the country and all the banks are still closed. I'll give it to you, all of it, if you take us home."

This time the driver didn't need to confer with the other man. "Okay," he said. "Get in. But we will only stop long enough to get your wife and the tickets."

The three of them got into the back of the car. Mitchell leaned over the front seat and directed the driver to Dr. Tamir's house. This is the last time I'll pass this corner, he thought. I'll never see this street, this house, again. He felt strangely forlorn.

The driver pulled up at Dr. Tamir's house. Mitchell had half expected the Sozranis to be back, but the streets were still deserted. He ran up the porch, opened the door and called out, "Claire!"

In another of his nightmares Claire would be gone, and all the strange masks and swords would wink at him maliciously from the wall. But Claire was still at the kitchen table where he had left her, a fat book opened in front of her. "We've got to go," he said. "We don't have much time. Pack only what you absolutely need—we're going to the airport. Oh, and give me all the money you have."

Claire stared at him without comprehension. She looked only slightly more alert when Casey and Angie came into the room after him. "How did you—?" she said.

"There's no time," Mitchell said. "Get everything you think you might need. You too," he said, turning to his children.

If Claire was surprised at his new decisiveness she didn't show it. "Everything—" she said vaguely, but Mitchell was already hurrying down the corridor to their bedroom.

In ten minutes he and Casey and Angie were packed and heading out the front door. Claire trailed after them, holding only her purse and her book, fingers carefully keeping her place. The car had waited for them, though the driver swore in Lurqazi when he saw the three suitcases the family had brought outside.

Mitchell took out a bundle of notes, conscious that the stack was not as thick as it might have been. The banks had been closed since Cumaq's takeover. Claire fumbled in her purse and brought out a few more bills. The driver counted them and then, satisfied, ordered his passenger from the car. The passenger began to argue in Lurqazi.

This is it, Mitchell thought. One of us will have to stay behind. There's not enough room for all of us. And we were so close—But luck was with them even in this, and at last the driver gave the other man about a fourth of the notes and the man left the car.

Mitchell got in front, balancing his large half-empty suitcase on his knees, careful to avoid the rifle. Claire, Casey and Angie sat in back. The driver pulled away from the curb. The last thing Mitchell saw as they turned the corner was the bronze statue of the man holding the egg. He realized he had never found out who the man was.

Twenty-fifth November Street: 5

*M*ama sat in her bedroom in a chair she had taken from the kitchen, carefully watching the man who slept on her bed. His breathing was regular now, and his complexion, though still pale, seemed healthier. The wounds on both shoulders, under the sterile white bandages Rafiz had wrapped around them, had finally stopped bleeding.

Her work was ended. She sat back in her chair and closed her eyes, hardly hearing the excited voices of her neighbors outside in the street. Seventeen years ago a tourist had come into her store carrying an old rusted piece of metal with one end strangely carved. Seventeen years ago she had recognized the pitted metal for the Jewel King's sword and bought it from the man immediately. And seventeen years ago Blue Rose had come running into her store, demanding the sword back, claiming that it was she who had sold it to the tourist in the first place. The two had not spoken to each other once in the intervening years, not until the day last week when Mama had thrown the sword to Casey.

The man on the bed stirred and she leaned over and felt his forehead. With the recognition of the sword had come further understanding, the knowledge that she had somehow been appointed the sword's guardian, that her task was to see the sword handed over to the people who would care for it. She didn't know who those people would be, but she knew she would recognize them when they finally came to the street. And so she had guarded her prize for seventeen long years, watching as nearly everyone on the street moved on, as she and Blue Rose advanced toward the middle of the street from opposite sides until their stores stood next door to each other.

She had had her first child shortly after the man had sold her the sword. As the sword's guardian she was afraid that something might happen to her, that she would not always be around to protect it from Blue Rose. Two children didn't seem to be enough protection, nor did six, nor did ten. By the third or fourth the people on the street had started calling her Mama, and by the fifth or sixth no one could remember her real name. Sometimes she had trouble remembering it herself. The twelfth child had been born some time ago; she had not felt the need for more children after that one.

Outside the sun was going down. As they had done all during the past week, the shopkeepers had closed their stores and gone outside to talk about the latest events on Twenty-fifth November Street. Mama stood slowly and turned on the light. Now she could hear her neighbors as they gathered wood and junk that no one had been able to sell for a bonfire, their excited voices drifting up to her.

"She was from the United States, you know. Mama told me."

"Amazing. She lived here all these years and we never even suspected."

"I think she heard about the sword while she was living in the United States. And she knew she had to have it, and moved here."

"Yes, when she opened her store she claimed to be an expert on swords. I remember someone told me that. Whenever someone wanted a sword or had one to sell people sent them to her."

"And then someone must have sold her the Jewel King's sword. But it looked like an old piece of scrap metal, so she got rid of it."

Someone laughed. "I wonder how she felt when she found out she'd sold the Jewel King's sword."

"The sword she'd come to Amaz for."

"And what about when she learned that Mama bought it?"

"And just last week, when she found out that Mama hadn't sold it after all?"

Everyone laughed. This was the kind of story they all enjoyed, evil and evil's punishment, the wheel of justice coming around slowly to work retribution. And if a few of them looked uneasy because Blue Rose hadn't been all that evil, had, after all, been neighbor to all of them for longer than they could remember, they didn't see fit, in the glory of the bonfire, to say anything in her defense. Everyone knew that by the time the street was finished with Blue Rose she would have become one of their legends, that everything that went wrong on the street would be blamed on her, that parents would use her name to frighten their children into behaving. Already two or three people were looking over their shoulders, trying not to imagine they saw her approaching the fire out of the darkness.

"And Mama. Just think of her keeping that secret to herself. Keeping it for seventeen years."

"I have to admit I misjudged her. I always thought she was far too cold to Blue Rose. I never understood what she had against her."

"We could start the antique dealers' association again."

"That's true, we could."

"And we could elect Mama to be president."

"Hey, that's a great idea!"

Mama, sitting upstairs by the bed, heard them call out her name and shook her head. She would have to stop this idea before too many people took it up. She had better things to do than be president of some organization.

Outside a young woman, not more than twenty, stood and

stretched. "Sorry I can't stay any longer," she said. "I still have some cleaning to do."

"Hey, sit down, Calano."

"Sorry," Calano said, walking away from the circle. Everyone watched as she left the protective light of the bonfire and blended into the darkness around them. After a while they saw light flare out from the door of Blue Rose's shop as she opened it and stepped inside.

"I still think she's too young to take over Blue Rose's store all by herself," someone said, almost whispering.

"Oh, you're just jealous. Everyone knows you wanted that store for yourself."

The circle of people around the fire grew quiet. Then someone said, "I wonder where she is now."

"Blue Rose? She went back to the United States, I bet."

"Maybe she got carried off by the same birds that took Harhano's wife."

"And where's Harhano? I haven't seen him since last week either."

No one suggested that the birds could have been responsible for Harhano's disappearance too. Although the speculations of the people on the street were frequently unlikely, they stopped short of the ridiculous.

The man in the bed opened his eyes, cried out once and then was silent. Mama hushed him and tucked him back in bed, careful not to touch his bandages. He has beautiful eyes, she thought, watching as he sank back into sleep, brown like a doe's and surrounded by long black lashes. What would a child fathered by him look like?

The thought surprised her. Hadn't she just finished telling herself that her guardianship was over, that there would be no more children? And yet she knew she was still fertile. Perhaps she had been lying to herself. Perhaps the children were the most important thing, after all. And where would the young man go after he healed? She had heard him tell Casey that he had been with the Sozranis since he was twelve. Wouldn't it be better to keep him here with her?

She bent over the man in the bed. Her long black hair brushed his face and he woke, this time completely. He lay still, marveling at the woman's abundance, her beauty.

Rafiz sat downstairs in Mama's store, hardly listening to the cries and laughter of his neighbors in the street. He knew all the colors now, could name each of them correctly and without making embarrassing mistakes. The world was crowded with color. He had not turned off the lights and each one pressed against him insistently, red, blue, green.

With the ability to see colors, he knew, would come the ability to see Death. He had seen Death a few times already, only briefly because he couldn't bear to look directly at it. Death was a skeleton each of whose bones was painted a different color, like the xylophone Mama had sold the other day. He had once told himself that he had had a long life and would not be unhappy when it ended, but now that the time of his death was at hand he could not help but think that he was unready.

The colored skeleton grinned at him from behind a jumble of open cartons. He tried to stand but his legs would not hold him. If he could only get to Mama perhaps the skeleton would disappear, daunted by having to face someone it had not come to claim. But the climb up the stairs to Mama's bedroom seemed impossible. The skeleton beckoned to him.

"No," Rafiz said weakly. "I'm not—"

The skeleton came out from behind the cartons. With a long wave of one bony hand it gestured to Rafiz. Come to me, the hand seemed to say. Its fingers were blue, red, green, yellow.

Rafiz pushed his chair back. Its legs scraped loudly against the floor. The skeleton came closer. "I'm not ready!" Rafiz said, summoning up the last of his energy.

The skeleton shook its head. You are ready, it seemed to be saying. I have been waiting a long time for you.

Rafiz slumped in his chair. It was true, he had been given a longer life than anyone he knew, perhaps longer than anyone in the world. And there was nowhere to hide. At least he had been granted the knowledge of colors before his death.

The skeleton beckoned to him again. Haven't you had time to do everything you've ever wanted? it said to him without words. Casey, he thought. I just wish I could have said good-bye to Casey. He rose to follow it, leaving his old, old body behind.

The look in the wounded man's eyes was the same one Mama had seen in the eyes of the twelve men before him. He tried to rise, but he was too weak and fell back onto the pillows. Later, Mama thought. She rearranged the blankets around him and listened to his breathing become regular again.

Outside the night had deepened. The only light came from the dying bonfire and the high stars. One by one the shopkeepers left the circle of the fire and went to their stores, leaving only three or four people who would talk through the night and leave the "Closed" signs on their doors the next day. The voices quieted, made a soothing murmur that became the background for Mama's thoughts.

In a way she was sorry the sword had been found. The sword had been the source of all magic on Twenty-fifth November Street, and the slow seepage of that magic had gradually spread to the rest of the city. She had once heard Rafiz call the street the center, the heart, the dry river that runs through the dry city, and she thought he had spoken her feelings exactly, though she didn't know how he had come to understand them so clearly.

But now all that would change. She didn't think the people on the street would even notice: all of them except Blue Rose had come to the street after she had received the sword, and the magic had become as familiar to them as breathing. They had come to think of people like Zem and Rafiz—people who had arrived on the street, drawn unknowingly by the sword—not as odd or eccentric, but as people like themselves. They had come to think of the strange events not as magic but as part of the regular patterns of their lives. And those patterns would go on, but with one strand missing.

Only Mama would know what was gone, and only she would regret it. She stood heavily and went to get ready for bed. Her children, who had been running up and down the street finding wood for the bonfire, would be home soon. Ah well, she thought. Maybe a new baby would make up for part of the loss she felt.

Someone in the street called her name. Mama wrapped her embroidered shawl around her and went ponderously down the stairs. Rafiz was still in the store, slumped in a chair, his eyes closed. She wondered if something was wrong with him. "Mama!" a woman's voice called out in panic, and Mama hurried past him and went outside.

"Mama!" the woman said for the third time, and now Mama recognized Calano, the new occupant of Blue Rose's store. What could have happened to her? "Mama, come quick! There's a blue rose growing through the floor in my store!"

Mama breathed a prayer of thanks to all the gods she believed in and went next door as quickly as she could. The magic hadn't left her yet.

Home

The soldier dropped them off at the airport. The small terminal was deserted; their footsteps echoed as they crossed it. Mitchell hurried to an airline clerk and handed him their tickets.

"All foreigners must leave the country," the clerk said.

"Yes, we're trying to," Mitchell said. "When's the next flight to the United States?"

"It is—the next flight leaves now."

"Now? What gate?"

"Oh, you will never make it. Probably it is gone already. You must stay until the next flight, which is—" the clerk consulted a printed list taped to his counter. "The next flight leaves tomorrow. One flight a day to the United States."

"What gate?"

"You will not—"

"What gate?"

"Eleven."

Mitchell lifted two suitcases and nodded to Casey to take the third. He raced down the hallway, glancing at the odd-numbered gates on his right. One, three, five . . . He looked back, saw that Casey and Angie were hurrying too. Angie was holding one of the straps of Casey's suitcase. Claire followed at a fast walk.

A loud sound came from outside Gate Eleven. Mitchell tossed his tickets to the clerk at the door and hurried down the gateway. The sound was coming from propellers, he saw now. A prop plane.

"Sor," the clerk said, calling after him. "Sor! The dates on these tickets are wrong, sor!"

Mitchell ignored her and ran for the plane. There was no stewardess at the open doorway. He went inside and glanced down the aisle. Only one other passenger had taken a seat.

He lifted his two suitcases to an overhead bin, saw Claire and his daughters to seats and then sat himself. The clerk had not followed them.

The door closed, and Mitchell relaxed enough to look around him. The other passenger was a young man wearing a clean new suit and several days' growth of beard. He had opened his briefcase and was checking over a long list of numbers with a pocket calculator. Once he took off his glasses and started to cry. Mitchell wondered how much money he had lost when Cumaq's forces took over the country.

A stewardess walked to the front of the plane and began to explain the seat belts and oxygen masks. The plane taxied down the runway. It separated from the ground, lifted high, higher. Mitchell saw Amaz below them; each building and roadway stood out sharp-edged, clear.

The clarity matched the way he felt; the understanding he had gained from the sword was still with him. He thought of his time in Amaz, felt that he almost grasped the pattern whole. But a few answers, a few lines of the pattern, still eluded him.

He turned to Casey in the window seat next to him. "Who was that woman at the window in the junk shop?" he asked. "The one who threw down the sword, remember? I thought she called your name."

"That was Mama," Casey said.

For a moment, startled, Mitchell thought that Casey was talking about Claire. But Casey would never call her own mother "Mama." With his new insight he saw that Casey's pattern had led her to this woman, had caused her to seek out substitutes for her own mother. And not just the woman in the junk shop but others as well: hadn't she said once that she had met another mother, a woman who wanted to sell her baby?

Now he realized that Casey had thought of herself as the mother of their family ever since Claire had abdicated. No, ever since both parents had abdicated. She had taken on all their problems; had been the only one to worry about Claire and Angie. Mitchell could not help but think that the strain of that would almost certainly break her. He felt his old love for her, and another, newer, feeling: a determination to help her put down her burden.

"But why were you at Twenty-fifth November Street in the first place?" he asked. "Weren't you kidnapped by the Sozranis? And how did Angie get away?"

"I was," Casey said. "But I escaped. And then—"

Angie leaned over from the seat across the aisle and interrupted. "I went to Twenty-fifth Street to get Casey—"

"She knew where I was because I'd asked her to come with me one time—"

One by one the daughters told him their stories. He had never realized that they could talk so much. He drew them out, asked them questions, expressed his concern—carefully, very carefully, feeling his way cautiously toward a new relationship with them. Words had uses outside old manuscripts, he thought.

He joined his story to theirs, telling them how he and Jara had come to the sword. Their voices overlapped; they laughed as they spoke. His daughters sounded like chimes, Angie slightly lower than Casey.

Turbanned men and junk shops, a woman with twelve children

and a woman with roses on her palms. Pastry shops and policemen, straight and jagged letters, the Jewel King and his age-old enemy. Narrow escapes, new reunions; a word written on the streets of Amaz and a new pattern forming in the midst of the city.

The hours passed. Mitchell felt hungry but he could not see the stewardess anywhere; she must have gone into the cockpit. "I looked in your notebooks, Angie," he said. "I'm sorry, but I had to find out where you were. Where on earth did you find the epic of the Jewel King? Jara and I had the only manuscript, and I never translated it."

"I thought I was making it up," Angie said. "I thought I was writing a story of the Two Kingdoms."

"I'd like to see your notebooks when we get home."

Angie shook her head. "I didn't bring them. It's time to move on to other stuff."

"The city used you to write its story, I think," Mitchell said slowly. "Just as it used me to spell out a new word on its streets." He glanced at Casey, his practical daughter. "Do you believe any of this?"

Casey was looking out the window. She said nothing, and at first Mitchell thought that he had lost her once again, that his insistent questions had pushed her too far. Then he saw the even rise and fall of her breathing: she had fallen asleep.

He yawned. It had been a long day for all of them. They were flying over ocean now, limitless gray water. He looked out the window past Casey, smiling, and never knew the moment he dozed off himself. He woke to hear the stewardess over the address system, telling them to put their seatbelts on.

Just before they landed the stewardess passed out customs declaration forms to Mitchell and the young man. Under nationality Mitchell wrote "American," studied the word for a minute and then crossed it out and wrote "United States."

The family went through customs, still yawning from their sleep on the plane, and took a taxi home from the airport. Everything looked strange, elongated, as if seen in a funhouse mirror. The people were too pale, the cars too new, the houses too angular.

The road home seemed too straight, too obvious, seemed to declare for the Sozranis instead of for the Jewel King. As they neared their house they thought it impossible that they had ever lived on such a street, in such a home.

When they got inside they stood for a while, stupefied. For a moment they felt they had returned to Amaz. The smells of Dr. Tamir's cooking shimmered in the air: cinnamon, coffee, fish. Even the furniture had been placed to remind them of Dr. Tamir's house, the two couches facing each other instead of at right angles as they had left them, all the chairs taken to the kitchen and grouped around the table.

Tamir had left a note on the table. "Sorry I could not be here to greet you," the note said. "Pressing business called me back to my country." Mitchell, who had expected to deliver the bad news to Tamir that he would not be able to stay for the entire year, read the note and laughed aloud. He wondered how much of Tamir's "pressing business" had to do with the Sozranis, irate because the sword had slipped away from them. He hoped that Cumaq's forces would give Tamir and the rest of the Sozranis as much trouble as Tamir had given him.

Claire opened the refrigerator and took out fish and vegetables. "There's enough here for dinner," she said. "But it'll be pretty small."

"That's fine," Mitchell said.

In the kitchen cabinet Claire found half a dozen spice boxes and took them out one by one. The word *araraq* was stamped in red on one of them. A strange word, Mitchell thought, as out of place in the sharp fluorescent-lit kitchen as a herd of lowing cattle. He brought the tin box to his nose and then put it down, briefly disoriented.

He went upstairs to unpack. Half an hour later the smells of dinner brought him down again. He found he was starving; they had had nothing to eat on the plane.

His daughters had come down as well. They sat at the table and ate. The old silence welled up around them, and for a moment Mitchell thought they would return to their earlier habits, that this house where they had been so unhappy would force its patterns on them.

Then Casey spoke. "I heard what you asked me on the plane, Dad—whether I believe any of the things you told us. And the answer is that I've changed my mind about a lot of things. I don't think I have any choice. I've seen things with my own eyes that— Well, it doesn't seem possible to deny anymore that some things exist, things I never could have imagined."

His two daughters, once poles apart, had started to close the gap between them, Mitchell saw. Angie was willing to believe in the real world, in what she saw outside her notebooks, and Casey had started to accept the existence of things she had rejected before.

He felt replete, delighted beyond words. No man could possibly have such satisfaction from his family. He looked around the dinner table and saw Claire. She lifted a small bite of fish to her mouth and took a sip of wine.

Hadn't she and Casey quarreled about something the day Casey ran off? The family had made an art of avoiding arguments so it must have been serious, bad enough to make Casey leave the house after all the warnings he had given her. Had they ever made up?

"How are you doing, Claire?" he asked.

Claire stopped eating and starred frankly at him. Was that the first time he had ever asked her that question? "You found the sword, didn't you? No one tells me anything, but I heard you and the kids talking on the plane. I suppose I'll see even less of you now. You'll be famous, in big demand. The man who found the Jewel King's sword."

"I'm going to try to spend more time at home," Mitchell said. "Something happened on the streets just before we found the sword—some kind of shift—"

"I know," Claire said. All the belligerence had gone out of her, one of those sudden changes of mood that used to surprise him the first few years they had been married. She's had a lot to drink, he thought. When did she find the time? "I felt it too. The air went all shimmery. I looked up from my book—I thought I was hallucinating, but it didn't go away. It was hard to move. And then suddenly it stopped."

"That was us," Mitchell said. "We were—we were forging new streets. Creating new patterns as we got closer to the sword." How much of the story was she going to believe? It seemed absurd to state it as baldly as that.

"I know. The city used to open for me too. I used to be able to find anything I needed. And then it stopped—it closed me out, deserted me. And you—you three—"

Mitchell nodded. His new understanding, the clarity he had gained in Amaz, enabled him to see even this. He and Casey and Angie had followed the maze to the center, to Twenty-fifth November Street. They had traced their own story on the streets of Amaz, had turned the crooked writing of the Sozranis into the fluid letters of the Jewel King. The three of them had drawn together in a new configuration. But his wife hadn't been there. She had been home reading and drinking.

"Claire," he said.

"Maybe we can talk later," Claire said. "I'm tired, and I have a headache from the plane."

She stood up and left the table. They heard her go upstairs and close the door to her bedroom, and then the noises stopped.

In Amaz Mitchell had rescued his daughters from forces he didn't altogether understand, and he had rescued them too from their cold cities of silence with his words. Claire had said that she had once felt the city's magic, that Amaz had sheltered her within its embrace. Perhaps he could draw her back into that warmth, into the new pattern of the family. Perhaps, now that he understood how much had been his fault and how much he could change, he could rescue his wife as well. Maybe it would be more difficult, but he knew he had to try.